Finding Lacey
Moon

Also by Donya Lynne

Finding Lacey Moon

A Hope Falls Novel

Donya Lynne

Finding Lacey Moon
Donya Lynne
Copyright © 2014 Donya Lynne
ISBN: 1938991109
ISBN 13:9781938991103

Cover art by Mae I Design.
Edited by Laura LaTulipe

Acknowledgements

First, thank you to my fabulous, talented beta readers. Adriana, Alana, Dawn, Leann, Martha, Sandy, Tami, Toni, and Kathy: Your feedback helped make this book better than I could make it by myself. An extra special thank you to Liz for giving the manuscript a final read after I rewrote half the book, because you know how I love to rewrite my books. Ha!

To my readers, I couldn't do this "writing thing" I love so much if not for your enthusiasm and dedication to the worlds I create. I hope I can continue creating many more worlds for you for years to come.

To my husband. You pick up so many pieces for me so that I can focus my creative spirit on making my stories "just right." I love you. Thank you for supporting my dream.

"No one gets up or down life's mountains unscathed."
-Anne Lamott

Chapter 1

It's okay to fall. Falling down teaches us how to get back up.

Lacey stood at the mouth of the halfpipe, recalling the words her coach had said to her the first time she took a hard spill during a training run. That had been thirteen years ago. Why was she thinking about that now, when she was eyeing the icy tube and preparing to make her run for gold?

Shoving her coach's words aside, she bobbed her head to the up-tempo music pumping through her earbuds. Music usually calmed her before a competition, but not this time. And not just because this was the Olympics. Something within her competitive spirit had shut off in the last twelve months.

She used to be a fearless, gushing spigot, ready to tackle any run down the pipe, no matter the situation. Now, she was a closed, dry well, completely tapped out. There was no fire in her belly. No hunger. Instead of the rush she used to feel as she stared down the pipe, she felt...

Nothing.

Nada.

Zilch.

Well, and dread. She definitely felt dread. But there wasn't a glimmer of the old Lacey anywhere in sight.

Okay, so maybe that was why her coach's words were echoing inside her thoughts.

I'm in trouble.

Five years ago, Lacey Moon would have stood atop this hill with ice in her veins. Hell, even a year ago, when snowboarding had still held a snowflake's worth of fun, she would have ruled this bitch. She was a two-time Olympic gold medalist, for God's sake. She'd won the X Games three times. She'd medaled every year since she started competing. She was practically the Shaun White of women's superpipe and slopestyle. Nowhere near as high profile as the Flying Tomato, but still, she was no chump.

But sometime in the last year, things had changed, and now she wanted to be anywhere but here. Anywhere but facing the tube of ice carved out of the snowy mountainside.

Except the official had just given her the sign to get ready. With time ticking down before her run, she peered at her coach, who made a fist and nodded once. His mouth formed the words "Crush it, Lacey," but she didn't hear him over Ed Sheeran commanding her through her earbuds to "Sing."

Swallowing, she faced the pipe, adjusted her goggles, and smacked her leather-gloved hands together as she did before every trip down the pipe. But this run was anything but routine. It was for the gold. All the marbles.

The truth was, she hardly cared.

I'm in serious trouble.

At her third Olympic games, with the pressure on, when she should be flying on adrenaline and gold medal pandemonium, snowboarding had lost its luster. She put on her happy face for the media, said all the right things in interviews, and even mustered the illusion that she was hungry for her third gold, but snowboarding was no longer fun. Now it was more like work. A business. A machine that churned her in its cogs and spit her in ten different directions.

She dreaded training, dreaded the constant swarm of media outside her hotel at every competition. Fans heckled her as much as cheered her, eager to see her fall off her perch.

Then there were the sponsors and endorsements. It seemed that every week she was tugged to consider a contract for one product or another. Energy drinks, sportswear, even a makeup line. A goddamn makeup line! When had she turned into a model instead of an athlete? When had this transformation taken place? When had she lost control of herself so drastically that she had become a glamour puss instead of a kick-ass snowboarder with a thirst to win?

Her heart hammered against her ribcage as she stared down the pipe like it was her enemy and no longer the best friend she'd had since she was eight years old. She needed to get her head in the game...needed to do what her coach said and crush it...needed to focus on her tricks, flips, and speed. If she didn't, she could get hurt. She could *fall*. The halfpipe was brutal on those whose heads weren't locked in.

It's okay to fall. Falling down teaches us how to get back up.

Of all days, this wasn't the day she needed to remind herself how to get back up after a fall. Falling wasn't an option in the Olympics.

But she couldn't shake the boiling sense of panic, which hovered just under her skin at the top of her spine.

Her life had become a business, not an adventure...pulled in too many directions, especially now. And everywhere she turned, the knives drove into her back. Her own teammates had been making cracks about her for days. Some even whispered under their breath that they didn't care who medaled as long as she wasn't anywhere near the podium.

What had happened to team spirit and supporting one another? Years ago, these same competitors had cheered for her. They had been like family. Now they were estranged.

At twenty-five, Lacey was flirting with old age in the snowboarding universe. Younger competitors not yet tainted by the machine came in hungrier, saucier, throwing more tricks. And their nubile bodies weren't as beat up as hers. They didn't have to worry about the bum knee or the numerous ankle sprains, which had plagued Lacey throughout her long yet decorated career. Sure, older competitors could still throw down the smack and medal, but they had to work a lot harder for it and suffer through more pains than a younger one did.

And while many boarders still rejoiced for each other in the spirit of the games and friendship, despite national affiliation, Lacey increasingly found herself on the outside looking in. The outcast. The one everyone else wanted to knock off the top of the heap.

That's what happens when you're on top, though, and Lacey had been on top for almost ten years. She was the one everyone was gunning for, aiming their vitriol at, wishing failure upon…wanting to divest of her title. They wanted what she had. They wanted the media, the sponsors, the fame. And honestly, right now she wanted them to have it. She didn't want the attention anymore. She wanted to fade away, disappear, crawl inside a cave and stay there for about five years.

When was the last time she had been able to do anything without having at least six other people around? She couldn't even go shopping without a legion of paparazzi tagging along. And don't even get her started on stalkers. She'd had her share of those. She'd even had to hire a team of bodyguards a few years back. Bodyguards, for Christ's sake! How had a girl from her humble background grown into a woman who needed goddamn bodyguards? Lacey wanted to go someplace where no one knew who she was. Someplace where she could simply…breathe.

But first, she had to complete her run. She was the last one to take the pipe. All her competitors had finished their final runs, and currently no boarder from the United States sat on the podium. She was the only one who could land a medal for the States. And not just any medal. Gold. Everyone expected her to win gold. Anything less would be a failure and plummet her toward obscurity.

Obscurity. That sounds good.

With the weight of an entire country on her shoulders, she tried to shove panic aside for the next sixty seconds. That was all that stood in her way. One short minute and a world of panic that threatened to consume her.

She received the signal to go.

She blinked, and the white landscape briefly faded out and back in.

Deep breath. Just breathe, Lacey. It'll be over soon, and then you can rest.

She pushed off, approached the left wall, flew down into the pipe and up the ramp on the other side, grabbing big air.

The cheering crowd sounded far away as she kissed the landing and glided back across to the other side of the pipe to fly above the heads of the press lining the deck. Cameras clicked by the dozens as she grabbed the back of her board and straightened her back leg.

Landing, she pushed through the bottom of the pipe to gain speed. On the way up the opposite wall, her heart began to race. She couldn't breathe. Her biggest trick was coming, and she suddenly couldn't see through the spots clouding her vision.

She felt her board leave the surface, felt herself twist and flip in the open air, sought the surface of the pipe by rote, but the world was a blur of dots and blotches. Panic clawed her and refused to let go.

Gravity buddied up to panic and formed a terrible duo, pulling her down hard and fast. A sinking feeling clutched her gut, the collective breath of the crowd held, and then...

CRASH!

Lacey slammed into the flat of the halfpipe. The edge of her board caught and threw her forward, and she tumbled like a slingshot ragdoll over the hard, icy surface, bashing her head against the ground. A crack rang out from her helmet as it whacked the ice.

The crowd gasped. Several people screamed. Lacey heard one stifled squeal of joy, and right before she passed out, she thought, *Be careful what you wish for, because you just might get it.*

Chapter 2

Seven months later...

Lacey crawled out of bed and dragged herself downstairs to the kitchen. A note from her mom sat on the counter.

> *Lacey,*
> *Trent called to check on you. He heard about Doug. Wants to make sure you're okay. I ran to the store. Be back around lunchtime.*
> *Love,*
> *Mom*

She tossed the note in the trash and turned for the fridge. How pathetic was it that she was living at home again?

After breaking her leg and dislocating her shoulder during her unofficial farewell to snowboarding at the Olympics, she'd been forced to move back home, where her mom, dad, and Tory, her younger brother, could help her get around and keep an eye on her. She'd spent the better part of the first four months in a splint, cast, or boot, and the better part of the last three months rehabbing her leg.

At least her helmet had saved her head in the fall. Things could have been a lot worse.

Still, that was little consolation. The mental shitstorm she'd experienced during those final seconds before her fall had yet to let up. If anything, the claustrophobic, assiduous panic had worsened through the media swarm after the Olympics. It had continued to decline during her recovery, through the endless hours lying in bed staring out the window through her tears, finally cresting during her breakup with her longtime boyfriend, Doug, two days ago.

Ha! Boyfriend. Doug was a downhill skier from Colorado with an ego the size of Mt. Olympus. They'd been an on-again, off-again item for three years, but Lacey had finally had enough. Enough of his philandering. Enough broken promises. Enough horseshit.

He thought their breakup was because she'd found out about the Russian figure skater he'd hooked up with during the Olympics. Lacey hadn't even known about that. She'd ended the relationship because she didn't see a future with him. For her, cutting him from her life was akin to putting out the trash. Sort of like cleaning out her closet and tossing everything that no longer fit.

Of course, after hearing about Irena or Ivanka or whatever her name was, Lacey wasn't sorry about kicking him to the curb. The Russian was just the last in what Lacey was sure was a long list of infidelities. Longer than she previously thought, anyway. She knew he'd messed around, but if he could hide figure skating's silver medalist from her for seven months, what other women didn't Lacey know about?

Ignoring the platter of cold pancakes in the fridge, Lacey grabbed the milk and poured a bowl of Trix, sticking her tongue out at the rabbit on the box.

"Silly rabbit, Trix are *not* just for kids." She defiantly shoveled a spoonful into her mouth, turned her back on the box as she exited the kitchen, and made her way back upstairs.

At least she could walk on her own again. No more crutches. No more walker. No more cane. But the doctors wanted her to take it easy for a few more months and continue doing her physical therapy exercises.

No problem there. She had no plans of going anywhere near a halfpipe, a snowy slope, or even her snowboards, for that matter. They still sat in the back of her blue Ford Escape, untouched from when she returned home in February.

She yawned then ate another spoonful of cereal as she pulled a pair of jeans and a sweatshirt from her closet then flipped on the shower in her bathroom. She packed the last few bites of cereal into her mouth as the water heated up then climbed in and leaned forward against her outstretched arms under the falling water. With her head bowed, her long red and brown hair hung almost to her knees. She hadn't cut or colored her hair since June. It was now September. Her blond roots were way past showing, but she didn't care.

In fact, she didn't care about anything. She hadn't for months. It was as if she were still stuck in that tragic moment. The one that had hit her mind right before she hit the ice. The one that filled her with desperation. The one she couldn't figure out how to get rid of. What was wrong with her? Why did she feel so lost, so stagnated, so...hopeless? She felt like she didn't know herself anymore.

Was she suffering from depression, or was she simply burned out? Did burnout normally last upwards of a year? She couldn't shake the absent feeling that she was wasting into oblivion like a block of ice that melts in spring, evaporating into nothing, as if it were never there at all.

The only thing worse than being overwhelmed by the media was falling into complete obscurity and being labeled a has-been. She could hear it now. "Remember Lacey Moon? One-time champion. She'd been a contender once, but where is she now? What has she done lately? Looks like another of the older generation has fallen to make room for the new."

Lacey didn't want to go out that way. The last thing people would remember about her was that she fell during the most important run of her life, ending the quest for a three-peat. It was hard enough to win two Olympic Golds. To win three was a history-making statement. It said, "I'm for real, y'all! Catch *this*!"

Climbing out of the shower, she gave her hair a cursory rub with the towel, got dressed, then put in her new contacts. They were brown. She didn't know why she chose to get colored contacts. It had been a whimsical, spur-of-the-moment decision, but one she'd been driven to make.

She lifted her gaze to the mirror and froze. The eyes staring back at her weren't the light blue she'd come to know as hers. They were someone else's. She'd only wanted a change when she ordered the brown contacts, not a total transformation. But just changing her eye color gave her face an entirely new dimension.

Feeling almost playful for the first time in months, she pulled her hair back, and, for a moment, she imagined she was someone else. Not the icon. Not the former queen of the superpipe. The brown-eyed stranger staring back at her led a simpler life. She had bigger dreams, because she hadn't been tainted the way Lacey had. She could go to the mall and not be recognized by a single person. She could eat at Appleby's and not be hassled for an autograph. She could go to the beach and disappear in the sea of exposed flesh just like everybody else. She could trust that when a man showed interest, it was because he really wanted to get to know her, not that she was a celebrity he could use to give him his fifteen minutes of fame.

This brown-eyed woman staring back at her was a nobody. A regular person.

And Lacey envied her.

Within seconds, her playfulness vaporized, and she began to cry. Then sobbed. Then bawled uncontrollably as rivers of tears flooded her cheeks and dripped off her chin. She wanted to be that woman in the mirror. She wanted to be her so damn badly! Unencumbered by the shackles of her public persona. She wanted to be anyone but herself even though she didn't have a clue who she really was.

Lacey Moon had been a champion snowboarder. That was what defined her and made her notable. Other than that, who was she? If she never snowboarded again, what would she do?

Not even twenty-six years old, and she was already in the middle of a cataclysmic identity crisis, and didn't that just piss her off? Who the hell was she? More importantly, who did she want to be?

It was time to change. Time to take control and figure out exactly who she was. Screw the machine. Screw Trent. Screw everything!

Spurred by a force that felt like it was coming from outside herself, she yanked open the top drawer of her vanity as she angrily slapped the tears from her cheeks. She shoved the contents side to side, looking...frantically searching.

Scissors! Damn it, where are the scissors?

Not finding them, she slammed the drawer shut, opened another, then another, until finally, success!

Snagging the shears from the bottom drawer, she threw them on the counter and dug an elastic band from the glass dish beside the sink. She couldn't work fast enough. Now! This had to happen now. More tears gushed from her eyes, making her vision blurry. But her mind was clear. Finally, clear.

She knew what she had to do. It was as if seeing her new brown irises had awakened her. Inspired her.

Stretching the elastic band around her fingers, she cranked her wet, multi-hued hair into a ponytail then snapped the band in place and tugged her trademark long tresses through. The wet ends fell and slapped her lower back.

She snatched the shears in a death grip.

No more. She was done being Lacey Moon. Done being a puppet for the media, her sponsors, the *machine*. Just...done!

Grabbing her ponytail with her free hand, she yanked it taut and poised the open blades around the bundled, damp mess just below the nape of her neck. Then, with a war cry to rouse the dead, she began sawing. Over and over, she squeezed, sliced, and ripped. She was closing the book on this part of her life. Lacey Moon, the puppet who did everything she was told, was no more.

Gone.

Over.

Dead and being buried this very moment.

After several gut-wrenching seconds of aggressively sawing through her hair, the final strands severed. She'd been pulling so hard on her ponytail that her head flew forward. She had to drop the scissors and slam her palm against the counter to keep from nose-diving into the faucet.

Gasping, she pushed herself up. Her cheeks were soaked. Her eyes bloodshot. And in her hand hung almost two feet of dark-brown and red-streaked hair. What was left attached to her head was half brown, half blond, and a couple inches longer than shoulder length.

She felt lighter than she had in years. Not just

physically, but mentally.

She'd read somewhere years ago that hair holds energy, and that the best way to shed negativity was to cut your hair. That by doing so, you eliminate the negative influence from periods of antagonism and adversity and can gain a fresh start.

With the sublime lightness infiltrating her mind, Lacey believed it was true. Without a doubt, she had just chopped off at least ten years' worth of poison. She could already breathe more easily. Hold herself taller. Feel a glimmer of excitement reaching up from the depths of her soul. She almost seemed to be vibrating...like she was tuning into a great cosmic energy field humming with hope.

But she wasn't finished. If she was going to make this transformation complete, she needed more than just a new eye color and shorter hair. She needed to ditch the brown and red, as well.

Tossing the ponytail in the trash, she flew from her bathroom into her parents' bedroom, into the master bath, and rifled through her mom's cabinets until she found the box of hair coloring Mom used to hide her greys.

Back in her own bathroom, Lacey haphazardly dried her hair then applied the blond dye. She hadn't had blond hair since she first covered her natural color at sixteen.

Twenty-five minutes later, she rinsed her hair, trimmed the ends, dried it again, and then stared in the mirror.

She couldn't recognize herself. Not only was her hair shorter than it had ever been, but even with brown contacts, her eyes appeared brighter. She fingered the blond strands falling just past her chin and grinned, her tears long since dried. If she went shopping right now, not a single person would know it was her. How terrific would that be? To go out among the people and not be recognized? To be just another common, everyday citizen going about her normal life. She could drive cross country, stop in every major city, stroll openly along any major thoroughfare, and no one would be the wiser.

Finally, she could actually get away if she wanted to. Take a vacation. Today. Now.

With a gasp, her mouth fell open.

That's it!

She knew what she needed to do. And the open road was the answer.

Chapter 3

Lacey parked and hoisted her bag from the backseat and made her way inside the hotel on the outskirts of Boise, Idaho. She'd been driving for five hours and needed a break.

"Welcome to Fairfield Inn, may I help you?"

Lacey smiled at the young man behind the counter. This would be her first test. Would he recognize her? "I'd like a room for the night, please." She set down her bag and fished out her wallet.

"Certainly." With an amenable air, the man tapped a few keys on his computer. "King or double?"

"King, please." Lacey nibbled her bottom lip and absently raised her hand to twirl her hair, which she did when she was nervous. Only there was no hair to twirl. Feeling foolish, she dropped her hand to the counter.

The man slid a keycard across the counter toward her. "That's ninety-nine dollars plus tax. How would you like to pay?"

"Visa." She handed over her card. Thank God her credit cards showed her first name. Lacey was her middle name, but she preferred it to Mathilda, which she hadn't gone by since first grade. The only people who still called her Mathilda were her family, and even then, only rarely. Everyone knew her as Lacey now.

Except the credit card companies. To them, she was Mathilda L. Moon.

She signed for her room, and with a relieved sigh that she'd passed her first test, headed for the elevators.

Once settled, she called her mom.

"Lacey? Honey, oh my God, where are you? I came home, and you weren't here, and—"

"I'm fine, Mom." In hindsight, she really should have left a note so her mom wouldn't have worried. But she'd been in such a hurry to split and get on the road she'd forgotten that part.

Her mom exhaled heavily. "What's going on? Where are you?"

"I'm just..." What? Running away? Adults didn't run away. That was something kids did. "I'm taking a vacation." Much better.

"A vacation?" Mom made a noise that made Lacey envision her shaking her head and pinching the bridge of her nose. "Now? Why?"

Of course Mom wouldn't understand.

Lacey flopped back on the bed. "Because now seemed like a good time, Mom."

"Lacey, what's going on? Are you okay?"

How could she explain something she didn't fully understand. She just knew she had to leave. Get away. Go somewhere no one knew her. Call it intuition, but hauling her ass to God knew where—literally, because she was driving without a map or a destination—seemed like the right thing to do.

"I just need a break, okay? I just need..." She sighed. She couldn't sum up in a few short words what she needed. The list was too long. "I'm tired, Mom." She stared up at the white ceiling. "I'm tired and confused and...I don't know who I am, anymore."

Long pause.

"Honey..." It was the tone Mom used when she consoled her or was about to make an attempt at talking her out of something. But right now Lacey didn't need to be consoled or talked out.

"Mom, I need to do this or I'll lose my mind."

Mom sighed. "I'm worried about you."

"Well, don't be. I'm an adult. I know what I'm doing." Or at least, she *should* know what she was doing. Having been coddled by a staff for so long, she'd never really had a chance to learn.

And, honestly, wasn't the anxious yet exhilarating hum that skittered like static along the edges of her nerves a good sign? Like she was alive for the first time in years? Riding out this thrum of energy to see where it led felt like the right thing to do.

"You *have* been through a lot this year, honey," her mom said. "But don't you think—"

Lacey didn't want to hear where her mom was going with that thought and cut her off. "This isn't just about the past year, Mom. It's about everything. My life hasn't been my own since I was twelve."

She'd missed out on so much. Half her childhood had been spent practicing, traveling, competing. Like a gerbil in an exercise wheel, she'd been running forever but going nowhere. The machine had become her life. How could she figure herself out when she was never given the time or a chance? From the moment she began training, someone else—usually her coach Trent—had controlled everything. What she ate, when she slept, school, conditioning. When had she had a chance to just be a girl? Once she began competing in the big events, she hadn't even been able to attend a normal school. Most of the time, she'd had tutors.

"I'm sorry, honey, I thought you were happy."

"So did I." It wasn't that she'd been *un*happy, but year after year, the hole in the center of her soul where her identity was supposed to be grew larger and larger. She'd reached a breaking point.

"I wish you would have talked to me before you ran off, though."

Lacey closed her eyes. "I need to do this on my own, Mom. If I'd told you, you would have tried to talk me out of it."

For once, she needed to experience what life was like standing on her own two feet without an overlord watching her every move. She wanted to experience life without fans and paparazzi following her everywhere. She wanted to eat junk food without hearing her coach's voice in her head. She wanted to laze around for a week without feeling guilty that she wasn't training. She just wanted to...*be*!

"So, where are you going?" Mom said.

"I don't know. Away. Somewhere I've never been." She didn't know her destination, but her intuition told her she'd know it when she got there.

"For how long?"

"As long as it takes, I guess." She wasn't going to put a deadline on this.

"You know, you can't just run away. The problems will still be here when you get home."

Lacey frowned resiliently. "I'm not running away. I'm *getting* away. There's a difference. And the problems won't be there once I figure things out. That's the whole point of this trip."

"What are you trying to get away from?"

She didn't need her mom lecturing her or planting any seeds of doubt. For once, she just wanted her mom's unquestioning support. "Mom, can't you just tell me to have a nice trip? You know, give me your blessing? I mean, God, I just want a little support for once."

"Well then, help me understand this, Lacey. This isn't like you."

And that was the point, wasn't it? This wasn't like her. At least not like the Lacey Moon everyone had come to expect. She needed to stop being what people expected and start being who she was. But she couldn't until she figured that out.

"I'm trying to get away from everything, Mom. The media. My broken leg. Doug. Trent. The constant badgering. *Me!*" She slapped her palm on her chest. "I need to get away from this person I've become and don't know, anymore. I need to find myself, Mom. I need to remember why I started down this path and decide if I want to stay on it. I can't do that at home. I can't do it with you and Trent and everybody else constantly hanging over my shoulder!"

"Okay, okay." Mom huffed. "Calm down."

She'd gotten carried away. But that was a good thing, right? She was finally passionate about something again. Okay, so maybe she was channeling that passion like a bulldozer, but still. "I'm sorry. I just—"

"It's okay. I don't fully understand what's happening with you, but I get what you're trying to do. I just wasn't ready for all this."

"I know, Mom. I'm sorry."

"You've thrown me off, honey." Her mom chuckled, but it was an uncomfortable sound, as if she were trying to shift gears and wrap her mind around the situation. "It's been a while since you surprised me."

"That's a good thing, right?"

"I don't know. Ask me again in a few days."

Lacey laughed drily. "I will."

After a moment of awkward silence, her mom said, "Lacey, I love you. Do what you need to do. Just be safe and make sure you call me, okay? I'll worry if you don't."

"I will. I promise."

After saying their goodbyes, Lacey lay back on the bed, her hands cradling the back of her head, and stared up at the ceiling. Where would this journey lead? She had no idea. But that was what excited her so much about it.

The next morning, Lacey made her way farther north, deeper into Idaho along Highway 55. The longer she drove, the more the landscape began to resemble something out of the old west. The architectural motif was more or less rugged log cabin chic, and many places had foregone paved parking lots in favor of plain old dirt or gravel.

Around lunchtime, she saw a sign for Hope Falls. She liked the sound of that. Hope Falls. Would she find hope there?

Even if she couldn't, could she at least find lunch? She was starving. Her stomach had been rumbling nonstop for the last five miles.

Following the highway into town until it dead ended at a lake, forcing her to turn either left or right, she turned left and searched for a place to park. She needed to gather her bearings and decide whether to backtrack or search for a route to the nearest interstate. Or stay.

After parallel parking along the side of the street, she plucked her jacket and handbag from the passenger seat and hopped out into what really did strike her as a Wild West town, only with cars instead of horses, although she was sure horses were around here somewhere. The place was too rustic not to have a horse farm or two.

The buildings lining both sides of the street had the same feel as those in one of the many spaghetti westerns she'd watched with her grandpa as a kid. One even looked like a converted saloon, with an upstairs balcony where she could imagine the working girls in their full skirts and low necklines waving to the cowboys below, beckoning them to come up for a romp.

Damn, there was a lot of brown. Brown paint, brown shingles, brown brick. Brown roads. It looked as if a constant stream of muddy water melted down from the surrounding mountains during every rain, staining the pavement, and the locals had just learned to accept it.

In the direction she'd come from was Hotel Hope Falls, which seemed to be the most updated building in the area. Of course, it was still brown. She crossed the street toward it and began walking south along the sidewalk. She'd passed a bunch of restaurants just a short ways back.

The sidewalk steadily inclined away from the lake, and after a couple of blocks, her leg began to ache. Even though she'd been in physical therapy for months, she'd never exerted herself this much in the real world. Still, it was surprising how weak her leg still was. She would need to start walking more and build up her strength.

Another two blocks later, she came to a cozy corner diner named Pappy's. Black, wrought iron tables and chairs dotted the front patio, and a large pink and green neon sign was centered on the front. The motif reminded her of something out of the fifties.

Once inside, she felt like she'd stepped back half a century. Old school rock and roll played from a jukebox, and a large U-shaped counter dominated the center of the room. Booths lined the perimeter and white Formica tables dappled the remaining space. This had to be what the old malt shops of the fifties looked like.

"Have a seat wherever you like, sugar. I'll be right with

you." A waitress holding a coffee decanter winked and gestured toward a nearby booth. Her nametag read "Shirl."

Lacey bit her bottom lip and brushed back the blond strands hanging around her face as she slid into a booth with red, pleather seats.

A moment later, the jukebox changed songs to "Runaround Sue," and Lacey smiled. She liked this place. When she was little, she'd spent a lot of time with her grandpa. He had always listened to the oldies. Had said that music these days was weak and not really music. Music from the fifties was fun, carefree, something to tap your feet to. True to form, she was tapping her sneakers against the black and white tiled floor and drumming her fingers on the table. In a way, it felt like Grandpa was sending her a sign.

This is where you'll find yourself, Mattie.

Grandpa had never called her Lacey. He'd always insisted on referring to her by Mathilda. Or Mattie. That had been his nickname for her.

She had loved those times with him. He'd died the year before she won her first X Games, so he'd never gotten to see her compete. Now she realized just how much she missed him. How much she longed to spin and dance to those oldies but goodies again.

"Hiya." Shirl returned with a smile. She was slim, maybe in her early fifties, with coiffed, red hair. Her darker roots showed traces of grey. She handed her a menu and held up the decanter of coffee she was still holding. "Coffee?"

"No, thank you." Lacey had never been a coffee drinker. "Do you have tea?"

"Sure do. Be right back, honey."

Lacey watched her shimmy away then looked out the window at the—yes—brown stone and wood three-story office building across the street. Evergreens jutted skyward all around. Fir trees were definitely the dominant vegetation in Hope Falls.

There was something serene and homey about the town. Congenial. Relaxing. No one seemed to be in a rush. If Grandpa was giving her a sign, he'd picked well. She could definitely find herself in a place like this.

"Here you go." Shirl set a Lipton tea bag, a small metal pot of hot water, and a glass of ice water on the table. "You need more time to look things over?" She gestured toward the plastic-covered menu with her yellow number two pencil.

Lacey glanced down and scanned her choices. "Um..." She'd been so busy reminiscing she hadn't even looked at the menu. "What's good here?"

Shirl perked up as if eager to educate a newcomer. "Pappy's is known for our burgers, sweet potato fries, and shakes." She pointed to a blackboard on the wall behind the counter. Over twenty flavors were written in brightly colored chalk of all hues, the lettering fat and bold. "We've got the best veggie burger this side of the Mississippi, too."

Wow. That was saying something since California was the predominant culinary force in the western states, especially when it came to veggie burgers.

"Okay, um...I'll try the veggie burger then. And the sweet potato fries. And an Oreo shake. Can I get caramel in that, too?" Might as well break all the rules. She was finding herself, right?

Shirl scribbled on her pad, nodding. "Sure thing, sweetie. Anything else?"

"No, thank you."

Shirl collected the menu with the practiced movements of someone who'd been waiting tables all her life. "Be right up, honey." She scuttled off to put in the order, and Lacey scanned the inside of the diner.

Locals gave her curious glances but otherwise paid her no attention. As if she were just another passer-thru and nobody special. Not Lacey Moon, Olympian and X Games champion.

A thrill shot through her. She might just be able to pull this off. Be an invisible nobody. Walk down the street without anyone running after her for an autograph or photo op.

While she waited for her food, she pulled out her phone and did a search for a place to stay while she was in town. Because, yes, she'd decided to give Hope Falls a shot. She'd stay here a few days, maybe a week, see how it went.

Hotel Hope Falls looked nice, but she wanted something more obscure. Someplace that felt like home and offered extended stays, but was more isolated. Surely, there was a cabin rental place around here. Places like Hope Falls always had cabin rentals.

Within minutes, she found two that looked promising.

McCord Cabin Rentals and Evergreen Cabins. Both had availability, and both were close enough to Hope Falls not to be in the sticks, but far enough away she wouldn't feel crowded.

Okay, Grandpa, if you really want me here, you decide which cabin place I should stay at. Give me a sign.

Bobby Darin's "Dream Lover" cranked up in the jukebox just as the bell jangled on the door. She looked up, her index finger still poised over her phone's touch screen, and her jaw dropped.

The specimen of tall, dark, and handsome that entered stole her breath, along with her motor skills and ability to form coherent thoughts. All she could do was stare as he crossed to the counter and swaggered onto one of the barstools in an easy way that bespoke he'd done so a thousand times. And from the way the others in Pappy's reacted to him, he was a regular. Several of the patrons nodded, waved, or grinned in greeting, and the waitresses all seemed to brighten, as if they'd simply been waiting for him to show up.

"Hi, Scott," Shirl said with a wink.

"Hey, Shirl." The deep timbre of his voice overruled every conversation in the place, traveling to Lacey's ears as if it had been made just for her.

He wore a perpetual scowl, but not in a way that made him seem unfriendly, just...intense. Guarded maybe. As if he'd gotten so used to pushing people away with just a look that the expression had taken up permanent residence on his face.

He glanced up and down the counter, returning the greetings of those around him, and then unfolded the newspaper he'd carried in and began to read.

She was still studying him a moment later when his gaze lifted and met hers as if he'd felt her staring. Sucking in her breath, she buried her face in her phone again, absently tapping her finger on the link for McCord Cabin Rentals.

Decision made. Thanks to the handsome, brooding man at the counter who had forced her to look busy instead of gaping at him like a starstruck groupie.

As she finished making her cabin reservation, Shirl returned with her food on a large oval-shaped plate.

"Here you go, sugar. I'll check back in a few."

Lacey hadn't expected such an oversized spread, but it looked and smelled mouthwatering, and before she knew it, she had inhaled half the burger and the fries. She'd been hungrier than she thought.

"Here's your order, Scott."

Lacey was chomping out another bite of her veggie burger as one of the waitresses handed a to-go bag to Mr. Gorgeous. He pressed his lips together in what she imagined was his attempt at a smile, took the bag, and stood. As he made his way to the door, he glanced sideways at her again. This time, instead of looking away, she sat a little bit taller. This might be the last time she saw the guy, and she kind of wanted to commit that striking, brooding face to memory.

His pace slowed as he neared the door, and his

expression softened. The faintest of smiles touched his mouth. It wasn't much as far as smiles go—almost imperceptible really, but that didn't matter.

He was smiling. At her.

She smiled back, still holding the burger in front of her mouth.

With a subtle nod in her direction, he pushed open the door and exited.

She continued to stare after him as he walked toward the parking lot on the other side of the restaurant and climbed into a dark grey Dodge extended cab truck that looked like it had seen its share of salt spray and muddy puddles.

"Don't get your hopes up, honey."

Lacey snapped from her daze and looked up at Shirl, who winked down at her. "Oh, uh...what?"

Shirl bobbed her head toward Scott's truck as it pulled from the parking lot. "Our Scott there." She waved as the truck drove past. "Don't get your hopes up for that one."

"I'm not...I wasn't..." She glanced out the window then down at her mangled burger.

Shirley laughed. "It's okay, honey. We all have our dreams about Scott. Even an old grandma like me." She propped her hand on her hip, holding her ever-present coffee decanter in her other hand. "After all, he's just about the handsomest thing ever to happen to Hope Falls. A young thing like you can't help but notice an eligible bachelor like Scott, am I right?" She giggled and continued without waiting for an answer. "But I feel it's my duty to tell you not to waste your time. Scott hasn't dated anyone in ten years. Tragic story. Just tragic." She shook her head, but it was obvious she was simply waiting for an invitation to spill all.

"Why do you say that? What happened?" And just that quickly, Lacey took the bait, even though every bone in her body loathed her for it.

As a victim of gossip more times than she cared to remember, she hated the shit, but her desire to learn more about the man-god who had just walked out the door was stronger.

Shirl's eyes twinkled, obviously pleased she'd found an audience who hadn't yet heard the story. Lacey made a mental note to watch what she said around Shirl.

"It all started ten years ago," Shirl said. "Scott was the biggest football star Hope Falls had ever seen. Earned a football scholarship to Oregon. Everyone was sure he'd go pro after college. A few pro scouts even tried to talk him into going straight into the big leagues, but Scott was too smart for that. A lot of talent *and* brains in that one." She paused, shaking her head regretfully. Then she inched closer and lowered her voice. "He would have been a star if not for what his girl did to him."

Chapter 4

"Daddy!"

Scott set his bag of food on a bench overlooking Hastings Skatepark and knelt to catch his daughter as she launched herself into his arms.

"Savannah, be careful," her mom said.

Scott shook his head at his ex, Theresa, as he hefted Savannah and stood. "No, it's okay." He kissed Savannah's cheek. "You're not big enough to hurt your dad, yet. Are you, birthday girl?"

"No!" Savannah giggled.

"That's right." He hugged her and pinched her nose.

Someday Savannah would be too big for him to pick up and rest on his hip. Too old to indulge him his doting, fatherly love. But not yet.

Theresa tucked her brown hair behind her ears and crossed her arms. "How are you?"

Scott grinned blankly at Savannah as he set her down and watched her grab her skateboard and dart back to her friends. "Are you still planning on moving in two weeks?"

"Yes."

"Then how do you think I am?"

In two weeks, Theresa was taking Savannah away from

him. Well, not really away, but two hours south was far enough to feel like away.

Theresa shifted her weight and averted her gaze back to the dozen or so friends who had joined Savannah for her birthday party at the park.

"I'm sorry, Scott."

He stabbed his fingers through his hair. "I can't believe you're doing this to me all over again, Theresa. Destroying my world without even consulting me. Without even getting my input first. Just like before, when..." His jaw clenched as he watched Savannah skateboard down a slope to the other side, where she zoomed up the incline, pulled a u-ey, and rocketed back down to the flat. He hated thinking about the past.

"That's not fair," Theresa said. "This is nothing like what happened when I got pregnant." Her face reddened with guilt.

Theresa didn't like talking about how Savannah came to be any more than he liked to think about it. But even though they'd dealt with all that crap years ago, it sometimes still felt way too fresh.

Scott blew out a defeated breath. "I know. I'm sorry. I shouldn't have said that. But, damn it, Theresa, it feels exactly the same. I feel like this is a nightmare and I'm going to wake up and realize this has all been a huge mistake and that you're not really taking her two hours away."

Theresa sighed and lowered her head. "What do you want me to say, Scott? I can only say I'm sorry so many times."

He turned and snatched his bag of food off the concrete bench, more to expend his frustration than because he was hungry. "Why can't Brian move here?"

But Scott already knew the answer. Theresa's fiancé Brian was a big-time potato farmer. He couldn't move. His business was south, so if Theresa was going to marry him, that's where she had to be. And she was taking Savannah with her.

In less than two weeks.

"Scott, you know Brian can't move here."

He sat on the bench and dug out his to-go box of burger and fries. "I know, but damn it, Theresa. You know how much Savannah means to me."

"And you'll see her every weekend if you want."

"Two hours one way, Terry." He gave her an affronted look. "I can't take eight hours to pick up and drop off my daughter every week, and you know it." He had work. Not just at the cabins, but at the high school, as well as for the park if they needed him for volunteer maintenance. And what about in winter? Two hours was how long the drive took without snow and ice piled on the roads. Not to mention, the drive would get old for Savannah fast.

Theresa made a noise of capitulation as Scott bit into his burger. "We'll figure something out. Okay? I know how much Savannah means to you. I won't keep her from you."

Ten years ago, the last thing Scott had wanted was a daughter, but Theresa had had other plans. Without warning him, she'd stopped taking the pill and gotten pregnant. She'd said it was because she was scared of losing him when he went off to college.

The betrayal of trust had destroyed their relationship, but not his love for his daughter. The first time he held her, he knew he would never love anyone or anything more. She was his life. His world.

And now Theresa was taking her away.

The knife drove into his heart again. And just as before, Theresa was the one holding it.

He frowned against the memories of the domino effect Theresa's actions had stirred into motion that night ten years ago. The night he learned what she'd done, he'd been so angry, so hurt. He couldn't comprehend how someone who claimed to love him—who he had loved with all his heart—could pull such a devious, life-changing trick on him.

In a heated flurry, he'd left her house and driven home, stunned, eyes misty with tears.

He winced as he remembered the impact. The sound of crumpling metal.

The way life as he knew it ceased to exist in the blink of an eye.

Feeling pain in his heart, he lifted his gaze to his nine-year-old daughter as she threw another trick on her skateboard. Losing her now, after she'd become his entire life, made him feel like he was reliving the car crash all over again.

The crash that ended his football career.

The crash that had almost killed him.

Chapter 5

Lacey pulled the blanket she was snuggled under farther up her body, hugging the bowl of popcorn she was munching on against her chest.

For a week, she'd remained mostly secluded in her cabin except for a trip into town for groceries. The place was fully furnished, so it had all the comforts of home. And the lake view from the private back patio was breathtaking.

She liked the place so much she'd extended her rental contract for another month.

At midnight, the movie she was watching ended, and she returned her empty bowl to the kitchen. As she rinsed it out, she shivered. Was it her, or was it colder inside the cabin?

A check of the thermostat sent a shard of alarm through her. The heat wasn't working. And with the temperature outside near freezing, heat wasn't a luxury she could do without.

Damn it. Pulling on the chunky, light-blue sweater she'd bought in town after leaving Pappy's that first day, she hustled to the bedroom, where she pulled the rental paperwork from the bedside table and turned on the lamp. Surely, there was a maintenance number.

Within seconds, she found the phone number along the bottom margin and grabbed the phone.

"McCord Cabins answering service."

"This is La—er, Mathilda Moon in cabin thirty-six. My heat isn't working."

There was a brief pause, and then, "We'll send someone out. He should be there within the half-hour."

"Okay. Thank you." She hung up and paced back to the living room, where she waited on the couch, cuddled under her blanket, distractedly watching the late movie. Some horror flick. Why did they show these kinds of movies at such a late hour? Anyone who watched them wouldn't get any sleep. But maybe that was the point. Anyone up this late wasn't sleeping anyway.

Twenty minutes later, headlights flashed on the wall, and she hopped up to see a truck pull into the driveway.

Hurrying toward the door, she pulled it open as the service tech made his way to the porch.

"Thank you for coming out so late. I—" Her words caught in her throat.

The maintenance tech who had come to save her from freezing her ass off was none other than the man she'd drooled over at Pappy's five days ago. Scott. The man who'd suffered more than anyone should ever have to suffer at such a young age, according to the story Shirl told her.

He wore a puffy, green Oregon Ducks coat, grey knit scarf, and a green and yellow Oregon skullcap with a pom-pom on top. Dark brown—almost black—hair peeked out in tufts from under the cap, and dark scruff covered his proud, square jaw.

His gaze met hers and his steps briefly faltered as recognition lit his eyes. "Are you Mathilda?" He spoke as if he couldn't quite believe it.

Lacey looked away. She hated lying to this guy. "Um, yes. But everyone calls me Mattie." If Grandpa could be considered "everyone," it wasn't a total lie.

"Pleasure to meet you, Mattie." He stepped in front of her, and she lifted her gaze to his once more.

He looked like he was trying to put together a puzzle, studying her as though he wasn't sure what to make of her. God, he was tall. As in way tall. She had to crane her neck to meet his gaze.

"So..." Scott's eyes narrowed then he glanced over her head into the cabin. "I hear your heat's not working."

She was plenty warm enough now, thanks to him, but that wouldn't sustain her through the night unless he stayed. Which no way would that happen. Lacey hadn't come all this way just to hook up with a piece of hot man flesh. This trip was about finding herself, not her libido, even if her libido was currently making a persuasive argument about being found.

"Yes." She stepped aside to let him in. He towered over her as he crossed the threshold and beelined for the utility room. He moved like a jungle cat, sleek and silent, but full of purpose.

She followed, pulling her sweater more snugly around her, recalling the story Shirl had told her. Who would have thought the man in front of her, who carried himself with such strength and control, had once been a mangled mess of broken bones, lacerations, and bruises? Was the crease jutting up from the inside edge of his left eyebrow a scar or just a product of too much scowling?

Scott had plenty of reasons to scowl, too, if what Shirl had told her was true. If Lacey thought she had problems, Scott had her beat. Going from being a promising wide receiver with the entire world at his fingertips and nothing but success in his future to having his dreams yanked out from under him in less than a second was way worse than anything Lacey had ever faced.

And how do you trust again after being lied to about something as important and life-changing as a baby? No wonder Shirl had told her not to get her hopes up.

She hovered nearby as Scott inspected the furnace.

"Looks like your pilot light went out." He glanced over his shoulder. His gaze softened once it met hers.

She didn't know a pilot light from a flashlight.

"Is that hard to fix?"

"No. Shouldn't be." He faced the furnace again, turned something off—or on, she really didn't know—then checked his watched as he faced her. "Let's give this a few minutes and try and relight it." He settled against the open door. "You were in Pappy's the other day."

He remembered. A thrill ran through her. "Yes."

"You're not from around here." He spoke so matter-of-factly. Like a cop who'd taken her in for questioning. Was that a by-product of having been stripped of emotion or just the way he was?

"No." She squirmed under his intense, scrutinizing stare. Did he recognize who she *really* was? Was her cover blown? "I drove up from Utah."

"Just passing through?" He crossed one ankle over the other.

With a shrug, she glanced at the floor and raised her hand to play with her hair, only to drop it when she remembered her long tresses were gone. There was nowhere to hide.

"Just taking a break from life," she said.

Scott nodded and checked his watch. "How long you plan on staying in Hope Falls?"

"I don't know. I haven't really thought about it. Right now, I'm set for a month."

Regarding her again with a nod, he glanced out the nearby window. "Hope Falls is a good place to take a break."

"Oh?"

"It's quiet here. The people are friendly." He pushed away from the door and glanced at the furnace. "And if you can handle the cold, it's a pretty place to lose yourself if what you need is to be lost."

Was he reading her mind or regurgitating his own thoughts? Thoughts that had helped him get through losing his football career before it even started.

"Getting lost sounds about right." Lacey brushed her hands up and down her arms and hunched forward in an effort to warm herself.

"Complicated life?" His gaze sliced into hers.

"You could say that." She pulled herself up and hugged her arms around her waist to keep her sweater in place.

"And you think spending time in Hope Falls can uncomplicate it?" His knowing eyes softened as he studied her in such a way that made it clear he thought she was in the right place.

The easy yet truncated conversation felt nice. Like ice breaking kind of stuff that could lead to friendship. "Yeah, I think it can. I drove into town five days ago and knew this was where I needed to be." At least she could be honest about that.

"How did you know?"

"I had a feeling." Talking to him was surprisingly easier than she thought it would be.

The corners of his mouth lifted slightly. Was that a smile? For her? Scott gave the impression he didn't smile much, but she'd gotten two out of him. One at Pappy's and now this one. Okay, sure, they were tiny smiles. Almost microscopic. But a smile was a smile.

She leaned back in the chair. "When I entered Pappy's, I felt..." He cocked his head to one side, waiting for her to continue. She felt her cheeks heat. "Never mind, it's silly."

"No, tell me. What made you decide to stay?" He appeared almost hopeful.

She blew out a breath. "Pappy's reminded me of my grandpa. When I was a kid, we'd listen to the oldies together and dance and sing." Those were such fond memories...from a time before she'd been turned into a brand. "Hearing those old songs at Pappy's took me back. It was almost like my grandpa was there with me, telling me I should stay here for a while."

Another smile. Bigger this time. Like he'd let down his shield for a moment.

Scott had a wonderful smile. It completely changed the construction of his face. Instead of a brick wall, he became a window, revealing a piece of his soul. In that instant, his heart and goodness shone through.

"You and your grandpa were close?"

She nodded. "Yes."

Scott nodded then checked his watch again. "Okay, let's try this." He turned toward the furnace, manipulated a couple of switches, then struck a match. A flame lit and he stepped back as he blew out the match. "There you go."

Lacey stood as he closed the door. "That's it?"

"Yep. Unless it goes back out. If that happens, I'll need to clean the line. Hopefully that won't happen, but if it does, just call us back."

"Thank you."

"Just doing my job." He zipped his coat.

"So, you work here then?" What were the odds that she'd seen him at Pappy's right before randomly choosing to rent a cabin here. Maybe Grandpa *had* been there. Maybe he *had* been telling her something.

Scott started for the door. "You could say that. My brother and I own this place."

"You own it?" She hadn't seen that coming.

He nodded as he opened the door and stepped onto the porch.

"And you do the maintenance?" Call her silly, but she couldn't see the owner fixing the breaks.

He adjusted his Oregon Ducks skullcap with its out of character fluffy pom-pom. "Only when the regular maintenance guy calls in sick."

Lucky me for colds and flu.

She hugged her sweater around her. "Sorry you had to come out. You were probably sleeping, huh?"

He grinned. The biggest he'd shown her yet. "It's just sleep. I'll be fine. I couldn't let you freeze to death." His grin grew into a smile, and he actually looked like he was about to tell a joke. "That wouldn't look good for business."

His gaze lit on hers. She felt like he'd just given her a gift. Like maybe he was flirting with her. But that didn't coincide with what Shirl had told her. She'd said Scott was a quiet, guarded man. Private. Not interested in "girls." But his guard sure felt like it had fallen in the last fifteen minutes. Reserved men bent on avoiding romantic entanglements didn't strike her as the type to joke and flirt with women they didn't know.

With a soft giggle, her face warmed, and she glanced away. It was hard not to feel enraptured under his attention. "I suppose you're right. A frozen guest would probably put a kibosh on cabin rentals."

When she glanced back up at him, his mouth worked as if in amusement, then he reached into his pocket and pulled out a business card. "Here." He held it toward her.

"If your pilot light goes out again, or if anything else needs fixing, call me direct. That's my cell." He pointed to the card as she took it.

"Thanks." She stared down at it.

Scott McCord, Owner and Chief Financial Officer. So he worked the books, too. Talk about having a hand in every pot.

"I'm available twenty-four seven. You need anything, just call."

Lacey got the feeling Scott didn't offer his personal assistance to just anyone.

"I'll keep that in mind, but I'm sure everything'll be fine now. Thank you."

Offering a tight smile, Scott nodded once then turned for his truck. "Night, Mattie."

"Good night."

She waved as he backed down her driveway. When she returned inside, heat poured from the vents again.

And as she tucked his business card inside the palm of her hand, heat poured through her body, as well.

Life had just gotten interesting in Hope Falls.

Chapter 6

"Hi, sugar!"

Lacey smiled at Shirl as she took a seat at the counter inside Pappy's. "Brown Eyed Girl" by Van Morrison was playing on the jukebox.

"Hi, Shirl."

"Coffee?" Shirl held up the decanter as if she could goad her into a cup.

"No thanks. Just tea, please."

Shirl busied herself behind the counter then returned with a small metal pitcher of hot water and a tea bag. "Thought you'd left us days ago, sugar."

"Just catching up on some 'me' time." Lacey poured water in her cup then ripped open the packet, pulled out the tea bag, and dunked it.

"Nothing wrong with that, honey." Shirl winked and left her to peruse the menu as she waited on another patron.

Spending time by herself had hit the mark, but after a week tucked inside her cabin, Lacey had begun to go a little stir-crazy. For once, she wanted to get out. Go shopping. Sightsee. When was the last time she'd gone sightseeing without a gaggle of paparazzi and fans tagging along? And she really needed to get a professional haircut to fix the tragedy she'd made of her hair by unceremoniously whacking it off.

"You ready to order, honey?" Shirl held her pad and pencil at the ready.

Lacey ordered a Cobb salad but stopped Shirl before she could scoot away. "Is there a hair salon nearby?"

Shirl's smile lit up the diner. "Sure is, sugar. You'll find Marian's Salon three doors up on the other side of the road. But why do you want to cut your hair? It's plenty short already."

That was something no one had ever said about her hair. Then again, it had always been over two feet long. At least for as long as she could remember.

She ran her fingers over the back of her head. "I just want a trim."

"Well, Marian'll do you right." Shirl winked and took off with her order.

Two hours later, Lacey turned her head left and right, inspecting Marian's handiwork in the mirror. Not only had she shaped up the ends so they weren't so uneven, she'd also fixed the color so it wasn't as brassy. The result was a warm, honey-dipped blond with muted highlights.

"I love it." She'd never thought she'd have short hair, but now that she saw how fun short hair could be, she couldn't see going back to long.

Marian unsnapped the cape covering her clothes and flipped it to the side. "It's a new you, dear." She leaned on the back of the chair and winked at Lacey's reflection.

What a hoot Marian had been. Only marginally more discreet than Shirl, but clearly part of the heartbeat of Hope Falls, the owner of the salon had regaled Lacey with humorous anecdotes about townsfolk she didn't even know. Another lady getting her hair cut had laughed as Marian relayed a story about her and how she had fallen off a snowmobile last winter and broken her arm, all because she'd been chasing her cheating husband into the mountains.

"Yeah, well, he nearly lost his big toe to frostbite, so it was worth it!" The lady had said, laughing. "The cheating bastard."

Lacey had gotten a kick out of the way the women bantered back and forth like old friends, feeling as though they'd welcomed her into the fold without even knowing who she was.

Scott had been right. The people in Hope Falls were very friendly.

After paying, Lacey wandered back out into the lovely weather. It was unseasonably warm for the last week of September, so she took off her jacket and tossed it in the passenger seat of her car before driving off in search of adventure.

A few minutes later, she drew in her breath as she turned the corner and saw a skate park. A big one. Kids were enjoying the last gasp of summer, zipping up and down the sloping sides on their skateboards, grabbing air and grinding the rails.

A sign out front read Hastings Skatepark.

The name sounded familiar. She'd heard of this place. Tony Hawk had been there years ago. She'd been just a kid, but in the skateboarding community, news like that made the rounds. And even at ten years old, she knew who Tony Hawk was. After all, she'd gotten her start on a skateboard.

Parking, she plucked her jacket off the seat, made her way into the park, and sat down on a concrete bench.

So many kids. So much laughter. The memories of her own escapades on a skateboard filtered into her mind.

Parents milled the outskirts, some holding up phones to record their kids. One little girl with dark brown hair zoomed fearlessly down the far wall toward a short tunnel. She flew up and around the concave doorway and back toward the wall, arms out, eyes alert. So intense. She couldn't have been more than nine or ten years old, but she had the practiced focus of a professional.

The little girl reminded Lacey of herself when she was that age. So determined. Hungry. Ready to conquer the world. How things had changed.

"Hey, how's your heat?"

Lacey tore her gaze from the little girl and looked up, shielding her eyes against the sun. Mr. Tall, Dark, and Handsome was walking toward her, sans the Oregon Ducks coat and skullcap from the other night. Today he was wearing a navy-blue T-shirt and dark-blue jeans that hung just low enough on his hips to make him look like a hipster, even if that hadn't been his intention.

And wow! Scott had serious arms. Until now, she'd only seen him in long sleeves. In short sleeves, it was clear he took care of his physique. But she didn't miss the scar slashing his thick biceps. A remnant of the car crash?

He stared at her expectantly. Only then did she realize he'd asked her a question.

"I'm sorry, what?"

"I asked how your heat is. You know, in your cabin?" His dark eyebrows raised in amusement as he angled his head curiously.

"Oh, um, yeah. It's fine. Not that I need it today." She lifted one arm as if to catch rays of sunshine in her palm.

He glanced toward the blue sky then back to her. "Summer's last hurrah. It'll be plenty cold in a couple of days, though. Storm's coming."

"How do you know?"

He bent and patted his knee. "My knee says so."

"Oh." The reminder of what she'd heard about his accident made her glance away.

Now that she was getting to know him, she hated that Shirl had revealed so much of what had happened to him ten years ago. It put her in a delicate position. She already knew all about his past, which made things awkward. Should she pretend not to know about the car crash that ended his football career? Should she pretend she didn't know about how his high school girlfriend tricked him by getting pregnant? Or did she fess up and tell him the truth? But doing that would make him think she'd been inquiring about him, even though she hadn't. Shirl had volunteered everything. Lacey just hadn't stopped her.

"Your hair's nice." He gestured toward her hair.

Her fingers shot up to the back of her head. "Oh, thank you. I had it done."

"I like it." He took a seat beside her. "So, what brings you out here?" He nodded toward the skate park, which to non-skateboarders probably looked like an elaborate swimming pool without water.

How much should she tell him? "I used to skateboard. When I was a kid."

Scott's eyebrows rose. "Really? I never would have imagined that."

"It's true."

"Were you good?"

Good enough to transition to snowboards and win three X Games and two Olympic gold medals.

"I could hold my own. How about you? Did you ever skateboard?"

He blew out a puff of breath. Lacey imagined that was as close to a laugh as he got. "No. I played football. I wasn't coordinated enough to skateboard."

"It takes as much coordination to play football as to ride a skateboard."

He regarded her with a sideways glance, his hard stare liquefying as one corner of his mouth lifted. God, those tiny smiles felt like precious gifts.

"Maybe," he said. "But skateboards and I...?" He squinted at the concrete hills and valleys. "We never got along." He paused. "I think it's the height." He looked back at her. "Being six four is a bit of a detriment when it comes to sports that require riding around on something with wheels. I think it's easier for shorter people to keep their balance on a rolling surfboard. Me? Not so much."

Was he flirting again?

"I guess you're right. Six four *is* a bit tall for a skateboarder." And was she flirting back? Yes. Yes, she was.

She turned her attention back toward the little girl sailing around the park like a mini-Lacey Moon.

"So, Mattie, what do you do?"

It took her a second to register that he was talking to her again. She wasn't used to being calling Mattie.

"I'm sorry, what?"

"I asked what you do for a living."

Ice flew down her spine. She hadn't been prepared to answer questions about herself. "I'm in sales." The lie flew out of her in a panic. In a way, though, it was true, because didn't she sell herself to the devil every day as a competitive snowboarder.

"What do you sell?"

"Sporting equipment." She was a piece of sporting equipment, wasn't she?

Scott's face showed his surprise. "You don't strike me as the sports equipment salesperson type."

She longed for this line of questioning to end. "Well, I'm not sure I want to do it, anymore. I'm taking some time off to decide whether I want to continue doing this for a living or if I want to try something else." At least that wasn't a lie.

"Like what?"

Like continuing to live a lie in Hope Falls for the rest of my life to see if these feelings I have for you will pass or grow stronger.

She knew life would catch up to her sooner or later, though, which meant she needed to tread carefully with Scott.

"I don't know," she said. "I used to work as a snowboard instructor in Utah." It wasn't a total fib. As a teenager, she'd run a couple of snowboarding workshops for kids out of Park City as part of a community campaign. She'd helped teach some of the local children the basics of snowboarding. "I really enjoyed that," she said.

"Why'd you stop?"

She shrugged, not able to come up with a good enough lie. And since telling the truth wasn't an option, keeping her mouth shut seemed the best course of action.

Scott's head bobbed up and down, anyway, as if he understood completely where Lacey was coming from, despite her lack of an answer. "So, you're here to figure things out."

"Yes."

A faraway look briefly glazed his eyes. "I had to do that once." His gaze drifted to the skating area. "About ten years ago my whole life did a one-eighty. Hell, maybe you could say it took a three-sixty." Resigned content washed over him as he drew silent.

But Lacey could tell he was reliving the past in those long, pensive moments.

Then he straightened abruptly as he pressed his palms

up his thighs. "At any rate, Hope Falls helped me figure things out. It's a good place to do that. Maybe it'll do the same for you." He glanced at her with eyes so brown they looked almost black. Even so, they held a gentle warmth that wrapped around her like a protective blanket. "You know how you said the other night that you felt your grandpa had given you a sign that this was where you needed to stay?"

She nodded.

"Well, maybe he did."

"You really think so?"

"What I think doesn't matter. What matters is whether or not you think so?"

They stared at each other. No words, no movement, just an intimate meeting of eyes. The rest of the world faded. The laughing children disappeared. For a moment, it was just the two of them, and it felt as if they were suspended inside a private bubble shielded from everything else.

Then a high-pitched screech pulled Scott's attention around. In a flash, he was on his feet.

"Savannah! Oh my God, honey, are you okay?" He leapt into the bowl and rushed to where the girl with dark hair lay on her side. Her board flipped and flew across the concrete, landing upside down.

That was his daughter? The girl with the mad skills and wicked lines was Scott's child?

Lacey shot up and hurried down the wall. She retrieved the girl's skateboard then joined him. "Is she all right?"

He was helping her sit up.

"I'm okay." The little girl sounded like she was trying to reassure her dad more than herself. "Just fell."

She looked shaken but uninjured.

"You need to be more careful." Scott helped her to her feet.

"I was. I—"

But Scott wasn't having it. His controlled demeanor was gone, replaced by panic. "You could get hurt, Savannah. This isn't like snowboarding. There's no snow to cushion your fall. Here, you hit concrete. You could break an arm or a leg or—"

"She looks okay," Lacey said, touching his hand, trying to calm him.

She didn't want to tell him that hitting snow wasn't as "safe" as he thought. Snow hit back just as hard as concrete, especially when it was packed over a layer of ice.

But his thoughts seemed to have taken him to a darker place. One that was scary and too close to his own past.

Lacey jumped into calm-down mode. "Nothing's broken. Not even a scratch, right?" She knelt and winked at Savannah. "You're all good, right?"

Savannah nodded, her eyes filled with worry as she glanced up at her dad. "I'm sorry, Daddy."

Scott paced away and blew out a heavy breath.

Lacey tapped the tip of Savannah's nose and gave her a conspiratorial smile. "Don't worry, he's just having a daddy moment. He'll be fine. My dad used to react the same way when I fell." Her dad had nearly had a heart attack many times until he got used to seeing her fall and get back up.

"Are you a skateboarder?"

"I used to be." She stood.

"Really?" Savannah's eyes opened wide, and for a moment, Lacey feared Scott's daughter had recognized her.

"Uh-huh. A long time ago, though." She helped dust off Savannah's clothes. "Trust me, your dad will get used to the falls. Mine did."

"I don't think I'll ever get used to seeing her fall." Scott raked his fingers through his hair, still agitated.

Lacey offered him a reassuring smile then turned back to Savannah. "You've got major talent, kiddo. Mad chops. I was impressed watching you."

Impressed? Try inspired.

Savannah beamed as if Lacey had paid her the highest compliment imaginable.

Scott planted his hands on his hips and blew out a frustrated exhale, but he finally looked relieved.

"By the way, Savannah, my name's Mattie." Scott's cheeks reddened as if he was embarrassed for failing to introduce her. But, really, could Lacey blame him? This was his kid. He was in the midst of a fatherly crisis, which meant he didn't need to expend mental faculties to remember his manners. "You sure you're okay?"

Savannah nodded. "Are you a friend of my dad's?" She looked between her and Scott.

"Mattie's renting one of our cabins." Scott brushed his hand down his face as if he was still trying to pull himself together.

Skateboarders continued to whir around the park but blessedly stayed out of the bowl so Scott could tend to his daughter.

"Maybe we should get back up top," Lacey suggested.

"Yeah, okay." Scott absently nodded. "You're right." Scott took Savannah's hand and guided her to the wall.

In the few times Lacey had seen Scott, he'd been quiet, calm, and collected. Seeing his daughter wipe out had drawn out a different Scott. One who was flustered and upset. Probably experiencing a flashback to his own traumatic accident, even if falling on a skateboard was nothing like being hit by a car. But try and explain that to his overstimulated mind.

Once topside, Lacey handed the skateboard back to Savannah.

"I think it's time we head home, hot shot." Scott knelt and unfastened Savannah's helmet. He sounded like he was feeling better, if not still a bit unsteady.

"Can we stop by Pappy's for a shake first?" When Savannah pulled off the helmet, long dark hair the color of her dad's spilled over her shoulders.

"I don't know." Scott tucked her hair behind her ears. "Do you think scaring your dad like that merits a marshmallow shake?"

"Daddy, pleeeeeaaase."

Scott stood and sighed. "Okay, but only a small one.

No ruining your dinner."

Savannah beamed and turned toward Lacey. "Wanna come with?"

Seems the friendly townsfolk extended to the children, as well.

Lacey's gaze shot to Scott's. "Oh, not me. I ate there for lunch and already had my daily quota of milkshake."

"You sure?" Scott tucked Savannah's helmet under his arm. He sounded more than down with his daughter's invitation.

She smiled. "No, thank you. I'm fine. You two have fun, though." The last thing she needed was to get too close to Scott and his daughter. Not when she couldn't be honest about who she was.

"Okay. Another time maybe." His warm, dark eyes held hers for a moment as his cheeks colored. Then he motioned for Savannah to head toward the exit.

Lacey followed them out.

Once he got Savannah settled inside the cab of his truck, he took a step back, out of his daughter's line of sight. He halfheartedly lifted his arm toward the skate park. "Thank you for helping out back there."

"No problem." Lacey had plenty of experience handling worried dads. She'd mastered her own.

"I guess I kind of lost it. I've never seen her fall like that. I do volunteer work here and see kids fall all the time, but—"

Lacey touched his arm, quieting him. His gaze dropped and landed where her skin met his. "It's okay. You don't have to explain a thing. I totally get it. She's *your* kid. Seeing her fall isn't like seeing other kids fall."

His skin was warm, his arm firm. He felt like coiled power ready to pounce, making her draw in an unsteady breath. As his gaze met hers again, the muscles in his forearm flexed under her fingers, rippling as if responding to her touch. She gulped and gently disengaged, drawing her hand back to her side.

Awkward silence followed until he cleared his throat and blinked several times. That same expression from the other night was on his face. The one that made her feel like a riddle he was trying to solve.

Finally, he inhaled and straightened. "You're right." He gave her another of his tiny smiles. "Thank you for...well...just thank you."

"Any time." The southerly breeze blew the ends of her hair over her face, but she hardly noticed, too transfixed by his stare.

His heavy brow ticked inward above the bridge of his nose. "Well, I'd better go." His boots scuffed the pavement as he stepped back.

"Yeah, me, too." She started for her car.

He walked around to the driver's side of the truck. "See you later, Mattie."

She waved as she unlocked her door.

If her life wasn't already so complicated, and if she didn't need time to sort her shit out, Scott would make a nice diversion. But she had already lied to him about her name and her "job." She didn't want to lie to him about anything else, and lies were all she had to give if she wanted this trip to achieve what she'd intended, which was to find herself, not a man to share a bed with. Scott McCord seemed like too nice a guy to drag into her problems. He deserved better than she could give.

But damn her if she didn't want him in a way she'd never wanted a man.

As she watched him drive away, she shook her head. "Grandpa, what have you gotten me into?"

Chapter 7

The following Friday, Scott and his brother were performing routine maintenance and upgrades on one of their cabins. Every summer was a race against the next winter as they updated their cabins and prepared for ski season.

He parked beside Liam's truck and was greeted by his brother's yellow Lab, tail wagging and tongue hanging out.

"Hey Rosco." He rubbed the dog's head and started for the porch.

The Lab followed him inside to the kitchen, sniffing the takeout bag from Pappy's. Scott found his brother's denim-clad legs sticking out from the cabinet under the kitchen sink.

"About time you returned," Liam said. "I'm starved." He pushed himself to his feet.

Scott handed over the bag then knelt on his haunches and peered inside at the new pipe his brother had installed. "Sorry. Lost track of time."

"You? Lose track of time? Yeah, right." Liam set down his carryout and tested his plumbing by washing his hands.

No leaks.

Scott stood and grabbed a bottled water from the

counter. Liam had his number. He hadn't lost track of time. He'd dawdled at Pappy's on purpose in hopes he would see *her*. The petite blonde with the brown eyes and big heart. Mattie. Who he hadn't been able to stop thinking about since the first time he saw her almost two weeks ago, especially after bumping into her at the skate park.

"Well, the sink's finished." Liam's grit-splattered face turned toward him as he pulled out his container of food. "Hey, where's yours?"

"I already ate." Scott chugged a gulp of water and turned toward the living room so he didn't have to see the accusatory expression on Liam's face.

"Okay, what's up with you?"

"What do you mean?"

"You know what I mean."

Scott only ate at Pappy's when he had Savannah with him. Otherwise, he ordered his food to go. But today his need to see if he could bump into Mattie had overruled his desire to get back to work, so he'd made an exception to eat in, much to the surprise of every waitress and almost every customer in the joint.

"What are you? My dad? Come on, it's nothing." For ten years, he'd been able to resist falling for the opposite sex, but something about Mattie made him *want* to fall. Hard.

She was so petite, so lithe, so...beautiful. He loved the way her short hair curled over her shoulders, the way her smile warmed his heart, the gentle singsong melody of her voice. Everything about her seemed ideal. As if she'd been made to tempt him. And tempt him she did. For the first time in a decade, he actually...*wanted*. Not just sexually, but in a way that felt deeper than anything he'd felt before. And he hardly knew Mattie. Not even Theresa had made him feel this way, and he'd been prepared to marry her until the truth came out.

Liam jarred him from his thoughts. "You've been off your game for days, Scott. What's going on with you?"

"Nothing. Drop it." Scott tossed a frown Liam's way. It must have gotten the message across, because Liam held up his hands in surrender.

"Fine. Dropped. Jesus, you don't have to be a dick about it."

Shit, had he come off that gruff? He hadn't meant to, but then again, he was torqued. This was his last weekend with Savannah before Theresa took her two hours away to a new home. So, not only was he jonesing for another dose of Mattie, but he was twisted up inside over losing what had been his life support after the accident and throughout his long recovery. It was a wonder he hadn't literally bit Liam's head clean off.

"I'm sorry, Liam. I'm just..." He couldn't even say the words.

"This is your last weekend with her, I know."

Scott's frown deepened, and he propped his hand on the wall as he lowered his head. "What am I going to do without her? She's everything to me. Damn Theresa for fucking up my life all over again."

"Theresa's a bitch." Liam crunched into crisp lettuce

on his burger. "I've never forgiven her for what she did. I can't believe you did." He spoke around a mouthful of food.

Scott tossed the empty bottle in the recycle bin. "I only forgave her for Savannah. As messed up as that whole situation was, I did get something good out of it." Good? No, something *great*. Something fabulous! A daughter who had been the key to bringing him back from the brink. If not for Savannah, Scott might not have come out of the accident as clearheaded as he had.

Liam seemed to sense the direction his thoughts had taken, because he quickly changed the subject. "Why don't you start pulling out the fridge while I eat? When I'm done here, I'll help you move in the new one."

"Sure, yeah."

He and Liam had co-owned McCord Cabin Rentals for the last six years. Before that, it had just been Liam. He'd bought the property from their parents straight out of college and converted it to a resort. Scott had moved here his sophomore year to help out and be closer to Theresa, who he'd met the summer before. He'd thought they would always be together. How wrong he'd been.

Their parents, who ran a potato farm a few hours southeast, had originally bought the property in Hope Falls to use for family vacations. They'd sold only a portion of their total acreage to Liam, so they still held family gatherings here a couple times a year at their parents' cabin, which was more like an estate. But even Scott's younger sister had transplanted to Hope Falls permanently, even though she was spending a few months back home now that fire season was pretty much over. She was a smokejumper trained out of the Hope Falls base.

There was just something about this place that called to the McCord children.

He couldn't deny that he hoped Mattie would feel the same pull. There was something magnetic about her, and even though it was irrational to expect her to abandon her prior life, he wanted her to stick around.

Liam finished lunch, and the two of them moved in the new refrigerator, cleaned up, and headed off to clear a fallen pine along the back edge of the property where Scott led nature hikes in the summer.

As they drove along the gravel road, throwing up water from the puddles left over from yesterday's storm, Mattie's blue Ford Escape approached from the opposite direction.

Scott perked up and craned his neck as she passed without even a glance their direction.

"Who was that?" Liam said suspiciously, throwing Scott a curious look.

Scott quickly turned front. "No one."

"Uh-huh." Liam's eyes narrowed. "That's why you nearly climbed over me to get a look at her."

"Shut up. I did not." Scott scowled out the window.

"Yeah, whatever. She's the one renting cabin thirty-six, isn't she? Mathilda Moon?"

"Mattie."

"Ooohh, Mattie, is it?" Liam chuckled. "So, you do know her."

"She called for maintenance last week when Mike was

sick. Pilot light went out on her furnace."

"And I bet you lit it, didn't you?" Liam's sarcastic tone grated Scott's nerves.

"I *fixed* it, yes."

Liam said nothing for a few seconds then, "She's pretty." He harrumphed in that way that said he'd been checking her out, too.

The green-eyed monster rose in Scott's blood. The thought of Liam moving in on Mattie didn't sit well. The guy wasn't known to be the settling-down type. More like love 'em and leave 'em. And Mattie was too sweet for that kind of treatment.

"Keep your hands off that one, Liam."

"Why? You staking a claim?" Liam cast him a challenging sideways glance.

Scott glared at him. "No. I just don't want you pawing the guests."

"Bullshit!" Liam barked out a laugh. "You've never voiced concern before. Why now? What's so special about *Mattie*?"

"There's nothing special about her." Liar. Everything about her was special.

Liam pulled up to the fallen tree, threw the truck into park, and shut off the engine. "You're so full of shit, Scott." He pushed open the driver's side door. "It's been ten years, for God's sake. Stop being such a flake. If you want her, ask her out. If you don't, I will."

Liam saying he would ask Mattie out was akin to him saying he was going to fuck her. And that shit didn't fly.

Scott threw his door open, stormed to the back of the truck, and got chest-to-chest with his brother, who stood an inch taller than he did. But that didn't mean Scott couldn't kick his ass. "Stay away from her, Liam."

Liam's brown eyes narrowed as he smirked. "Thought so. You're hot for her."

Scott ricocheted back and blew out a derisive puff. "I'm not discussing this with you, so drop it. Just stay away from her." He reached into the bed of the truck for a chainsaw. "You're not good enough for her, anyway." He turned his back on his brother and marched toward the tree, already yanking on the cord to start the saw.

It buzzed to life, and he began trimming off the branches.

It was over two minutes later that he glanced up to find Liam standing a few feet away, wearing a sullen scowl.

Scott shut off his chainsaw and straightened, suddenly feeling like a chump for throwing that last insult at his brother. What had happened to his wife hadn't been his fault. But Liam had never gotten over her death, and his deviant behavior proved it. He'd turned into an unfeeling ass.

Liam stood rooted in place, a pillar of regret and seething emotion. "I may not be good enough for her. That much could very well be true." He paused and set his jaw, jutting out his chin. "But at least I still get out there. At least I try. You've just given up completely."

"You don't try," Scott said with a subdued shake of his head. Fucking every woman who remotely flicked his interest then bolting the next morning like he couldn't get away fast enough was not trying. It was hiding. "You've given up, too. You just think you haven't, which is way worse."

Chapter 8

Late Saturday afternoon, Lacey stood amid what looked like a culinary war zone in her cabin's kitchen. She had thought sautéing mushrooms and roasting a chicken would be easier.

What had gotten into her at the bookstore yesterday? At the time, buying Julia Child's cookbook had seemed like a great idea. Now, with the kitchen in disarray, she wondered what madness had persuaded her to think she could do this.

Okay, so maybe she was being a little dramatic. The stuffed bird was in the oven—*finally*—and smelled heavenly, but oh gracious! What it had taken to get it there. She'd never trussed a chicken before. Check that off her bucket list.

At least she'd had the common sense to make the salad ahead of time and stick it in the refrigerator. Now, she just needed to wait an hour and twenty minutes and start basting with cream then make the gravy. In the meantime, she could clean up this mess.

As she wiped down the counters an hour later, she noted that she hadn't heard the heat kick on in a while. Come to think of it, it was a bit chilly in the cabin. She hadn't noticed in the oven-heated kitchen. But when she checked the thermostat, sure enough, the heat wasn't working again. And with October upon them, the weather was taking a turn for the colder.

She pulled Scott's card from her purse and bit her bottom lip. Maybe she should just call the regular maintenance line. Then again, he *had* told her to call him direct if she had any more problems with the furnace. Who was she to ignore a direct order from the owner?

"This is Scott."

"Uh, hi. This is Mattie Moon. In cabin thirty-six?" Her words lilted like a question.

"I know who this is. How are you? Is anything wrong?"

"The furnace isn't working again."

"Damn. I'll be right there. You don't mind if I bring my daughter, do you? I've got her this weekend."

"I'm so sorry. I should have called the main line and—"

"No, no. I'll handle it. I just wanted to make sure you're okay with me having to bring Savannah with me."

"Of course. That's fine."

"We'll be there in ten minutes."

She finished cleaning the kitchen as she waited then sat down at the table with a cup of tea. At least the oven was keeping this part of the cabin warm.

She had just finished her tea when Scott arrived.

When she opened the door, he lifted his nose and inhaled. "What smells so good in there?" He held a box of tools in one hand, and Savannah's hand in the other.

"I'm roasting a chicken." She stepped aside to allow them in. "Hi, Savannah. Good to see you again."

"Hi." She waved and trailed after her dad.

"Smells delicious." Scott set down his tools, took off his gloves, and stuffed them in his pocket.

"You're welcome to stay. There's plenty for everyone."

Scott smiled at her. "Are you sure. I don't want to impose."

She laughed. "Believe me, you're not imposing. I don't know what made me think I could eat a six-pound chicken by myself."

Scott looked at Savannah. "You want to stay for dinner, Savvy? Sure smells good."

She liked his nickname for Savannah. Savvy was better than her childhood nickname. *Moon Pie*. Thank God no one called her *that* anymore.

Savannah giggled in that way little girls do when their single daddies are flirting with the idea of asking a woman out.

"I take that as a yes." Scott cleared his throat and threw Lacey a sheepish grin.

"Good. I'll set two more places."

While Scott went to work on the furnace, Lacey set Savannah up with cartoons then returned to the kitchen to prepare for the next phase of war. Hopefully, making the gravy wouldn't be as hard as the first battle with the stuffing and trussing.

She was bent in front of the open oven, removing the

fat from the roasting pan, when Scott entered the kitchen. "I think we're all fixed." He stepped forward. "Here, let me give you a hand with that."

She stood as he knelt and tipped the roasting pan so all the juices flowed to one corner.

"Thanks." Her gaze met his, and her face flushed with more than just the heat from the oven. She continued spooning the savory juices and fat out of the pan. "What was wrong with the furnace?"

"Just needed to clean the line. You should be fine now."

She set the bowl of drippings on the counter.

He placed the pan back on the rack and stood as she basted the chicken with cream and closed the oven.

"So…" He gestured toward the stove. "What motivated you to go to all this trouble?"

Sighing, she shrugged and shook her head. "Honestly, I don't know, but the idea sounded good at the time." She laughed at herself, and he chuckled. What a warm sound.

"Is this part of your search for what you want to be when you grow up?"

Cute.

"Something like that."

"Don't tell me you're thinking of becoming a chef."

She held up her hands as if warding off a crowd. "After what I just went through, hell no." She grabbed a pan out of the cupboard. "Today, I fought a chicken, and the chicken almost won. I don't think becoming a professional cook is in my future."

"I see." He crossed the kitchen to the window and glanced outside. "I always loved the view from this cabin."

"Me, too. It's worth suffering a little lack of heat for."

He grinned then glanced in the direction of the utility room. "Sorry that keeps happening to you, but it should be fixed now."

"I don't mind. I mean, it could be worse." Besides, if her heat kept going out, she could keep calling him over to fix it. That sounded like a fair trade, especially when just his presence was enough to turn up her body heat.

Savannah popped in, all smiles. "Daddy said you used to teach snowboarding. Is that true?"

Scott's face flushed. "I hope you don't mind. Savvy loves snowboarding even more than skateboarding. I might have mentioned that you used to be an instructor."

Lacey's heart picked up pace, but she forced herself to remain calm. Lots of people taught snowboarding. It didn't automatically mean they were international sports stars. And, honestly, knowing he'd talked about her to his daughter gave her a thrill. It shouldn't have, but it did.

She addressed Savannah. "Yes, it's true." Now she was lying to nine-year-olds. This just got better and better.

"Cool." Savannah beamed. "Have you ever met any stars? You know, like Lacey Moon?"

Lacey's heart nearly flew out of her chest. "Umm..."

"She's a huge Lacey Moon fan," Scott said nonchalantly. "Worships her."

"Is that so? Even after what happened at the Olympics?" She looked from Scott to Savannah and back.

"A lot of people jumped off her bandwagon after that." She hadn't missed the rumblings through the snowboarding community that she was past her prime and should leave the sport after such a horrific fall.

Part of her agreed. But a part of her still clung to hope.

Scott ruffled Savannah's hair. "That was tragic. But we're still Team Lacey, aren't we, Savvy?"

"Lacey's tough," Savannah added with an exuberant nod. "She'll be back. Just wait. She'll come back stronger than ever." The little girl took a step closer. "Your last name's Moon, too. Are you Lacey's sister?" Her voice rose hopefully.

If her heart didn't stop racing, she would pass out. "Um, no. I'm not Lacey's sister."

"Savvy..." Scott's voice took on the placating tone of a teacher about to explain a math problem. "Lots of people who aren't related share the same last name."

Savannah made a pouty face. "Well, she kinda looks like Lacey. Kind of." She turned toward Lacey. "You're really pretty, just like Lacey." She sounded pleased with herself.

"Well, thank you, Savannah. That's sweet of you to say." Lacey hoped her voice sounded normal, because inside, she was in a mini-panic.

"So, do you still snowboard?" As is often the case with young kids, Savannah darted off on another tangent, dropping the subject of Lacey Moon like it was yesterday's news.

"Not since last winter," she said truthfully.

"Are you good?"

"I'm fair." Lacey smiled at the little girl before glancing toward Scott. He had moved back to stand next to the window again, an introspective expression on his face as he watched her with his daughter.

"Will you teach me?"

Scott pushed away from the wall. "Mattie's here on vacation, honey. She didn't come here to teach snowboarding to precocious little girls like you." He ruffled her hair.

"Daddy!" She giggled and ducked away from his hand.

"Why don't you go watch cartoons while Mattie and I finish dinner? Okay, pumpkin? You can talk snowboarding with Mattie later."

She huffed and made a stink face at him as if he'd just told her to brush her teeth and get ready for bed so the grown-ups could be alone. Then, just as quickly, she broke into giggles and darted back to the living room.

Lacey heard her changing channels a few seconds later.

"Sorry about that," he said quietly, sliding up beside her at the stove as she turned off the oven and donned her oven mitts.

"Don't worry about it. She's just excited." She opened the oven, pulled out the chicken, and set the pan on the stove.

"Can I help?"

She pointed to the platter on the opposite counter. "Can you grab that?"

A minute later, the stuffed chicken rested on the platter, covered by aluminum foil.

"Now what?" he said.

"Pray I don't mess this up."

He laughed as she poured the drippings back in the roasting pan and turned on the burner.

He was a handsome man, appealing in the most primal way. But when he laughed, he became breathtaking.

"You have a nice laugh," she said, averting her gaze, feeling her cheeks instantly flush with heat.

When he didn't answer and grew silent instead, she glanced back up at him. The way his eyes burned into hers nearly stole her breath.

"Savvy was right about one thing." He moved closer, his full lips pressing into a thin line.

"What's that?" She sounded as dazed as she felt.

"You *are* pretty. Very pretty." He took a shaky breath, as if he was nervous. "Even prettier than Lacey Moon." He waited a few seconds as his face flushed crimson. Then he grinned awkwardly and turned toward the living room. "Savvy, get washed up, honey. It's almost time to eat."

In that moment, one thing was certain. She needed to break her furnace again in the very near future.

Chapter 9

The following Friday night, Lacey sat at the counter inside
Pappy's, sucking down the last of her mint chocolate chip
shake. Last Saturday's dinner with Scott and Savannah still
sat in the center of her mind, even though she hadn't seen
Scott since. But the evening had been...well...sort of
perfect. Conversation had been easy, and Scott had stayed
to help her clean up while Savannah watched a movie.

She'd thought he was going to ask her out, but despite
several leading looks and what Lacey thought were a few
false starts, Scott ended up leaving without making a date.

He was probably just nervous, but she couldn't blame
him. It *had* been a while since he'd asked a girl out. It was
bound to take time to work up the gumption.

She set her empty shake glass on the counter. She was
going to start gaining weight if she didn't get back to a
sensible diet. At least she'd been burning some calories by
doing her physical therapy exercises twice a day. And she'd
started walking every day, too, trying to build her strength
back up in her injured leg. She was mostly out of the woods,
but healing a broken leg took time, even if the fracture had
been a clean break.

The cook called from the back, "Shirl, Kim and Angie

just called in sick."

She glanced toward Shirl, whose face fell as she turned toward the parking lot as if she would see a deluge of water rushing toward them. "This isn't good, Jake. They'll be here any minute."

"I know. Just thought I'd better warn you." Jake turned back to his grill.

"Who will be here any minute?" Lacey asked.

"The kids." Shirl started bustling behind the counter. "It's Friday night, and there's a football game at the high school."

Another waitress named Rosie rushed out to bus tables as she said, "That means it's about to get real in here."

"Can I help?" She had no idea what made her volunteer, but it sounded like the right thing to do. Maybe all the niceness in Hope Falls was rubbing off on her.

Shirl and Rosie glanced at each other, and then Shirl gave a sharp nod. "Hop on back here. Here's an apron."

A blue and white flash of fabric flew at her. She quickly pulled it on and followed Shirl around as she gave her the five-minute tour.

"They'll want burgers and fries and milkshakes. There'll be a line out the door, but the rush will come fast and leave just as quickly. But for about an hour or two, it'll be mayhem. You sure you want to do this?"

Maybe she shouldn't have been so quick to lend a hand.

Lacey nodded. If she could handle years of her coach,

the paparazzi, and sponsors, she could handle this kind of pressure. "Just point me."

"If you get their drinks, Rosie and I will sweep around and take their orders. Then you can help clear the tables. The rest we'll make up as we go. You ready?"

Lacey nodded as a pair of cars full of teenagers pulled into the parking lot.

"Here goes."

For the next hour, Pappy's was a flood of adolescents stuffing their faces, laughing, and carrying on. Apparently, the home team won, leaving everyone in high spirits.

Lacey rushed from table to table, delivering drinks on the front end, bussing them on the back. It was exhausting, but exhilarating. Working as a waitress was about the furthest thing she could do from being a snowboard champion, but no one was the wiser. No one here recognized her, and she found herself laughing even as she worked harder than she'd worked since training for the Olympics. In some ways, waiting tables was even harder work than training. It definitely wasn't for the faint of heart. She developed a newfound respect for those who worked in the service industry.

True to Shirl's warning, a little over an hour after the rush started, Pappy's began to clear out. The worst was over, the calm settling in once more.

Lacey set about collecting the discarded plates, delivering drinks to the last wave of kids, and wiping down the U-shaped counter when a large set of rugged hands caught her attention as they eased onto the white Formica surface. The fingers crisscrossed, and she glanced up to see Scott sliding onto a barstool.

He was wearing that same Oregon Ducks skullcap and coat from the first time he fixed her furnace. He pulled off his cap and stuffed it in his pocket.

His dark brown hair stuck out in every which direction until he combed his fingers through it, settling it in thick waves.

"What happened?" he said. "Couldn't pay for your meal and they put you to work?" This time, the way his eyes twinkled made it obvious he was flirting.

She smiled and set a cup and saucer in front of him. "I was here finishing dinner when two waitresses called in sick. I sort of volunteered myself since it sounded like a mass of humanity was about to descend. Which, of course, it did." She looked around. "Where's Savannah?"

"She's with her mom. I normally get her on weekends, but Theresa moved south on Monday." An unreadable but pained shadow passed through his eyes, and Lacey's heart went out to him. Clearly, Savannah was the center of Scott's universe and he adored her.

"I'm sorry."

"It is what it is, right? Nothing I can do but try and make the most of it." He unzipped his coat and shrugged out of it. Underneath, he wore a black and white referee's shirt.

She gestured toward his shirt. "What's this? You're a referee, too?"

He glanced down at his attire. "Oh, yeah. I officiate the

games."

Lacey cocked her hip to one side and began ticking off on her fingers. "You're an owner, you do maintenance, you're an accountant, you volunteer at the skate park. Now you're a referee? Is there anything you don't do, Scott?"

The guy had a serious case of the busies. Did he even know how to relax?

"I run a summer football camp and do volunteer maintenance for the county park, too."

Was this guy for real? Did he ever just...stop? Smell the roses?

"What do you do for fun?"

An odd expression came over his face as if he didn't understand the question.

"You do know how to have fun, don't you?" She stepped closer and eyed him.

"Sure. Yeah. Of course." But the way he said it made it clear he was coming to the realization he hadn't experienced anything fun in a long time.

She could only guess that he'd buried himself in work to keep from thinking about the life he'd lost. The life that was ripped away against his will ten years ago.

"Hey, there's nothing wrong with being a workaholic," she said with a wink. "Just remember to have some fun once in a while." She handed him a menu even though he probably didn't need it then hooked her thumb behind her. "I'll go get Shirl to take your order."

Hurrying off, she realized how apropos her advice was. Wasn't her need to have more fun part of the reason she'd road tripped her way to Hope Falls in the first place? Because she'd been drowning in the residue of corporate America? Snowboarding hadn't been fun in years. Instead of feeling the thrill of trying a new trick, she feared wiping out, because that meant failure. Instead of the exhilaration of the brisk wind on her face, she felt only biting cold and a yearning for her pajamas, a blanket, and a fireplace.

When you began to resent the day in and day out of your career, it was time to look elsewhere for fulfillment.

After cleaning the rest of the tables, sweeping the floors, and fetching drinks for one last group of kids, Lacey returned behind the counter. She had felt Scott's eyes on her for the duration, and now was no different. As she approached with a decanter of decaf, he set his half-eaten burger down, watching her in a way that lit all kinds of fizzles in her belly.

"Need a top-off?" She lifted the decanter and nodded toward his cup.

He placed his hand over his mug and shook his head. "No, thanks. I'm good."

"Don't you normally get your food to go when you don't have Savannah?"

His cheeks lifted as he glanced down at his plate. "Shirl's been talking to you about me, hasn't she?"

He didn't sound angry, so why lie? "A little. You're quite the town's hero."

Puffing out an exhale, he shifted on the stool. "I wouldn't say I'm a hero. More like a casualty."

Lacey frowned, crossed her arms, and leaned against

the counter. "You're not a casualty. From what I've heard, you're a survivor." His gaze jumped to hers. "Shirl told me enough to know that much."

"I guess that's what I get living in a small town."

"What's that?"

"No secrets."

She arched one eyebrow. "Just because people gossip and talk about you doesn't mean you can't have any secrets. Just because they *think* they know the real you and what *really* happened doesn't mean they do. Only you know that stuff. You and whoever *you* choose to talk to about it. Those are the only people who really know the truth."

He watched her with the intensity of a hawk then said, "Why do I get the feeling you speak from experience?"

Lacey pushed away from the counter and fussed with a nearby display of salt and pepper shakers. "How does that saying go?" She met his eyes only for a second before dropping her gaze to her hands, hiding the windows to her soul. "Takes one to know one, right?"

After a brief hesitation, Scott said, "You know, you talk like a woman much older than you look."

Out of habit, Lacey lifted her hand to play with her hair only to find a lot of empty air. Even after three weeks, she wasn't used to her new hairstyle.

Scott's words hit close to home, though. She *had* grown up fast. She'd had no choice, giving up her childhood in favor of training before she turned ten years old. By the time she was seventeen, she had her own accountant. Not many teenagers earned as much money as a Fortune 500 CEO, and that sort of lifestyle had a way of abruptly ending any flicker of youth and frivolity.

Scott made a contemplative noise as he sipped the last of his coffee.

"What?" she said.

"I was just thinking." He set down his cup and popped a french fry in his mouth. "What do *you* do for fun, Mattie?"

"Me?"

"Takes one to know one, right?" This time when he smiled, his straight front teeth showed.

She bit her lip at the way he playfully threw her words back at her in a way she imagined was completely out of character for him. "Touché."

"That's why you've come to Hope Falls, isn't it? To find the fun that was missing in your own life. Tell me I'm wrong."

She sighed in surrender and offered a wan smile. "You're not wrong." But just because she could be honest about that didn't mean she could be honest about everything else. She still didn't feel comfortable revealing who she really was, no matter how much she wanted to.

The Everly Brothers' "Wake Up Little Susie" began playing on the jukebox.

"So, you didn't answer my question," she said, busying herself by filling a nearby napkin dispenser.

"What question was that?" he said before taking a bite of his burger.

"Don't you normally get your food to go?"

He tucked his bite of burger against his cheek. "Trying to get rid of me?"

"Just trying to make polite conversation."

He grinned as he chewed, watching her as if trying to decide how to respond.

After several seconds, he said, "Maybe I've finally got a reason to eat in." His trepidatious gaze burned into hers, making his meaning clear. "I mean, I'm kind of liking…" He drifted off, his cheeks shading pink. He shifted uncomfortably on the barstool as he glanced toward a group of laughing kids at the corner table. Then he seemed to find the second wind to finish what he'd started to say. Meeting her eyes again, he slid his elbows toward her on the counter. His gaze burned into hers. "I think I'm kind of liking the view here lately."

She bit her lip and felt her cheeks flush.

As "Wake Up Little Susie" neared its end, he fidgeted and cleared his throat. "You know, the last home game of the season is next Friday." His voice broke on the word "season."

His cheeks were full of color.

Recovering from his overt show of interest, she smiled coquettishly. "Are you warning me that I might have to volunteer my table-waiting services again? Or is this part of some covert football conspiracy?"

He chuckled, and the deep, nervous sound made her heart perform a little somersault. "No, I…" He cleared his throat again, pushing his fries around his plate. "I thought you might like to go to the game. It'll be…*fun.*"

He was asking her out. Very unexpected. "Are you officiating?"

"Probably, but afterward, maybe we could, you know, grab a late dinner." He gave her a crooked grin. "And hey, I can get you in to the game for cheap. I have connections."

She fought a smile and eyed him sideways. "Hmm, sounds shady. You sure this is on the up-and-up?"

The pink color in his cheeks deepened. "I promise." His eyes searched hers. "So, how about it? Would you like to come to the game? Maybe have dinner with me after?"

If she did this, she'd be crossing a line. Then again, she couldn't deny the way her heart and mind seemed to be on the same page, one pounding so hard it was a wonder it didn't fly out of her chest, the other screaming for her to say yes.

"Okay. Yes. Sounds like fun."

Relief blanketed Scott's expression. "I'll call you in a few days with the details."

The last group of kids gathered their things and left, toting Pappy's milkshakes with them, and she hurried off to clear the table, feeling Scott's eyes on her the entire time. She had a date. With him. Oh, God, what had she done? How would this work?

Hush, Lacey. It's just a date. You're not marrying the guy.

She needed to keep things in perspective and not freak out. If things progressed, she would have to tell him the truth about who she was.

Who was she kidding? Eventually, one way or another,

he would find out. Still, now wasn't the time to pull him aside and say, "Hey, by the way, I'm Lacey Moon. You know, your daughter's idol."

And what about Savannah? It wasn't just Scott she needed to think about, but his daughter, too.

When she returned behind the counter, he was pulling on his coat and smiling at her.

"You leaving?"

He nodded. "I've got a busy day tomorrow." He zipped his coat. "I'll call you soon, though." The determined look in his eyes put an exclamation point on his statement.

She waved as he headed out and made his way through the kids still hanging around outside to his truck.

It wasn't until she felt an elbow nudge her arm that she stopped staring out the window. She turned to see Shirl grinning at her like a proud momma.

"Seems someone has finally caught our Scotty's eye."

Heat blazed through Lacey's cheeks and down her neck. "No. That's...he's...you see—"

Shirl laughed and held up her hand. "Oh, honey, if you could see your face." She quieted and shimmied closer. "If you ask me, you're good for him, sugar. I know people, and I've had a good feeling about you since the moment I first saw you. Yessir, you and Scott'll be mighty fine together. How long you say you plan on staying in Hope Falls?" She gave her a wink then scurried off without waiting for an answer.

"Umm..." Despite the rush of excitement coursing through her, dread filtered in, too. She hadn't come to

Hope Falls to find a boyfriend. She'd come to find *herself*. She was messing with the whole dynamic of what had brought her here.

Still, she couldn't hold back where Scott was concerned. The more she was around him, the more she liked him.

And now she had a date with him next Friday night. She needed to tread lightly. This could blow up in her face if she wasn't careful.

Chapter 10

Scott's knee ached as he stood on the sideline during a timeout. A storm was coming. A big one from the feel of it. Not even the first week of November, and the season's first big snow was upon them.

And Savannah wasn't with him to enjoy it. She was settling into her new home with Theresa and her fiancé. New home. New school. New everything. If only there were something he could do to keep Savannah with him, but it just wasn't feasible. He worked too much, and Theresa would never agree to giving him full custody, anyway. And, despite the trickery behind how Savannah was conceived, Theresa was a good mother.

He glanced toward the stands where Mattie snuggled under the green and navy blanket he'd given her. Her blond hair poked out from under her fuzzy, light-blue cap, which matched the oversized sweater and scarf she wore under her dark-green coat. She pulled the blanket farther up her lap before cupping her gloved hands around her mouth and letting out a cheer as the teams took the field again.

Only ten seconds left, and Hope Falls High was down by three points on Mason's four-yard line. With no timeouts left, this was their last chance to win the game.

Scott blew his whistle and willed his knee to hang in there.

The center hiked the ball. The quarterback dropped back.

Scott kept his eyes on the players, watching for fouls.

The quarterback pumped, pulled the ball back in, rushed to the right. All the receivers were covered. But there *was* a gap. A small one, but if the quarterback didn't wait, he could make it to the end zone.

Scott rushed toward the action, remembering the thrill of a buzzer beater. He had played in several back in the day.

The quarterback saw the gap, tucked the ball, caught a lucky block, and broke into the end zone with only one second left on the play clock.

On the inside, Scott pumped his fists, but outside he remained stoic as the officials covering the end zone raised their arms straight in the air.

Touchdown!

Hope Falls had pulled out a win for their last home game.

He couldn't play favorites when officiating, but he was always happy to referee a game Hope Falls High won.

After the extra point sealed the game, Scott made his rounds to both sidelines then limped toward the home stands, where Mattie stood with the folded blanket in her hands.

"Why are you limping?" She hopped to the bottom bleacher. "Did you hurt yourself?"

He shook his head. "No, there's—"

She held up her hand. "Wait. Don't tell me. A storm's coming, right?" Her gentle smile, as well as her chilled-pink cheeks and nose, warmed his heart.

He glanced down at his leg then back up at her. "My knee makes me a better weather forecaster than the guy on the news."

She stepped down to the ground and smiled up at him, her brown eyes almost doe like. She was beautiful. He'd never seen such a breathtaking woman. Mattie made him feel things. Made him think he might be able to trust again, start fresh...fall in love. He'd given up on feeling that way about another woman a long time ago. But here came Mattie, and even though he barely knew her, and despite not knowing how long she would stay in Hope Falls, he found himself falling. He wanted to lose himself in her eyes. Wanted to kiss her pretty pink lips and run his fingertips over her porcelain skin to prove it was as smooth as it looked.

She glanced around. "No Savannah again this weekend?"

He shook his head. "No. But I'll get her for her fall break from school, so it's all good."

He missed his daughter, but looking into Mattie's kind eyes took some of the edge off his heartache.

Mattie stepped closer. "I love how close you two are. It's unfortunate she had to move."

He shrugged and took the blanket out of her hands. "I'll still see her. I'm just not used to her being so far away."

He was used to seeing Savannah almost every day. Now he would be lucky to see her twice a month. "I'm glad you're here, though." Before he could stop himself, he placed his gloved hand on the side of her face.

For a second, she appeared startled. Then her gaze lowered shyly as her cheeks shaded pinker than they already were from the cold.

Clearing his throat, he pulled his hand away and fought back a smile. God, but he felt like he was back in junior high again, putting the moves on the prettiest girl in school. "So, uh...you ready to go?"

She looked up at him and nodded, pressing her lips together. "Sure. Are you?"

"I just need to change." He held out his hand and felt his chest puff up a little higher when she slid hers around it, their gloved fingers lacing together.

He led her inside, and while she waited in the hall, he hurried into the locker room and changed from his referee uniform into a navy-blue sweater, blue jeans, and boots. With a nervous glance in the mirror, he straightened his hair and brushed his palms down the front of his sweater.

He hadn't been on a date in over a decade. He still didn't know *why now*? Why Mattie? What was it about her that drew him in as if she were his favorite addiction? He couldn't get enough of her.

"Here goes..." he murmured under his breath.

An hour later, after a pleasant dinner and a lot of small talk, the waitress cleared their plates and brought a piece of carrot cake for them to share. He'd decided to take her somewhere other than Pappy's. Too many familiar faces there. Too many nosy waitresses. Not that he didn't like Shirl and the others, and not that they wouldn't find out sooner rather than later that he'd taken her out, but he hadn't wanted to endure their stares and hushed whispers on their first date.

"Mmm, this is good." She licked frosting off her lip.

He took a nibble off his side of the cake. "Best carrot cake in Hope Falls."

"Best carrot cake anywhere."

He smiled at the blissful expression on her face.

After a couple more bites and a sip of decaf, Scott set his fork down and wiped his napkin against his mouth. "So, you're from Utah, right? I think that's what you mentioned before."

A subtle shadow fell over her eyes. "Yes."

"Whereabouts?"

"Salt Lake City." She kept her gaze averted.

"Have you lived there long?"

"Pretty much all my life." The shadows seemed to lift as if she'd forced them away.

He swiped a fingertip of cream cheese icing and licked it into his mouth, studying her. Just when he thought he was getting a feel for who she was, another wrinkle unfolded. She was like a Russian doll, with layer upon layer to open to get to the next.

Rather than push her for more—because, really, didn't he hate when people pushed him?—he turned the subject around. "So, what did Shirl tell you about me? I can guess, but it's better just to get it out there, don't you think?"

Her eyelashes flickered and she almost looked...guilty?

"Hey, it's okay," he said. "I'm not mad. I've known Shirl since I was a kid. She's a notorious gossip. Always has been. You don't need to feel bad because she told you stories about me."

"No, it's just..." She sighed and offered a benign smile. "I just feel weird about it. I'm not a fan of gossip."

And didn't that statement make Mattie's stock rise even higher? The more he learned about her, the more he liked her.

He'd misinterpreted her reaction. He thought she was upset because she'd indulged Shirl's gossip. And while, yes, she was a bit ashamed of that, she was more agitated because his words hit too close to the mark for comfort. *...it's better just to get it out there, don't you think?* How prophetic. It felt like Grandpa was giving her another sign, telling her to fess up.

"I'm not a fan of gossip, either," he said, before she could seriously entertain the idea of coming clean.

She played with her fork. "It's always made me uncomfortable."

"Me, too." He crossed his forearms on the table. "But I've learned to live with it."

"I can't see how anyone can learn to live with gossip." She recalled all the nasty things she'd heard and read about herself along the competition circuit and in celebrity rags found in the checkout lane at the grocery store.

"You sound like you speak from experience."

She stared at the half-eaten piece of cake. "You could say that." She swirled the tines of her fork in the icing before slicing off another bite.

He gave her a moment to finish the cake then pushed the empty plate aside, folding his hands together in front of him. "So, do you want to hear my story? The real story? Not Shirl's version, but mine. All the holes filled in."

"I don't want to pry."

"You're not prying. I'm offering."

She bit her bottom lip. "But...why? I mean, why me?"

"Why not you?" His gaze swept her face as though he were amused.

"You barely know me." She swirled her straw in her iced tea. "And Shirl implied you've never talked to anyone about what happened."

He shrugged. "Maybe it's time I did. And you're easy to talk to. That's 'why you.'" He paused and rotated his thumbs around one another. "I like you, Mattie." He hesitated and seemed to hold his breath. "Probably more than I should."

The hard angles of his features evaporated. The rugged man still dwelled within, but he wore a much softer expression now than when she first met him. One filled with affection.

"I like you, too." Her breath trembled as she quietly added, "And, yes, probably more than I should." What a gross understatement.

He took her hand. "Then let me tell you my story, just so there's no question about what really happened. And maybe because, finally, I need to put it behind me. Maybe talking about it will do that." He grinned. "And then, hey, you'll know all my secrets."

As she stared at his fingers around hers, she recalled what she'd told him at the diner last week, about how just because someone talked about him it didn't mean they knew him or his secrets. "I can't believe you've never told anyone about…" She sighed, letting her words drift off with a subtle shake of her head.

"Nope…never. I've never discussed what happened with anyone. Not really, anyway."

"Why not?"

"I don't know. I mean, after the accident, I was in the hospital for weeks. At the time, there were more important things to deal with, and I wasn't in any kind of shape to talk about much of anything, I was so hopped up on pain meds. By the time I was released, almost a month had passed, and I was more focused on dealing with and rehabbing my injuries than in rehashing that night, so it just kind of faded into the back of my mind." He hesitated and glanced down at his hands. "And maybe I didn't want to talk about it because I wasn't ready to let it go."

"And you are now?" Lacey said softly.

His lips parted as he glanced up and maintained eye contact. "Yeah, I think I am."

She was moved that he'd chosen her to be his sounding board, but at the same time, she knew what this meant. Scott saw her as more than just a passing infatuation, even though they'd only just met and were on their first date.

But it didn't feel like a first date. They'd seen each other so many times. At the skate park. At her cabin—twice. Once for dinner. At the diner the other night. All those times had felt sort of like dates. They'd been slowly getting to know each other, the undeniable attraction growing between them as the weeks passed.

He was easy to talk to, easy to be around, and damn easy on the eyes.

As she held his hand and listened, heart and mind open, he proceeded to explain how he'd come to Hope Falls the summer after his sophomore year. He told her about his parents' land, how his older brother, Liam, had bought a portion of the land and opened McCord Cabin Rentals. How he had moved in with Liam and helped him out on weekends. That he had come to Hope Falls because of Theresa and ended up staying because of Savannah.

Then he got to the gritty part. The part Shirl had summarized in dramatic flair. The part about what had happened before Savannah was born.

"My senior year, I was awarded a full scholarship to play for the University of Oregon. I had my ticket. My dreams had come true." His gaze lit on a faraway memory. "Everyone was already looking ahead to my professional career." He paused. "Then Theresa told me she was pregnant. I was stunned. We'd been so careful, and she was on the pill. Or so I thought." His lips pressed into a thin line as he took a deep breath through his nose. "We'd talked about getting married, but after I got accepted to Oregon, I'd begun to have doubts about our relationship and wasn't sure I wanted to stay with her. She'd grown so clingy and dependent. Going off to college, where I could see if what I felt for Theresa was real or whether there was someone else in the world who fit me better, was coming at a good time. But after she told me she was pregnant, my decision was made. I'd been raised better than to leave her like that. I was nothing if not responsible. So, I agreed to marry her the summer after graduation and take her to Oregon with me. I would make it work."

Lacey sat quietly as he gathered steam to continue.

"But a week before our wedding, Theresa told me the truth. She admitted that she'd gotten pregnant on purpose so I would have to stay with her. She knew the kind of person I was and that I wouldn't abandon her if she was carrying my baby."

Lacey squeezed his hand.

He smiled as if to reassure her. "I couldn't believe she'd lied to me. That she'd made such an important decision without considering my feelings. That she was so selfish she would lie to get what she wanted, all the while changing my life forever. She used me." His tight voice was edged with anger and disgust. "She ruined everything. One lie destroyed our lives. And it almost got me killed."

Lacey swallowed past the lump in her throat as he frowned down at their joined hands.

"Something snapped in me that night. I couldn't look

at her the same way. She betrayed my trust, and there was no way I could be with her after she did that. I would step up and be a father to my baby, but she and I were over."

He stopped as if preparing for the next phase of the story.

"But I was so angry. So messed up." He frowned and pointed to his temple. "In here. My head was a jumble of chaos and emotion. A disaster. I never should have driven home. I should have waited until I was more clearheaded."

"Scott..." Lacey tightened her grip on his hand. It was never good to look at the past like that...as if you could go back and change the course of events.

He held up one hand and nodded. "I know. What's done is done." His thumb caressed the backs of her fingers. "But in hindsight, I know I should have waited. But I didn't wait. I got in my car and started for home. It was late, and I was mentally drained. I never saw the drunk driver coming. I pulled up to the stop sign, barely glanced side to side, and then pulled into the intersection. He hit the driver's side square on at forty miles per hour. That doesn't sound fast, but believe me, it was. My left leg suffered the worst of it. Tore my ACL. I suffered multiple fractures. Broke my left arm. Concussion. Numerous lacerations and bruises. I was in the hospital for weeks and spent the next twelve months rehabbing my leg."

"And Oregon?"

A lopsided grin curled his lips. "They rescinded the scholarship. My football career was over. What good was a football scholarship to someone who couldn't play?"

"I'm sorry." She wrapped both her hands around his. He'd suffered so much. More than any person deserved.

"I ended up going to work for my brother while I took night classes and earned my business degree. Then I went in with him to become a fifty-fifty owner. Things have turned out the way they should have. I love my daughter." He snorted and shifted in his seat. "Hell, without her, I'm not sure I would have turned out half as good as I did. She was the only thing that kept me going. The one thing I looked forward to every day. I vowed I would be there for Savannah, to give her piggyback rides and be an active father who could take her places and do things with her."

"And you do."

He nodded. "But I've got a lot of battle wounds to show what I went through."

"Scars?"

"Both physical and mental." His brow furrowed. "I'm not so clueless that I don't know the effect Theresa's actions had on me. I know I have trust issues now because of her, and that I've struggled with..." He took a deep breath and slowly blew it out as his face flushed. "I've struggled with being comfortable enough to ask a woman out." He fidgeted and cleared his throat, his gaze flicking to hers as he gave a sheepish grin. "But I'm working on that."

She fought back a smile. "Well, that's a step in the right direction."

After nodding and gazing at her meaningfully for several seconds, he forged ahead. "And I no longer blame Theresa for the accident. At one time, I did. But that was irrational. She wasn't driving me home. I was. I should have paid more attention. I'm just thankful the accident wasn't worse than it was. I easily could have been killed."

"That's one way to think about it. At least you're still here for Savannah."

"Exactly." He leaned back with an air of finality. "So there you have it. My story, straight from the horse's mouth. Was it anywhere near the story you got from Shirl?"

"Close, but better. A lot more detail. More personal. Shirl only hit the highlights."

"Ah, the juicy highlights." He glanced down at the check the waitress had dropped by their table a while ago. "Shirl's good for dishing the juicy highlights."

They continued chatting about his past, the effect Theresa's deception and the accident had had on him, Savannah, his recovery, and his lost dreams for another hour. He seemed to be purging all the black sludge from his soul, his face growing more compassionate and softer the longer he talked. It felt nice to be the one he'd unburdened himself to.

Finally, he stopped talking, grinned, and glanced out the window as if he could feel the lightness enveloping him. Kind of like the way she had after chopping off her hair. Then he gathered the check off the small plastic tray as he met her eyes again. "It's getting late. I should probably take you home, huh?"

She'd completely lost track of the time. Checking the clock on the wall, she was surprised to find it was almost midnight.

"Wow, I had no idea it was so late." Pushing back from the table, she gathered her coat, and as they stood, she took his hand, drawing his attention. "Hey, thank you for sharing your story with me. I know it couldn't have been easy."

His gaze dropped to her mouth. "Something about sharing it with you made it a lot easier than I thought it would be."

After paying, they drove back to the cabins, neither of them saying much. He had laid a lot on her tonight, but instead of scaring her away, she felt drawn further in. If only she could reciprocate and tell him her secrets. She had a feeling he would understand, but enough fear still resided in her heart to hold her tongue.

He pulled up outside her cabin and helped her down from the truck's high passenger seat.

"Thank you for listening to me tonight," he said, following her up the steps of her porch. "It felt good to finally get that off my chest."

She unlocked her door then turned, lifting her gaze to his. "I'm glad." It had been nice to be talked *to* for a change, instead of talked *about* or *at*. She and Scott had had an actual conversation, one where she'd felt like an equal participant and not an icon. "And thank you for dinner."

He took a step closer and his gaze dropped to her mouth the way it had right before they left the restaurant.

He wanted to kiss her.

And she would let him. To hell with caution.

As he bent forward, she raised onto her tiptoes. In the

middle, their lips met, and she closed her eyes, savoring the firm, masculine caress.

The air seemed to whoosh out of his body, and he pressed closer. As his lips slowly parted and closed over hers again, his hand skimmed around her waist to the small of her back.

Thought ceased. All that existed was this moment. His mouth flirting with hers.

More.

Warmth spilled like a cascade of explosions through her body, starting at the nape of her neck, working its way down her back, between her legs, and down her thighs. All the way to her feet. Had she moaned? Yes. That was her making that soft, breathy sound as he opened and closed his mouth more forcefully over her bottom lip, his arm tightening, pulling her closer, drawing her against his body.

If she'd thought he was easy to talk to, he was even easier to kiss. The chemistry between them apparently didn't stop at the end of conversation. If anything, it intensified.

He gasped as he released her lip and pulled away just enough to look into her eyes.

For a breathless heartbeat, they just stared at each other, their breath quickening. He appeared almost in awe. Surprised maybe. As if he hadn't expected to feel what he was feeling.

Did she ever know how he felt. She was breaking the rules. She should have stopped him. Should have erred on the side of caution. Never should have kissed him. But now that she had, she just wanted him to do it again.

Then the damn broke. As if he'd surrendered to some unseen force, he pushed forward with such determination he practically threw her against the door. Her back slammed into the wood, her feet left the ground as he lifted her, and she wrapped her legs around his waist just as his mouth crashed down on hers again.

Lacey's body lit up like she'd been doused in kerosene and he'd thrown a lit match on her. She'd never felt anything like this. Such blazing passion. And the focal point was smack between her legs, right at the heart of her. Good thing they were dressed in layers, or she would have broken *all* the rules then and there.

His tongue delved into her mouth, seeking, plundering, fanning the fire. All she could do was grasp the back of his coat in her gloved fists and latch her legs around his hips so she could enjoy the ride longer.

Bliss.

Ecstasy.

Just from his kisses and the way he groaned deep inside his chest.

Finally, after what felt like not nearly long enough, his hold loosened, his kisses grew less frenzied, and his breathing stabilized.

Whatever pent-up energy had risen like an explosion had either expended itself, or he'd gained control over it.

From the molten yet restrained expression on his face when he pulled back and lowered her until her feet hit the porch, it looked like a little of both. He appeared tremulously in control as he inhaled deeply through his nose and rubbed his lips together as if still tasting her.

Flustered and a little speechless, Lacey blew out a heavy breath, nearly stumbling backward as he let her go.

"Okay, so...wow." She steadied herself by gripping the doorknob.

His lips worked into a pleased grin, and he shuffled his feet as he glanced away. "Yeah...well, um..." His gaze drew impishly back to hers, making her giggle.

He chuckled and inhaled a hearty breath as he stood taller, shoulders proud, as if he'd just roped his first calf.

"Thank you for um..." For what? Blowing her mind? Soaking her panties? Making her feel things she'd never felt? She'd already thanked him for dinner, so doing so again would be awkwardly repetitious.

Warmth poured into her face.

He placed his hand over hers on the doorknob. "Yes, thank you." His eyes flashed knowingly, as if he understood she was lost for words and could commiserate. "Good night, Mattie."

And just like that, with the reminder that he was totally unaware of her true identity, the magic blew out of the moment. Too guilt-ridden to maintain eye contact, she bowed her head. To him, she probably appeared demure, but inside, she was anything but.

He squeezed her hand then turned and practically skipped down the steps to the walkway.

As she watched him back out of her drive then pull away, she knew she was in trouble. Whatever this was with

Scott felt real. More real than anything she'd ever known. But how could it be real when she still hadn't told him who she was?

Chapter 11

Lacey vowed to tell Scott everything. But as October gave way to November and the days ticked by, the moment never felt right. A voice in her head told her there would never be a "right" time and that she just needed to spill the beans, but every time she tried, something stopped her, and the moment passed.

Despite the lie sitting between them, they continued to grow closer. But he was ever the gentleman, never inviting himself into her cabin or her into his after a date. While the front-door good-night kisses became more intimate, more familiar, more like horny teenagers making out, he never pushed for sex even though his body clearly wanted it.

Of course he would be cautious. Hadn't he said as much during their first date? He had admitted that he had trust issues. That dating was an awkward matter for him. And after what Theresa had done to him, the idea of having sex again had to make for a huge mental leap. Not one to be taken lightly. In fact, some men might have even been rendered mentally impotent after being tricked in such a deeply personal way. So if he wanted to take his time, Lacey was okay with that.

But as their relationship slowly progressed, something

else happened. Something almost as magical. Snow began to fall.

A lot of snow.

And for the first time in years, Lacey felt a whisper of her old passion for snowboarding reawaken deep in her soul. Each morning, she stood at the sliding glass doors that led to the back patio—and sometimes she even stepped outside—and stared longingly at the thickening white blanket. And each morning, the desire to retrieve her snowboards from the back of her Ford Escape, where they had remained buried and untouched for almost ten months, stirred a little more vigorously in her soul.

If she could rekindle her love of snowboarding, could she return to competition and remain in love with the sport? Or would she just get sucked dry again?

She was going on twenty-six, but she felt so much older. Or at least she had before coming to Hope Falls. Now she was starting to feel her age again. Her youthful spirit was returning, and the weary lines and dark circles she'd begun to notice on her face last year had given way to a fresh, smooth glow. Was that because of Scott? Or was it because she was beginning to feel like her old self? Free. Unencumbered from puppet strings.

With a rebellious tug, she slid the heavy glass door open and stepped outside. It had snowed again last night. Was still snowing, although not at what she assumed had been a fever pitch in the overnight. The fresh powder hit above the ankle of her well-worn Uggs, even up close to the cabin where the accumulation wasn't as heavy as farther out. From the looks of it, at least eight inches had fallen, and now big fat snowflakes drifted lazily from the grey sky, eking out every last ounce of moisture from the atmosphere.

She took another step into the snow-insulated cold. Absolute silence. The thick snowpack gobbled up every snick of noise, soundproofing the world. Hugging her mug of tea within her palms, Lacey felt like the only person on the planet, and for the first time in what felt like more than two years, she took a full, lung-expanding breath. Tension melted away, her shoulders relaxed, and she took yet another step away from the open door into what had once been her sanctuary. The magical, wintery landscape of white ice and packed snow that had fed her dreams since childhood.

"I've missed you," she whispered to the white world as she lifted her cup to her lips and sipped. "I've missed you so much." She knelt and dug her fingers into the cold, lightly packed powder with the same fascination she'd possessed as a kid.

When she was younger, she had lived for mornings like this, when fresh snow coated the slopes where she rode her board. Packed snow was what she needed for the pipe and slope style, but fresh powder was strictly for fun. There was something about hitting a pristine slope after a heavy snow, one where she was the first to touch it, the first to cut her track into the powder. She had always felt like she was discovering a run all over again at times like that, taking what the mountain gave her and finding a new path to the bottom.

Lacey looked over her shoulder, past the open patio door to the front entryway. Not even ten feet outside the front door, in her SUV, her boards waited for her, almost calling to her. *Take us out. Cut the snow with us,* they seemed to be whispering. She looked back down at the snow melting in her palm and smiled.

Maybe. Maybe I will. But not today. She wasn't ready, yet. Her body was healed, but her mind wasn't. Soon, though. There was only so long she could resist when the snow beckoned every day.

Turning, she headed back inside just as the sound of a snowmobile whirred nearby. It grew closer, and she opened the front door just as Scott pulled up in front of her cabin, his Oregon Ducks skullcap hugging his head, the little pom-pom bouncing. A layer of semi-melted snow covered his snowsuit-clad legs.

"Morning," he called.

"Good morning." She hugged her arm around her stomach and lifted her teacup in greeting. It had been a few days since their last date, but the heated memory of the way he'd kissed her stirred warmth low in her belly.

He hopped off the snowmobile and approached. Vapor puffed from his mouth as he exhaled. "I'm making the rounds. Checking on the tenants after the snow." Clouds of powder sprayed around his feet and ankles as he made his way up the lawn.

"How thoughtful of you." She bit her lip at the look in his eyes. Determination and something else. Hunger. She felt like a target he was closing in on.

"I saved you for last." The distance between them quickly evaporated.

"Oh? Why's that?"

He took the three steps up to the porch in one giant stride. "So I could do this." His gloved hands closed against her cheeks as he bent and pressed his lips to hers.

The heat of his lips, his tongue, his breath nearly melted her. Even as cold as it was outside, she suddenly felt like it was way too hot.

Breaking away, he smiled. "*Now* I can say it's a *good* morning."

Her eyelids slowly opened and she was sure a goofy, dumbstruck smile was plastered on her face. "Uh-huh." It was all her mind could come up with now that he'd sent her body into the stratosphere.

He looked much too pleased with himself. "I just wanted to come by before I left."

"Left?"

He nodded. "Once the roads are clear, I'm driving down to get Savannah. We're going to head over to Sun Valley for the weekend."

Lacey was familiar with Sun Valley ski resort. They had a state-of-the-art superpipe and terrain course. A couple of the girls she competed against trained out of Sun Valley, and she'd been there more than a few times in her career. She'd even competed there a couple of times.

She glanced skyward. "With this snow, the conditions should be good. Great snowboarding weather."

"Yeah, well, she wants to become the next Lacey Moon."

Lacey laughed. "Does she now?"

"Yeah, she's even growing her hair out so it can look like Lacey's." Scott chuckled. "I just hope she doesn't start dying it. I don't think I could handle it if Savannah turned up with red-streaks in her hair."

Lacey ran her fingers over the back of her head, remembering all too well what red-streaked hair looked like and that a lot of young girls had emulated her hairstyle. In a way, that was fortunate, because other than her snowboarding skills, she was known more for her hair than her face. Obviously...since no one recognized her with her shorter, blond hair.

"Not that there's anything wrong with Lacey Moon's hair," Scott said. "I just prefer...oh, I don't know...a more natural look." He eased in front of her, wending his hands over the tops of her hips. "And it seems I've recently developed a preference for blondes."

"Don't let Lacey Moon hear you say that." How strange to refer to herself in the third person.

"I'd say it even if she were standing right here next to us." He gazed into her eyes. "She's not the one I'm interested in."

She's exactly the one you're interested in. You just don't know it. Because she's too chickenshit to tell you the truth.

"Scott, I—"

He held up his hand. "I know. It's too early to be this

serious, isn't it?" He broke away and took a step back. "But I just can't seem to help it. I like you, Mattie."

"I like you, too." *Which is why I really need to tell you the truth sooner rather than later.* "But I need to tell you—"

His cell phone blared from inside his pocket.

"I'm sorry. Hold on." He pulled out his phone and turned away. "Hey, Theresa. What's up?"

Lacey sipped her tea and shuffled her Uggs in the snow, trying not to seem like she was listening while at the same time cursing herself.

"Okay, thanks. I'll be there around five o'clock." He hung up.

"Anything wrong?" Lacey said.

"No. Savannah just got invited to a birthday party with some friends after school, so I need to pick her up a couple hours later than planned. No biggie." As he slid his phone back inside his pocket, his gaze shifted from her to his snowmobile, back around to the snow-covered porch, then to her face once more. "Well, I just wanted to stop by before I leave. I'll be gone a few days, and…um…" He seemed to be wrestling with his words, as if he wasn't sure he should vocalize his feelings. After toeing a chunk of ice away from the edge of the porch, he said, "I'll miss you."

Lacey's eyebrows shot up. Scott didn't seem the type to say something like that just to say it. Or maybe he *was* that type but had kept that side of himself buried for the last ten years. The gruff, scowling man she'd seen that first day at Pappy's had gradually faded over the past few weeks, replaced by someone who smiled more. A man who seemed to be opening up a little more every time she saw him. Maybe she was seeing the real Scott McCord, and the man she saw that first day had simply been a shield he'd put up to ward people—especially women—off.

He took a tentative step closer. "How much longer do you think you'll be staying in Hope Falls?"

The way his voice wavered and his gaze danced over her face through guarded eyes made it clear he was searching for an answer that would give him hope.

Truth was, she hadn't really thought about when she would leave. She'd already renewed her rental contract through Christmas. "I don't know." Her eyes locked to his. "There's still so much I haven't figured out, yet." And right now, she was looking at her biggest quandary.

She hadn't expected to encounter a man like Scott when she began her trek to find herself. He'd thrown a wrench into things. Now, not only did she need to figure out who she was and what she wanted, but she needed to determine where and how Scott fit in...or even if he should. She wanted him in the picture, but a lot stood in the way before that could happen.

Scott tilted his head to the side. "What about your job? Won't they miss you? You've been here a long time already."

Lacey hastily shook her head. "Uh, I'm sort of taking an extended leave of absence." *Way to bend the truth, Lacey.*

"That's nice of them to give you the time off. Not many

companies would."

She glanced down into her teacup. "Yeah, it's a decent gig."

Shit, but this lying garbage had to stop. She had to tell him. Now. She looked up at him, but all the words she'd gathered to blurt out the truth caught in her throat.

He towered over her, a monolith of hard muscle and rugged outdoorsman that stole not just her breath, but her thoughts, as well. And yet his face looked as serene as an angel's, despite the shadow of trimmed scruff outlining his jaw. Her confession locked down and wouldn't budge as he stepped closer, his gaze cutting into hers like a soul invasion.

"I have to get going," he said, but he didn't make a motion to leave. Instead, he eased his hands over the tops of her hips. "But let's have dinner one night next week. At my place." His dark-brown eyes sparkled expectantly. "You, me...and Savannah."

Gulp. Dinner with the daughter. Officially. This was a big step, because this dinner wouldn't be like the accidental dinner they'd all had together a few weeks ago when her furnace had stopped working. She and Scott were romantically linked, now.

"Are you sure you want to do that?"

"I think she already suspects something's going on between us. She's been asking questions." One side of his mouth curled upward. "She's seen how happy I've been and knows you're the reason."

Guilt knifed her gut. "Scott, I—"

His firm lips stole her voice as they gently caressed hers. It was just one tender, burning kiss, but his mouth lingered on hers for an eternity before he finally pulled away, leaving her floating speechlessly.

"Please say yes." His eyebrows cut inward.

He seemed so eager. As if taking this step to formally introduce her to his daughter as the woman he was dating had stretched him outside his comfort zone, and he couldn't stand the idea of her saying no.

The confession she'd been so close to voicing melted off her tongue.

Every time Scott kissed her, her vocabulary skills vaporized. His lips were seriously dangerous and should have come with a warning. *Will cause temporary lapses in judgment, reasoning, and language skills. Could cause confusion. Care should be taken when operating farm equipment, driving, standing, or making important life decisions such as coming clean about one's past.*

She sighed and offered a shallow smile, vowing to tell him the truth at the next opportunity. Once more, now wasn't the right time. "Okay. Yes. I'd like to have dinner with you and your daughter."

His face relaxed. "Don't worry. She knows this isn't anything serious." The unspoken "yet" hung in the air. Even though he hadn't said the word, Lacey had seen it on his face in the way he blinked and dropped his gaze.

Her face heated. She liked the idea that whatever was going on between them could become something more serious.

"Okay, well...I've got to go, but I'll call you." Scott took a forced step back, dragging his gloved hands from her hips.

Still speechless but smiling, she gazed after him as he tracked back through her yard and mounted his snowmobile.

With a wave, he sped off, leaving a blanket of hope and expectation in his wake.

Scott couldn't remember ever feeling this way.

Something about Mattie burrowed under his skin and sparked his heart back to life. When was the last time he'd felt so alive in a woman's presence?

But he had only just met Mattie. Well, not just, but it hadn't even been two months. And she hadn't even been inside his cabin, yet. Was it crazy that he was already this addicted to her smile? To the way she made him see hearts every time his gaze met hers. To the way his body heated every time he heard her voice.

Then again, Scott had always been a bit of a romantic. Before Theresa had blown his world apart, he'd worn his heart on his sleeve, giving her endless tokens of his affection. Flowers, tiny boxes of chocolate truffles, a homemade picture frame housing a photo of the two of them snuggled on the bleachers after a football game, him still in his uniform. And every time they went someplace that had those little gumball machines filled with trinkets, he ponied up fifty cents and let fate drop a gift in his hand by way of one of those clear plastic eggs. Theresa had amassed an entire shoebox of rubber balls, plastic rings, tiny tiaras, rubber spiders, and every manner of Made-in-China nothingness. At the time, those senseless trinkets had meant everything. Not just to Theresa, but to Scott, too.

Then she lied to him.

And while he lay in a hospital bed recovering from the accident, he removed his heart from his sleeve and hid it away.

Now his heart was making a comeback. He wanted to do all those little things he'd done with Theresa again, but this time he wanted to do them with Mattie.

It had been too damn long since he'd had a woman in his life to give flowers to. Too damn long since he'd held a woman. Now that he'd met Mattie, his body needed that. It needed the supple, warm curves of her body pressed against the hard plains of his.

And something about Mattie awakened his instinct to protect. Not that she came off needy or dependent, just a bit lost, as if she were running from something. The clues were in the way her gaze shifted away from his sometimes when their eyes met, and the way she combed her fingers self-consciously through her hair as if trying to brush it over her face.

But he saw strength in her, too, like an understated fire that stirred just beneath the surface. It made for an odd combination. She seemed both scared and excited.

He wanted to think he was part of what excited her.

But she lived in Utah. How would that work? He couldn't move there, and he couldn't ask her to move to

Hope Falls. Except maybe she would want to. She said she didn't have any immediate plans to leave town.

An unexpected rush of hope raced through Scott's veins at the idea she might want to stay around for a while. The thought really shouldn't have pleased him so much, but it did.

If she stayed, who knew how far their relationship could go?

Did he want it to go there?

His heart beat a little harder at the prospect.

Chapter 12

With Scott spending the weekend with Savannah, Lacey took the opportunity to do a little soul searching. She went for a long walk in the snow, relishing the brisk air on her cheeks and the crunch of snow under her boots.

The temptation to take out her boards and cut a track down one of the many available hills surrounding her cabin had grown stronger every day, and she wasn't sure how much longer she could resist.

On Saturday afternoon, she made her way into town and browsed the bookstore. When she spied a rack of journals with colorful skulls on the covers that reminded her of Mardi Gras, she remembered how, when she was a kid, she used to keep a diary. Journaling had helped organize her thoughts more than once. Maybe it could do the same now. She grabbed one notebook with a black cover, which was made of what felt like canvas fabric over thick particleboard, and added it to her stack of books, which included Apolo Ohno's autobiography. She figured he'd been where she was now, and who best to gain insight, wisdom, and inspiration from than someone who understood what she was going through.

After leaving the bookstore, she meandered aimlessly,

taking in the Thanksgiving decorations, as well as some early Christmas lights, letting fate pull her where it may.

And of all the places it could have pulled her, a Bingo hall was the last place she would have expected. But there she was, drawn in by the crowd and the warmth. And the restroom. Because that was what had really sent her into the single-story, brown-brick lodge.

"Well, hi there, sugar." Shirl carved her way out of a group of middle-aged women who appeared to be her gossip buddies. They all eyed her with renewed interest as Shirl made her way over.

"Hi, Shirl."

"You here to play, honey?" Shirl locked her arm around Lacey's elbow and began guiding her toward the bingo hall without waiting for an answer. "You can sit next to me."

Lacey's alarms went off. As sweet as Shirl was, the woman had loose lips and what Lacey imagined was an uncanny ability to put everything she heard through a filter to ensure when she retold the story it came out even juicier and more embellished than it went in.

"My friends and I are over here." Shirl pulled her to a table along the perimeter, by a window.

The next five minutes were a whirlwind of introductions and explanations about how to play. She knew how to play Bingo, but she went along with everyone fussing over her. It was easier that way.

Then the emcee called the crowd to order and everyone got serious. Seemed these ladies meant business when it came to Bingo.

For the next thirty minutes, focus was on the guy calling out the letters and numbers, interspersed with the occasional muttered curse as someone at another table yelled "Bingo!"

"So, Miss Mattie," Shirl said during a break while the others scuttled off to the restroom or to restock their refreshments, "how you settling in at that cabin of yours?"

Lacey shrugged as innocently as she could. "Okay, I guess."

"Scott sure has been smiling a lot since you came to town. And you seem to be smiling a lot, too, I might add." Shirl's eyes narrowed and one of her eyebrows arched as she tilted her head and gave her a look that screamed she was fishing for the juicy bits.

"Oh?"

Shirl lightly shoved her arm. "Don't you 'oh' me, sugar. You know what I'm talking about."

Trying to dissuade Shirl was like trying to put out a fire with gasoline.

"We just have a lot in common, that's all." Maybe if she gave Shirl a nibble, she'd drop it.

"Uh-huh. And having lots in common is the first step toward something more meaningful."

Or not.

"I'm not even sure how long I'll be in town, Shirl." Lacey really didn't want to get into this, especially not with Shirl.

"If you were gonna leave, you'd have been gone by

now, honey. Hope Falls is like that."

"Like what?"

"Once it gets into your blood, it won't let you go. Scott came here, and look at him. He stayed. Even after his accident when he could have moved back home, he stayed. Same as his brother. Same as his younger sister." She pointed to herself. "Same as me. And you, too. Hope Falls is in you now."

Lacey shook her head and picked at a chocolate chip cookie she'd snagged from the buffet table. "I've only been here a few weeks, Shirl."

"You've been here going on two months, honey, and that's plenty long enough for this place to get ahold of you."

Two months? Lacey stared at the bite of cookie in her fingers and thought back. It had been the last week of September when she'd arrived in Hope Falls. Thanksgiving was less than two weeks away. Shirl was right. She'd been there almost two months. Where had the time gone?

Shirl giggled. "I see your brain making the connections, sugar. You're one of us now, like it or not." Her thin, overly plucked eyebrows rose high over her blue-shadowed eyes as she nodded as if she knew all, saw all, heard all. And for all Lacey knew, she did.

Which made her uneasy. Because the last thing she wanted was for Shirl to figure things out before she had the chance to tell Scott the truth. If Shirl got wind that she was Lacey Moon, there was no way she would be able to hold that snippet in, and Lacey didn't want Scott to hear the truth through the grapevine. He deserved better than that.

"Um..." She checked the clock. "I think I'm going to head out. I was thinking about seeing a movie, and—"

"Now, sugar, I didn't mean to scare you off." Shirl offered a warm, almost-apologetic-but-not-quite smile.

"You didn't, I—"

"Oh, go on. You don't need to be playing Bingo with all us old folks, anyway." She gave Lacey a wink.

"You're not old." It was the truth. Shirl couldn't have been much older than fifty, which was young by most standards.

"Aren't you sweet." Shirl tapped her arm with her fingertips. "Now run on. You have fun. And give Scott a kiss for me when you see him. Lord knows that's as close as *I'll* ever get to kissing that handsome boy."

Lacey's cheeks flamed. "I...um...I'm not—"

Shirl laughed. "Thought so." She winked. "I knew you two would make a cute couple." She turned and headed back toward the Bingo hall, and Lacey blindly made her way to the door, mortified that Shirl was aware of her relationship with Scott.

When she glanced over her shoulder, she saw Shirl pull her friends together in a tight circle. One gasped, her eyes popping open. Another beamed and clapped her hands.

Great. Let the gossip begin.

Lacey sighed. She had a feeling that no matter how much of an expert she became at putting up boundaries, Shirl would find a way right through them. That woman was like water. She could find a way through a brick wall, even if only through a hairline crack.

But Lacey could learn a lesson here. Or relearn it as the case may be. Hadn't her coach tried to tell her countless times that sometimes things were simply out of her control.

"Sometimes people come along and start trouble, Lacey," Trent had said. "Sometimes that's not their intention, but sometimes it is. No matter the case, when that happens, there's no sense worrying about it. You can't control what other people do. You can't control the world. The only thing you can control is you and how you react."

Somewhere along the way, she'd forgotten that lesson.

She was still contemplating Trent's words fifteen minutes later at Pappy's counter, a pen poised over the first page of her new journal, when her phone rang.

She recoiled at the name on the screen.

"Doug?"

"Lacey, hey."

She hadn't talked to Doug since breaking up with him two months ago.

Two months. She still couldn't believe it had been that long.

When he didn't say anything further, she sighed. "What do you want, Doug?"

"Come on, don't be like that."

"Like what?"

"I miss you, Lace."

She'd always hated when he called her that. The nickname sounded perverted coming from him. Like she was a pair of panties or something.

"Well, I *don't* miss you." She tucked her face behind her hand and kept her voice as quiet as she could. No sense giving the locals anything else to gossip about.

Doug exhaled heavily. "Lacey, come on. I want to make this right. I want to get back together. Can't we work this out?"

"Why would you want to, Doug? You didn't seem to want to work things out when you were screwing Ivanka or Iyanla or whatever her name was."

"Ivanka. And that was nothing."

"Really?" She scoffed. "I've seen the pictures, Doug, and it looked like it was definitely *something*, not nothing."

"You're making too much of this, Lace."

"Am I? What about the other girls, Doug? What about all the rest? Am I making too much of those, too?"

"What do you mean?"

She shook her head, eyes shielded by her hand and fixed on the silver-speckled counter. "Give me some credit. I know there were others. And I'm sure there were some I never even knew about. For Christ's sake, Doug, you're so good at hiding your tracks that I didn't even know about Ivanka until the end of summer, and that shit had gone on since the Olympics. We're talking seven months, Doug. Seven!" She sucked in her breath, realizing she'd raised her voice. After a quick glance to the side, she gathered herself into an even tighter bundle and said, "You made a fool out of me, Doug. You were supposed to be my boyfriend, but you left me hanging when I needed you most. You ran off with your scags when I needed you."

She realized in that moment that Doug had been a big part of her problems. He'd dragged her down with his philandering and lies. She'd known all along he was being unfaithful, but she'd just put up with it. She'd been delusional to think they could make things work.

"I'm sorry, Lace, but...I'm here now. I'm ready. Come on, give me another chance."

"Another chance to what? What makes now so different, Doug?"

"Because I miss you, Lace."

"Stop calling me Lace. I hate when you call me that."

"It never seemed to bother you before."

She huffed. "That's because I never said anything."

"That's not my fault."

"No, but I'm saying it now. Don't call me Lace, anymore. I don't like it. I never did."

"Fine. Jesus, what's gotten into you? Why are you all of a sudden just now getting this goddamn hair up your ass?"

"I could ask you the same question. And besides, I didn't *just now* get this hair up my ass. It's been two months. *Two.* You haven't tried to contact me once this whole time. And now here you are, out of nowhere, wanting a second chance. And for the better part of the three years we were together, you didn't seem interested in making such an effort to make our relationship work. So, yeah, Doug. Why now? Why do you all of a sudden want to work things out with me now?"

"I just...Jesus, Lace—sorry...*Lacey.* Give me a break."

"No. Why now, Doug?"

Then it dawned on her. Ivanka had broken up with him. That was it, wasn't it? She'd taken her leave, probably because he'd begun to cheat on her, too. Now, he was alone. And for a habitual cheater who got his rocks off by stepping out on his steady girl, the excitement was gone.

She nearly gasped as the pieces fell into place. She understood now why they called it a lightbulb moment, because for so long she'd been in the dark about why he couldn't be faithful. Now she knew. She finally understood. Doug needed a girlfriend to skip out on so he could get off. For him, cheating was an aphrodisiac.

"Lacey..."

"Shut up. Just shut up, Doug." She paused to let the realization sink in that she'd just been a means to an end for Doug. She lowered her voice to barely above a whisper. "Ivanka broke up with you, didn't she?"

Silence.

"Thought so." She disconnected without waiting for him to reply then straightened on her barstool, gasping when she glanced to her left to find a man who bore a striking resemblance to Scott taking a seat on the barstool two down from hers.

"You're Mattie Moon." He wasn't asking.

"Umm..."

He extended his hand. "I'm Liam. Scott's brother."

Oh God. How much had he heard?

"Hi." She shook his hand, her face and neck hot.

Her phone began ringing again. Doug's name popped

up on the caller ID. Without thinking, she answered.

"Quit calling me."

"But, La—"

She hung up before he could say anything further then glanced back at Liam.

The way his eyes burned with suspicion made it clear he'd heard at least some of her previous conversation. Probably quite a bit.

"Here you go, Mattie." Rosie placed her to-go bag on the counter.

"Thanks." She hopped off the barstool and grabbed her bag as her phone started ringing again. She jammed it inside her purse without answering.

She didn't want to look like she was trying to get away from Liam, but that's exactly what she was doing as she hurried toward the exit.

"Off so soon?" Liam regarded her curiously.

"Yep." She lifted her bag as if providing evidence. The sound of her phone jingling out an inappropriate tune for an ex-boyfriend from inside her purse might as well have been a siren. She had forgotten to change Doug's ringtone from the sexy number she'd assigned him last year to something more fitting for a cheating bastard. She needed to fix that pronto. "Cold Hearted" by Paula Abdul would be a more apt ringtone for Doug now. "I'm heading back to my cabin."

"Well, maybe we can talk another time then."

"Sure. I'd like that." *Not.* "Nice meeting you."

"Yeah. Same here. Very...*enlightening.*" He chucked

his chin. "Have a nice night." He turned away and picked up his menu as if he didn't already know what he wanted to order. If he ate there as often as Scott, he had the damn thing memorized. But one thing was clear. It was the end of their brief discussion.

She hurried out to her car. When she hazarded a glance back inside, Liam was watching her. As in...like a fucking hawk.

Chapter 13

You can't control other people, Lacey. You can only control your reaction.

She'd been worrying all night about her encounter with Liam when her coach's words reemerged in her head. She'd been writing her first journal entry, a detailed account about why she'd started this journey in the first place, as well as her conflicted feelings for Scott, Doug's antics, his stupid phone call, and the fact that Liam had overheard at least part of her conversation. Basically, she'd been writing stream of consciousness for over three hours, which meant she'd run the gamut of topics. Wherever her thoughts led her was what she wrote. She could imagine that the pages read as helter skelter as the thoughts had felt inside her head.

But purging them to the page had helped make some sense of the mess. In an odd way, journaling her thoughts was like holding a conversation with herself. She was the speaker *and* the sounding board, which allowed her to hear herself and make connections she'd overlooked.

Which brought her back to her coach's words. She couldn't control Liam. She couldn't control what he'd heard. It was done, and dwelling on it would only tie her in knots. All she could control was how she reacted and what she did from this point forward.

She stopped writing to shake out the cramps in her hand and check the time. It was after eleven.

When had it grown so late?

She closed her journal and set it on her lap, laying her head back against the soft armrest of the couch. A crackling fire glowed from the fireplace, and what she called yoga music played through her Bluetooth speaker. She felt...peaceful. Zen. Quiet. Even the nagging voices that had plagued her mind for so long had shut up.

And how refreshing was that?

The only voice that remained was her coach's, but in a good way. All the lessons he'd taught her were bubbling back to the surface, finally freed from the clutches of all the crap she'd just expelled from her brain.

Fight, Lacey. Always fight. Never give up, and if you fall, get right back up and keep going. It's how we respond to adversity that defines us.

Trent's words. Words she had forgotten until now.

Everyone falls, Lacey. It's what you do after you fall that matters.

The message vibrated at the heart of her, deep down where her soul and will met.

How Lacey responded to her fall at the Olympics would define her from this point forward. What she did in this moment was all that mattered. She could let the Olympics defeat her, or she could fight back. She could spit in the face of adversity and find a way back to happiness, where she took control of her life, or she could give up and quit.

But, by God, she wasn't a quitter. Maybe she was down right now, and maybe she'd been overwhelmed by the chaos for a while, but she could feel her thoughts shifting into a better place.

What she needed were boundaries. Hadn't Trent tried to tell her that years ago? How wise and insightful he'd been. But she'd been young and unable to decipher wisdom from hocus-pocus. And, unfortunately, shit had already begun to go critical by then, and Lacey hadn't been able to see the forest for the trees even if Trent had taken her hand and led her through. So, Trent's words, wise as they were, had floated in one ear and out the other, never actually taking hold on her consciousness and sinking in. But now, with distance, she was beginning to understand what Trent had been trying to tell her.

Boundaries are like fences, Lacey. They let people know how far you're willing to let them go. They clarify where your space ends and their space begins. Not just physically, but emotionally, verbally, mentally, and professionally. And like fences, boundaries build strong, friendly alliances built on trust.

The tools to get out of the weeds had been there all along, but she had been too mangled within the cogs of the machine chewing her into pulp to catch her breath long enough to see them.

Problem was, she had been competing for so long, she didn't know much else.

Maybe it was time to find a little balance. Then maybe she could decipher what was important from what wasn't. Until now, others had spoken for her, which had prevented her from fully analyzing her own opinions to make decisions for herself. It wasn't that she didn't know what she wanted. She'd just never had much opportunity to figure that out and vocalize it. That was the hazard of starting training at such a young age. Nine years old isn't old enough to have the kind of real-world knowledge necessary to know what you wanted and how best to get it, so she'd relied on adults to guide her and speak on her behalf. That reliance had turned into a fifteen-year-long bad habit. One she needed to break if she was going to recapture her life.

If she decided to return to competition, she would do so on her terms, not someone else's. And she would take a more active role in defining how things operated.

But what if she decided to retire? What then?

At one time, she had loved snowboarding. But for the last two years, she'd hated it. No wonder she'd fallen at the Olympics. She'd lost the spiritual connection with the snow and ice. They'd been at war with one another instead of allies.

So then, how did she reconnect with the snow and ice on a spiritual level, recapture their alliance, and yet still compete? Could the two endeavors even coexist with one another? If not, what did that mean for her future? If her snowboarding days were over, what did she want to do with her life?

And that was at the heart of this vision quest she'd gone on, because until she found herself, she couldn't know where her heart lay.

She glanced over her shoulder to the front door. Maybe it was time to release her snowboards from their prison...and herself in the process. The only way to see if there was any hope that snowboarding was in her future was to reintroduce herself to her boards and the snow.

It was time. Tonight was the night.

Almost as if she were facing a rite of passage, she calmly strode to her bedroom, pulled out the khaki pants and patchwork jacket she'd worn at the last Olympics, and reverently stroked her fingers down the image of the American flag adorning the left sleeve. She was supposed to have won a gold medal with this uniform. Instead, she'd disgraced herself.

Well, no more. Her comeback started tonight. That was, if she eventually decided to make a comeback.

A few minutes later, changed and ready to go, she left the cabin, climbed behind the wheel of her Escape, and drove into the depths of the McCord Cabins property, toward a hill that was perfectly suited for a trial run. The trees were widely spaced, enough so that she could easily wind her way down without risking injury.

She parked along the side of the lane, pulled on her yellow goggles, which would brighten the terrain lit by the full moon, and fastened her helmet strap under her chin. With a glance toward the snowy incline, she opened the back hatch and tugged the board she used for freestyling from under the heavy quilt she'd wrapped it in.

After shutting the hatch, she faced the hill.

Cold, muffled silence welcomed her, and she smiled as a restless breeze teased the tops of the fir trees. It was almost as if the snow knew she was coming and stirred restlessly, impatiently, beckoning her to hurry.

"Okay, okay. I'm coming," she muttered, starting the long march up the hill.

Her feet sank into at least six inches of pristine snow with each step, and soon she was breathing hard, her leg bitching. For all the rehab and long walks—and even a few jogs—she hadn't hoofed it up such a steep incline since before her fall. But no way was she turning back.

The moon shone like a midnight sun overhead, lighting her way. Was this crazy? Was she crazy for what she was about to do? She didn't care. For the first time in a long while, the snow called to her. Or maybe it had been calling her all along, but she had been too swept up within the overwhelming chaos to hear it. All that mattered was she heard it now, and she didn't want to deny its pull, anymore.

Twenty minutes later, she stood at the top of the hill, out of breath. She turned in a circle, breathing in what smelled like victory, and gazed with awe at the beautiful vista, the frozen lake in the distance, and what Lacey had learned was the namesake for the town, Hope Falls. A narrow stream of water poured through the partially frozen falls, down from a jagged cliff to a slope below, where it had cut veins into the earth in its quest to reach the lake. Before long, the falls would freeze completely until spring. She closed her eyes, turned her face toward the moon, smiled, and listened to the screaming silence.

How glorious! Nothing but her own thoughts came back at her, which was sweeter than honey, because for once, her thoughts weren't rambling, fractured globs of rage and panic. They were pure, calm, peaceful. Loving. It had been so long since she had felt loving thoughts toward anything, including herself.

Opening her eyes, she turned and gazed longingly down the hill. The snow was still thick and relatively soft, as she suspected, so it had been the right call to bring her long board. She dropped it onto the snow, ritualistically secured her feet into the bindings, stood, and cut the back edge into the snow to hold her in place as she gave the hill one last glance.

The powder seemed to be crooking its finger at her. *Come, Lacey. Come to me. I'll catch you. I'll take care of you.*

She had always had a relationship with the snow, but two years ago, the voices had quieted and the relationship had soured. Now, the snow seemed to be eager to take her back and embrace her as though they had never gone their separate ways.

"I'm coming," she whispered with a smile, clapping her gloved hands together the way she always did before a run.

With one last glance, she turned her board and aimed it down the hill. The still air breezed past her, and she carved to the left, then the right, picking up speed as adrenaline broke in her veins. The moon looked on, smiling down on her as she weaved in and out of a loose stand of trees that dotted the hillside. A delirious thrill shot through her, and she shouted out a gleeful whoop as she flew around another tree. Faster still, she carved and cut, slicing a curved path in the snow behind her. Freedom. This was freedom. And it felt good. Like she was flying. Like she was soaring and looking down on herself from above.

At the bottom of the hill, Lacey threw her arms over her head, sliced to a stop, and then fell back-first into the snow. She was laughing like a maniac, whooping and pumping her fist toward the sky.

"Yes! My God, YES!" If she could hug the snow, she would.

And then she began to cry. Great heaves of racking sobs came out of nowhere, pummeling her and pounding against her chest. Tears flowed like rivers, and she pulled off her goggles. Cold air stung the wet trails, and she slammed her gloved hands over her face.

But these weren't tears of sadness. These were tears of joy.

Joy!

Releasing the bindings around her feet, she rolled to all fours and scooped up a handful of snow. She kissed it between tearful hiccups. "God, I've missed you. I've missed you so much."

Chapter 14

Scott pulled back into Hope Falls late Tuesday night. Savannah's head lay against the passenger window, her mouth open as she slept.

A weekend at Sun Valley ski resort had left her exhausted.

Him, too, but he had to make a couple of stops before he could collapse for a full eight hours—maybe twelve—of shuteye.

First, Pappy's. Priority number one was filling the void four hours of driving had left in his stomach.

He pulled into the parking lot, left the engine running, and rustled Savannah awake.

"Come on, Savvy, we need to eat."

She rubbed her eyes and blinked toward the lit windows as if she were seeing a dream instead of a restaurant. Then her eyes closed again, and her head lolled back.

Gone. She was passed out. He'd never seen anyone who slept as heavily as Savannah. When she was out, she was *out*. As in, not even a tornado, an earthquake, and a KISS concert could wake her. The only thing that woke her was her own internal clock.

With a sigh, he made a decision no one in a bigger city would ever make. But in Hope Falls, he knew he could leave Savannah in his truck and not have to worry about anything bad happening to her.

He quietly got out of the truck, locked the doors after tucking his spare key in his pocket, and went inside. He took a seat that allowed him to keep an eye on his truck, just in case. Because while Hope Falls was a safe, close-knit town, that was his daughter. He would keep her in his sights.

"Hey, Scott," Shirl said as she started to fill the mug in front of him with decaf.

He held up his hand to stop her. "Hit me with the hard stuff tonight, Shirl." Decaf wasn't going to get the job done.

Her perfectly plucked eyebrows shot up. "Oh? Planning a late night?" She exchanged decanters and filled his cup.

There was something in her sidelong expression that unsettled him. As if she thought his need to stay awake came with ulterior motives.

"No." He poured cream in his coffee and added sugar. "Savannah and I just spent the weekend in Sun Valley. I'm beat but still need to check in at the office before heading home." So yeah, a pick-me-up was essential.

She gave a little pout, shrugging. "Well, that's no fun. A young man like you should be having more fun, Scott."

"I'll keep that in mind." He wasn't in the mood for Shirl's games tonight. He adored her, but sometimes she could be too much for his patience.

"The usual, sugar?"

He nodded, sipping his coffee, and then lowered the cup. "Savannah's usual, too, please."

"Sure thing." Shirl headed off to give his order to the cook.

"Kisses Sweeter than Wine" started playing on the jukebox, and he grinned as his thoughts turned toward Mattie. She definitely had kisses sweeter than wine. Sweeter than any he'd ever known. He couldn't wait to taste them again.

"What're you thinking about to put such a smile on your face, sugar?" Shirl stood to the side, wiping down the already clean counter.

"Nothing." He fingered his coffee mug.

"You sure have been smiling a lot."

Shirl genuinely cared for him and everyone else in town, but that caring attitude more often than not came off as nosiness.

"Maybe I'm just happy, Shirl." He dropped his gaze into his coffee, hoping she'd take a hint and let the subject go.

No such luck.

She slid closer and leaned her hip against the counter. "Seems to me you've got plenty reason to be happy these days." Without skipping a beat, she added, "I saw your girl last night at Bingo."

Scott frowned. "My girl?"

Shirl let out a little laugh. "Mattie, sugar. She came to play Bingo with us last night."

"Mattie's not my girl." But he wouldn't mind if she were. He looked out the window to check on Savannah. She still had her head back on her seat, eyes closed, mouth open.

"Well, she sure seems to have the crazies for *you*." The insinuation in Shirl's voice and the way her eyes sparkled mischievously spoke volumes.

"Why? What did she say?" Jesus, he sounded like he was in junior high again, asking his best friend for the lowdown on the most popular girl in school.

"Oh, sugar, she didn't have to say anything. That girl's got major eyes for you, plain as day."

He exhaled heavily and turned his coffee mug in his hand. "Shirl, you've got to stop playing matchmaker with me."

He had gone through this with her before. For years, she had tried to fix him up with every eligible lady in town before throwing in the towel when he denied every one of them. Only, this time, he wanted to be matched. Mattie was special. He really liked her. There was something about her that tugged at his heart in a way he hadn't felt since he met Theresa. Even so, he didn't want Shirl interfering. He was doing fine with Mattie on his own, and Shirl would only get in the way and cause trouble.

"Just trying to look out for you, sugar."

He nodded. "I know you are, but I can handle this one on my own. So...I appreciate your help, but I'm a big boy."

"You're a man is what you are, Scott McCord." She waggled her finger at him good-naturedly. "And if it's one thing I've learned about men in my fifty-one years, it's that sometimes they need a little push to show them the obvious."

He glanced at her out of the corner of his eye. "I can assure you, Shirl, you don't need to point out the obvious to me on this one." He arched one brow to make sure his point got across that he was already caught in Mattie's web.

The realization spilled over her face like sunshine as her eyes lit up and a slow smile crept over her mouth. "Well then, I see." She glanced toward the kitchen. "Looks like your order's ready, sugar. I'll be right back."

Now that he'd handed her a nugget of gold, Shirl seemed momentarily content, but next time he saw her, she would want more. That was how she worked. Give her a small nibble here and there, and she was happy.

But Scott didn't want to put the cart before the horse and reveal too much until he knew where his relationship with Mattie was going. They hadn't done more than kiss. Sure, he'd wanted to, but after what Theresa had put him through, he wanted to take things slow, even if his body wanted to charge full steam ahead. But what if they reached that point and there was no chemistry? Unlikely, because, yeah, the chemistry they had when they were just kissing was off the charts. But it could happen.

And how would this work if she decided to return to Utah? He didn't want to put too much weight in what was going on between them if she was only going to leave.

There were just too many unanswered questions. All the unknowns were in the way of allowing him to think their relationship was anything more than two people enjoying each other's company. Could it be more? Yes. Would it? He didn't know.

He downed the last of his coffee as he took the bag of food from Shirl. After paying, he trekked back into the cold.

Savannah barely flinched when he climbed into the truck. But when she smelled the food her eyes peeled open, and she reached for her shake. Of course she'd want that first. He was too tired and bone-weary to tell her no. Tonight, she could have dessert before dinner.

Liam's truck was parked out front when he pulled in at the office.

"Come on, Savvy. I just need to go in for a few minutes and check my e-mail. You can eat while I do."

He led her inside and down the hall toward his desk in the back.

Liam glanced up from his computer in the office across the hall from his. "What are you doing here?"

Scott motioned Savannah inside, where she took a seat at the small round conference table in the corner and dug into her dinner.

"I could ask you the same thing. Isn't it kind of late to be working?"

"Says the guy who just got back from vacation and probably hasn't even been home, yet."

Scott shrugged out of his coat and hung it on the hook beside the door. "I just want to check my e-mail. My phone died while I was gone, and I forgot my charger."

Liam harrumphed, turning back to his computer. "What?"

Liam kicked back in his leather chair and crossed his hands over his stomach. "I ran into your girlfriend last night."

Scott glared at Liam and shook his head. What was with everybody? First Shirl, now Liam. He wasn't in the mood to be poked and prodded where Mattie was concerned. He was tired, hungry, and just wanted to check his e-mail so he could leave and eat his dinner. And after his last conversation with Liam about Mattie, he didn't like the way Liam glared back at him as if he were challenging him to a duel.

He turned toward Savannah. "Your uncle and I need to talk privately for a minute, honey, okay?"

Her mouth was full of hamburger, so she nodded.

"I'll be right back." He shut the door and crossed the hall, closing Liam's door behind him. "What is with everyone's sudden interest in my love life? And what are you doing messing with Mattie? I—"

"I didn't say I was messing with her. I said I saw her."

"Then why the smug-ass look on your face?"

Liam let out an exasperated exhale. "Scott, just how much do you know about Mattie?"

"Enough. Okay? I know enough." He paced to the window and glanced out at the snow-covered mountains.

"Really?" Liam rocked forward and laced his fingers together on his desk blotter. "Like what?"

"That's none of your business. What's it to you,

anyway?"

"I overheard her on the phone with someone. Sounded like a boyfriend." Liam paused to let that sink in.

Boyfriend? Scott raked his fingers through his hair. "You've obviously made some mistake." Mattie couldn't have a boyfriend. "Why the hell were you eavesdropping on her, anyway?"

"I wasn't."

"Then how did you overhear her on the phone?"

"I was at Pappy's. She came in. I recognized her. I was sitting at a table when she got a call. I only caught every couple of words because she was talking quietly, but it was obvious she was talking to a guy she'd obviously been close to. So I got up and took a seat at the counter near her."

"So you could eavesdrop. Like I said."

"Hey, I'm not the bad guy here, Scott. I'm just trying to open your eyes that there's more to this girl than you think you know."

"Well, it's none of your business, Liam. Jesus! I can't believe you." He paced left then right. "You're just pissed off, because for the first time in ten years, I'm happy. And since you're so goddamn miserable, you can't stand that. Everyone has to be just as miserable as you are, don't they? You can't just be happy for me."

Liam shot out of his chair. "Don't you dare make this about me."

"But isn't it? Ever since—"

"Do *NOT* go there, Scott. You hear me. This isn't about me. This is about you and what you may or may not know about the woman you're falling in love with." He straightened and puffed out a breath. "And you *are* falling in love with her. Don't tell me you aren't. And if you ask me, you're trying to turn this back around on me because you don't want to hear that your girlfriend might not be the angel you think she is."

Scott shook his head. "You're right. I don't want to hear it, because you're wrong, and it's none of your business."

"She was on the phone with another man, Scott. Someone who apparently called her 'Lace,' whatever that means. Sounds like he had a kinky bead on her, if you ask me, but whoever he is, she was upset with him."

"Then maybe he's not her boyfriend. You ever consider that? If she's upset with him, maybe they broke up."

"Or maybe she gets off on the drama and will go running back to the guy after she plays you as her rebound man. You ever think of that?" Liam challenged. "Maybe he's the reason she came here in the first place. To get away. Once she leaves and goes home, she'll be right back in his arms."

God, had Liam's past tainted him so severely against love? "You're talking out your ass on this one, Liam."

Liam shook his head and hitched his hands on his hips. "She's going to hurt you, Scott. That girl is carrying major baggage, and you're going to get caught in the crossfire when all this goes south. Whoever the guy was, she was close to him. Close enough to—"

Scott slammed his eyes shut and held up his hand. "I don't want to hear this, Liam."

"But you *need* to, Scott! Open your goddamn eyes before you get hurt again!"

"This is my life, not yours. Butt out and worry about yourself." Scott threw open Liam's door then shoved open his. "Come on, Savannah, we're going home."

From the look on her face, she'd overheard at least some of what he and Liam had said to one another. But she didn't question him. Just pulled her coat on and boxed up the rest of her food.

His dinner was likely cold by now, but who cared? It wouldn't be the first time he'd eaten a cold Pappy's burger and sweet potato fries.

After putting on his coat, hat, and scarf, he grabbed their bag of food and ushered Savannah into the hall.

"Scott…"

He shot Liam a warning glare. "No. Not another word." He shut off the light in his office. He would check his e-mail in the morning.

Liam followed him into the hallway. "Look, I—"

"No, Liam. This conversation is over."

Liam's past was just as painful as Scott's, but Scott was not his brother. Liam had fallen into a deep, hellish hole after his wife died, but that didn't mean Scott couldn't climb out of his own hole and find happiness again. He wouldn't let Liam get in the way of that, no matter how much he loved the guy or empathized with him. If Liam was going to find happiness again, it was up to him.

With a terse good night, he made his way back out to his truck and drove his daughter home.

As he passed Mattie's cabin, he noted her light was on. She was still up. That was good, because he really wanted to hear her voice. Especially after the run-ins with nosy Shirl and his paranoid brother.

At home, Savannah took their dinner to the kitchen while he detoured upstairs. After he plugged his cell into his charger, he grabbed the cordless phone and dialed Mattie's number.

"Hello?" She sounded pleasantly wary, as if she already knew it was him and wondered why he was calling so late.

"Hi." Just hearing her voice made him smile. She was the first truly bright spot other than his daughter he'd encountered all day. "I just drove by your cabin and noticed your light was on, so I took a chance and called."

"I'm glad you did."

"Me, too. I needed a smile."

"Hard day?"

He thought about Shirl nosing into his business and the argument with Liam. "You could say that."

"You sound tired."

"I am, but I'm feeling a bit more awake now."

She laughed. "Why's that?"

He chuckled and glanced over his shoulder to make sure Savannah hadn't come looking for him. "You just...uh..." His voice dropped lower as he pushed his bedroom door closed. It wasn't like Savannah could hear him from the kitchen, but he felt safer closing off his room from the rest of the house while he was on the phone with Mattie. "Something about you just wakes me up." He paused. "In every way imaginable."

He heard her exhale. "I know what you mean." Her soft, airy voice lilted introspectively.

"How about dinner Friday night?"

"You, me, and Savannah, right?"

"Yes." No hesitation.

"What time?"

"Seven o'clock?"

"Sounds perfect."

His heart skipped. "Then I'll see you Friday night."

"See you then."

"Good night, Mattie."

Pause.

"Scott?"

"Yes."

"There's something I want to tell you."

"What is it?" He tensed, thinking about what Liam had told him. He wasn't sure he could take it if Liam had been right.

Another pause.

"I...I'm..." She exhaled heavily. "I'm really looking forward to seeing you."

He breathed out a sigh of relief. "Me, too."

"See you Friday. Good night, Scott."

"Good night." He hung up and, with a renewed skip in his step, descended the stairs to the kitchen.

Savannah was already finished and lying on the couch watching a movie.

"Are you and Uncle Liam mad at each other?" she said, sitting up.

Scott fished his container of cold food out of the bag and set it on the table. "Uncle Liam and I just don't always see eye to eye."

"I heard you mention Mattie."

He tried not to smile at the mention of her name. "Yes."

"You like her a lot, don't you?"

He raised his gaze to hers. After a short pause, he nodded. "Yes, I do. Are you okay with that?"

She smiled, and her head bobbed up and down. "Uh-huh. I like Mattie. She's cool."

"You hardly know her." He sat down at the table and popped open the lid on his food container.

"She skateboarded when she was a kid. And she taught snowboarding. That's pretty awesome."

He chomped into a cold sweet potato fry. "There's more to her than just skateboards and snowboards, honey. She's really nice."

Savannah grinned. "Are you going to marry her?"

His heart fluttered at the thought. "I don't know. Maybe. Someday. We'll have to see."

Savannah's face beamed. "I hope so. I like her. She's fun."

Mattie *was* fun. And smart. And beautiful. But was he ready to start thinking about marriage? He needed to make sure he was taking this one step at a time, even if his heart could already hear wedding bells. "I'm glad you approve, because she's having dinner with us on Friday."

Savannah's smile cranked up another notch. "Really?"

"Yep." He took a bite of his burger as Savannah jumped off the couch, ran into the kitchen, and threw her arms around him. "Hey, what's this for?" he said, setting down his burger and scooping her onto his lap.

"You're happy, Daddy."

She was hugging him because he was happy? Had he really appeared so somber up until now that his own daughter was moved to hug him just because he'd smiled and was having dinner with a woman?

"Yes, I'm happy, honey."

"Me, too. I'm happy that you're happy."

He hugged her to him as she placed her cheek on his shoulder. Whether or not he and Mattie worked out in the long run, he needed to remember this moment. He couldn't let himself go back to the brooding man he had obviously become before meeting Mattie. Savannah deserved better.

"I love you, Savvy."

"I love you, too, Daddy."

Chapter 15

November 21

Dear Diary,

Next week is Thanksgiving. I've been in Hope Falls two months. I still haven't told Scott who I really am. Every time I try to tell him, either I chicken out or we're interrupted.

The longer this goes on, the harder it becomes to admit who I am. But he deserves to know, and I know that sooner or later he'll figure it out. It's inevitable. I can't stay hidden forever, and the moment I reenter society, he'll see it's me. If I don't tell him before that happens, and he finds out on his own, it'll hurt him. He'll be angry with me. I don't want to think about how he'll react, especially since he's already been lied to once. His ex lied to him ten years ago, and from what I can tell, it's taken him all this time to finally trust again.

And I'm the reason.

How ironic is that? I'm why he allowed himself to trust again, and I'm lying to him. How's that for a nasty twist of fate?

Shit, but I've dug myself into a hole. A big, fat, deep one.

I have to tell him. Tonight.

Lacey closed her journal with a sigh. Yes. Tonight. She was sure to get at least one opportunity to pull Scott aside during dinner and finally tell him the truth, even if she had to force it.

She had a few hours before it was time to get ready, so she decided to head back to the hill, see about taking another couple runs down on her board. The sizzle of excitement she'd felt after her midnight run the other night had yet to dissipate, and maybe communing with nature the best way she knew how would give her a bit of perspective—and courage—over her pending confession.

Two hours and four invigorating downhill rides later, Lacey was no more mentally ready to face Scott than she had been earlier. Apparently there were some things even meditation via snowboard couldn't solve. She packed up to head into town for groceries before going home to get ready for her date.

Sitting on the edge of the open back of her Escape, she

tugged off her snowboarding boots and pulled on her Uggs. She'd left the Olympic uniform at home this time. No sense risking exposure in the daylight. After packing her helmet and goggles in her duffle bag, she shut the hatch, hopped behind the steering wheel, and turned the SUV around.

On her way back to her cabin, she spied Scott's snowmobile parked alongside the lane and slowed to peer into the trees to see if she could see him. What was he doing out here?

About twenty yards into the trees, she caught a flash of color. A red coat against a navy one. Then she took a closer look. Scott was carrying Savannah, hurrying back to the snowmobile. He had a snowboard wrenched under his arm.

Lacey slammed on the brakes, slid a few inches on the snowpack, and tore out of the driver's seat.

"What happened? Is she okay?"

"She fell," Scott said, out of breath.

"Here, give me the board." Lacey took the board and scanned what she could see of Savannah, who was crying. Blood streaked her cheek, and her pants were torn. A nasty gash about two inches long stretched up the front of her calf. Blood was on her gloves as if she had grabbed her leg. When she raised her hand to wipe tears off her cheeks, Lacey realized that's where the blood on her face had come from as she left another crimson streak under her eye.

"I need to get her to the emergency clinic in town." Like the day at the skate park when he'd seen Savannah fall, Scott was in a panic. His eyes were wide, pupils dilated, his voice edged with tension.

"Stay calm, Scott." She hurried alongside him. "She's going to be okay."

"She could have a broken leg. Oh God, what if…" His mind was taking him down dark paths into even darker memories.

"Scott, ssshh." Lacey pulled open the back passenger door then hustled around to reopen the hatch. "Put her in the backseat." She placed Savannah's board on top of hers, grabbed the quilt, and rushed around to the side again. "She can lie down on this." She haphazardly spread the blanket over the seats and stood back to give Scott room.

He got Savannah settled as Lacey ran to the driver's side, slamming the hatch on the way.

"Tell me where to go," Lacey said as Scott shut Savannah in and jumped into the passenger seat. Instinct from a hundred past injuries kicked in, keeping her calm and levelheaded as she drove toward the exit.

Scott, on the other hand, was beside himself. "She just wanted to go snowboarding," he said, voice strained. "I wouldn't normally have taken her, but I didn't think it would be a problem. She's not used to boarding in such soft snow. God, I should have known better. I should have insisted that she wait, but she was so excited, and I…what if her leg is broken? I don't want her to go through what I did. I—"

"I'm sure she's fine." Lacey pulled out onto the main road then looked in the rearview mirror at Savannah, who was still crying, probably more from embarrassment than anything. "How you feeling, honey?"

She sniffled and caught Lacey's eye in the mirror. "I don't know," she sobbed.

"We'll get you taken care of." She glanced at Scott before putting her eyes back on the road.

Under the circumstances, Lacey didn't want to tell Scott that while a longer board was good for less experienced riders, as well as for soft snow, they were harder to steer. Savannah's board was long. If she had gotten into trouble and tried to steer clear, she might not have been able to and instead wiped out. Lacey would bet that's exactly what happened. But telling Scott that wouldn't make him feel any better.

"Scott, tell me where to go, okay. We'll take care of her. She'll be fine. It's just a little scratch is all." From the look Lacey had gotten at Savannah's injury, the cut was more than just a "little scratch." It would probably require stitches, but playing it down seemed the wiser choice if it meant she could ease Scott's panic and get him to give her directions.

Scott calmed down enough to direct her to the emergency clinic, but his memories had definitely taken him to a scary place.

She had barely parked before he was out the door, hoisting Savannah into his arms. Lacey ran ahead and opened the clinic's door.

Luckily, only one other person was in the waiting area. Thank God for small towns.

"My daughter's been in an accident," Scott said, rushing the nurse at the reception desk, who jumped to attention, startled.

"Oh dear," she said. Her name tag read "Gloria," and she wore lavender scrub pants and a top that was white with lavender, yellow, and mint green flowers on it. She darted to the door that led into the back of the clinic. "Bring her back and I'll get the doctor right in."

Scott led Lacey through, and she followed him into an exam room, where Scott laid Savannah on the table.

Gloria hustled back out and closed the door behind her, promising that the doctor would be in to see them right away.

Savannah whimpered, and Lacey took her hand as she stepped to the side of the table.

"It's not that bad," Lacey said, giving Savannah's hand a squeeze as she brushed her hair off her forehead. "Just a little cut and some blood." She smiled down at Savannah's tear-streaked face and bloodshot eyes.

"But, I crashed."

Lacey thought back to her crash in the Olympics, and suddenly it didn't seem so bad. For a little girl like Savannah, who hadn't had as long to take her knocks, this probably seemed like a catastrophe, but to Lacey, who had fallen countless times and suffered ten lifetimes' worth of bruises, sprains, and breaks, Savannah's accident seemed like no big thing. How quickly the world shifted to perspective under such circumstances.

"You know what? I've crashed a lot myself," Lacey said. "I've knocked myself around so many times on a course that sometimes I didn't know which way was up, but..." She looked at Scott, who had taken up residence on the other side of the bed and was watching her closely. "Someone once taught me a very important lesson about falling down."

"What's that?" Savannah said, sniffling.

Lacey combed the dark, sweat-soaked hair off Savannah's face, remembering her coach's words. "We all fall." She patted her hand. "We all fall, Savannah. But falling isn't what's important. It's what we do after we fall that makes all the difference." She didn't look at Scott, but she felt his grateful appreciation for how well she was keeping herself together for both his sake and his daughter's. "If you stick with snowboarding, Savannah, you're going to keep falling, and..." She hazarded a glance at Scott, knowing what she was going to say next would be harder for him to hear than Savannah. "I won't lie to you, the falls get harder. The longer you ride, and the more competitive you become, the more dangerous the sport becomes." Scott's face lost a little of its color. "But," Lacey said before Scott could interrupt, "if it's what you love...if it's what you want to do...then you have to follow your heart. Just go in knowing what to expect, and that will help."

It was advice she wished she had heeded a long time ago. Because hadn't she known early on that injuries were par for the course in snowboarding? For Lacey, the danger and injuries weren't what had thrown her into a downward spiral. It had been all the rest. The fame, the fortune, the constant press of the media, fans, sponsors, and endorsers.

Everyone had wanted a piece of Lacey Moon, and she hadn't known how to say no. She hadn't known where the boundaries were. That was the one thing—the hardest fall of all—she hadn't been prepared for, and it damn near stole her dream. And, who knew, maybe it had. The jury was still out. Maybe she would never return to competitive snowboarding. Perhaps she had attended her final Olympics, her final X Games, her final competition. If so, she needed to figure out while she was in Hope Falls what the next chapter of her life was going to be.

The door opened and a woman wearing a white coat entered the room. "Hi, I'm Doctor Taylor," she said.

Scott shot to attention and held out his hand. "I'm Scott McCord. This is my daughter, Savannah. She fell while snowboarding. Cut her leg pretty good on a rock under the snow."

The doctor pulled on a pair of latex gloves as she inspected what she could see of the cut. Then she glanced at Lacey. "Are you Mom?"

Lacey shook her head. Scott jumped in. "No. This is Mattie. She's a close friend and helped get Savannah here. It's okay for her to be here."

The doctor pulled a sterilized package containing a pair of scissors from the drawer and ripped it open. "I need to cut off this pant leg so I can see the wound and get it cleaned up."

Lacey joined Scott on the other side of the room and stood back to let the doctor work. A moment later, Scott's hand closed over hers and held on like she was a life preserver, the only thing keeping him afloat. She reached around with her free hand and closed it over his, letting him know she was there for him. The injury wasn't life-threatening or one that would require surgery or hospitalization, but from Scott's point of view, with his daughter cringing as the doctor dabbed the cut with alcohol-soaked swabs, Savannah's injuries may as well have been an amputation. His grip on Lacey's hand tightened every time Savannah winced or whimpered.

"You sure are making my first week in Hope Falls interesting, aren't you?" Doctor Taylor winked at Savannah, making her crack a smile for the first time in the last twenty minutes.

"Yeah, we're all about welcoming newcomers with a bang around here," Scott said, glancing at Lacey. He seemed to be calming down.

Doctor Taylor discarded her soiled cotton swabs. "This is going to need a few stitches." She turned back to Savannah. "But I'll take good care of you, sweetie. You won't feel a thing, okay?"

Savannah's face paled slightly, but she nodded as if trying to be a big girl.

The doctor began preparing her materials.

When Savannah saw the syringe of local anesthesia and the needle, she turned wide eyes toward Lacey.

"Are you nervous," Lacey said, stepping forward and squeezing her hand.

She shook her head.

"It's okay if you are. I was nervous the first time I got

stitches."

"You were?"

"Yep." She lifted her hand and showed Savannah the almost-imperceptible scar on the heel of her palm. "See that?"

Savannah squinted as Lacey pointed. Then she nodded. "Uh-huh."

"Shard of ice cut me," Lacey said. "I was twelve. Fell while snowboarding, just like you did today."

Savannah dragged the tip of her tiny, cold finger along the inch-long mark then looked down at her leg. "I'm going to have a scar, too, aren't I?"

Lacey took her hand reassuringly. "Probably, but think of it as a battle wound," she said with a smile. "A badge of honor that proves you were here. That you lived. That you said, 'Look at me, world, you hit me with your best shot, and I'm still standing.' Think of it that way, and it's not quite so scary."

Savannah grinned and gave a feeble nod.

A nurse joined them in the small exam room, and Lacey stepped back beside Scott once more as the doctor got to work.

Doctor Taylor patted Savannah's leg. "Don't worry, Savannah, I'll take good care of you. You'll be good as new before you know it. You'll just have a little reminder about how tough a kid you are."

As the doctor patched up Savannah's leg, Lacey turned to check on Scott.

He was watching her, gratitude pouring from his gaze.

"Thank you," he whispered.

Her heart nosedived at the enamored expression that consumed his face and seemed to be saying a lot more than just thank you. "You're welcome," she whispered back.

Forty minutes and one stop at the drug store for a bottle of children's Motrin and a box of bandages later, Lacey helped Scott get Savannah inside his cabin.

Savannah was drowsy now that her adrenaline had crashed, so Scott took her upstairs to bed while Lacey waited downstairs.

She'd never been inside Scott's cabin. It was open, airy...comfortable. His kitchen was twice the size of hers, with stainless steel appliances and oak cabinets. In the living room, a stone fireplace climbed one high wall in a majestic display of rustic decadence. The furniture was worn but high end.

Scott did well for himself.

She was inspecting the many pictures of him and Savannah on the built-in bookcase when he came back downstairs and joined her.

"How is she?"

"Asleep." His gaze shifted awkwardly to hers. "Sorry about tonight. This isn't exactly what I had in mind when I invited you to dinner."

"Are you kidding me?" She glanced toward the stairs then back to him. "You don't owe me any apologies, Scott. That's your little girl. She comes first."

If anything, she owed him for all her lies. Helping him get his daughter to the emergency clinic didn't even amount to half what she owed him for her deception.

He took her hand. "I know, but I really wanted tonight to be special."

"It *was* special." She grinned. "It's not every day that I get to be a Good Samaritan."

A crooked smile curled his mouth, and he lowered his gaze before meeting her eyes again. "You were terrific tonight. I don't know what I would have done if you hadn't come along when you did."

"You would have been just fine."

"I'm not so sure about that," he said with reservation. "My head went a little fuzzy for a while there."

She nodded. "I know. I could tell you were thinking about your own accident."

His eyelids fell, and his dark lashes obscured his eyes. "Battle wounds," he said quietly.

"What?"

He gingerly turned over her hand and ran his thumb over the small scar she'd shown Savannah, making her nerves spring to life. When he lifted her hand to his mouth and pressed a warm, gentle kiss on the place she'd injured as a child, she caught her breath, unable to tear her gaze away.

Then he took a step back and pulled his sweatshirt over his head so he was only wearing a T-shirt.

He pointed to the long scar on his left biceps then took her hand again as he closed the short distance between them. "We both have battle wounds."

Her mouth opened wordlessly as he kissed her palm

again, letting the tip of his tongue taste her flesh. She breathed harder, transfixed by the moist warmth of his breath, his firm lips on her skin.

Her gaze slid to the slender, pale line on his arm, right above his elbow. That was one of his badges of honor. One of the marks that proved he'd faced the worst life could throw at him and survived. How many more such badges did he bear in places she hadn't yet seen?

"You can touch it, Mattie," he whispered. His intonation made it clear he wanted her to.

Her gaze darted to his once more to find him staring at her. Desire. Yearning. Trust. All burned from his gaze.

"My scar," he said. "You can touch it." Then he softly added, "You can touch *me*."

Until now, she'd been more of a passive recipient of his affections, not an aggressor of her own. Clearly, he wanted more. And if the fiery curiosity that burned in his eyes was any indication, he wanted to know she found him as fascinating as he found her.

"Do you want me to?"

He blinked as if fighting hypnosis, and his eyelids slid heavily over his eyes. "Yes."

Pressing her lips together, she drew in an unsteady breath, letting her gaze fall to his broad chest. It rose almost instinctively...the way a male of any species puffs himself up to catch the eye of the female he's courting.

And it worked. She couldn't peel her eyes away. The thin material outlined the hard ridges of his abdomen, and his pecs pushed against the fabric, which stretched against the tight peaks where his nipples strained under her gaze.

Tentatively, she lifted her hands to his body, stopping just before touching him. She closed her eyes and inhaled. This was another line she was about to cross, but she didn't want to stop. For weeks, she and Scott had danced around each other, drawing ever closer to this moment, and she wouldn't let it pass. Kissing and making out like horny teenagers was one thing. What was happening between them now was something else. Something mature, intimate. Sexual.

As she opened her eyes again, she pressed her hands against his warm abdomen. He exhaled with her, caving to her touch as she skimmed her palms up to his chest, his shoulders, and down his arms, hesitating briefly so her fingers could caress his scar.

"Battle wounds," she whispered, smiling softly.

His body was as fine and hard as it looked, cutting in strong angles, sweeping in supple arcs.

A quiet groan rumbled from his chest, and a moment later, his hands closed on the sides of her abdomen. She could feel his restraint...could see it in the way he licked his lips as his breathing deepened.

"I've never felt this way," he whispered, running his hands around to her back as he inched closer.

"Me neither," she whispered back. The muscles in his arms bunched under her palms as she swept them up and back down his chest.

His hand rose to her face, cupped her cheek, his thumb stroking back and forth as his gaze sliced into hers.

Now. Tell him now. He needs to know.

"Scott..."

His mouth dove to hers before she could utter another word.

She gasped and clutched the backs of his arms, locking him against her. This was a kiss unlike any they'd yet shared. It was primal, infernal, and spoke to a need as old as time. One requiring a man and woman to connect at the most carnal level.

In a rush of heat, he hefted her off her feet as easily as if she weighed nothing at all. She wound her arms around his shoulders, her legs around his waist, and held on as he swung her around and pressed her against the wall.

His lips raced from her mouth and down her neck as he pulled her sweater aside. "God, this is crazy," he said on a breath before he assaulted her flesh again. "I can't stop thinking about you. Can't stop wanting you." His hands dug into her hips as he surged against her.

Her fingers were in his hair, gripping, hanging on for dear life as she ground herself against him. Arousal whipped through her body, sending her into a frenzied, lustful haze. All she could feel, see, hear, and taste was her need to have Scott inside her, on her, making her come again and again.

His warm, rough hands pushed under her sweater, stirring fire beneath her skin. Delicious, hungry fire.

He was hard all over. Hard inside his jeans. Pressing all that hardness against the juncture of her legs, making her moan. If he kept this up, she would come. God, she wanted that.

But a voice in the back of her mind edged through the pleasure consuming her body, telling her she shouldn't be doing this. She shouldn't be dry humping this incredible, sexy, maddening man against the wall in his living room. His daughter slept just upstairs. What if she woke up? What if Savannah came looking for her dad and found him bucking between her legs? What if she heard their moans, their inevitable cries, no matter how muted they tried to make them?

"Scott..." She stared up at the ceiling, breathless. She couldn't believe she was going to stop him. But she just couldn't do this. Not under the circumstances.

Scott continued invading her senses, mounting an offensive that if she didn't stop soon, she wouldn't be able to. Her body was on the verge of passing the point of no return.

"Scott, we shouldn't...we can't...we need to stop..."

His motions slowed, and he lifted his flushed face from the side of her neck. His hair stood out in tufts where she'd been gripping it. "What's wrong?" His eyes searched hers.

"Your daughter. What if...?"

Catching his breath, he glanced over his shoulder to the stairs. A moment later, he lowered his head in understanding, reluctantly surrendering.

"I just don't want her to—"

"I know." He turned toward her, still holding her against the wall. "You're right." The tone of his voice betrayed how much he wished she weren't.

Her body still flamed. Still screamed for release. "I'm sorry."

He closed his eyes and leaned in until his forehead kissed hers. "Me, too."

She clung to his shoulders, letting her body and his come down together.

Finally, he stepped back and lowered her to the floor. "I'm sorry. I shouldn't have—"

She pressed her index finger to his lips. "Sshh." She wouldn't let him diminish the power of what they'd just shared.

His eyes narrowed as the corners of his mouth ticked upward, but he didn't utter another word of apology.

"I'm not saying that—" she bobbed her head toward the wall "—wasn't good. And I'm not saying I didn't want it. Because I did." She paused to let her words sink in. "What I'm saying is that it just isn't the right time. That's all."

She brushed her hands down the front of his T-shirt, smoothing out the wrinkles their passion had created. She hated the distance between them, as short as it was. She wanted him pressed against her again. No clothes in the way. Nothing but skin on skin.

But that would have to wait until another time.

He brushed his fingers through his hair, glancing to the side as if his body was still recalibrating to the distance between them, too.

A moment later, he looked back toward her. "What are you doing for Thanksgiving?"

Her eyebrows rose in surprise. "Okay, that was a shift

I wasn't expecting."

He laughed and turned his eyes upward as he shook his head at himself. "I'm sorry. Sometimes, I just kind of say what I think when I think it."

"I like that. It's refreshing."

He took her hands, his gaze meeting hers again. "So, how about it. You want to spend Thanksgiving with me?"

"What about Savannah?"

"Her mom's got her for the holiday. I get her for Christmas."

Lacey nodded slowly. "What about the rest of your family?"

"I'd rather spend Thanksgiving with you. We could go sledding at the golf course in the morning, which is sort of a Thanksgiving tradition around here. You know, work up an appetite." His eyes glinted, and Lacey wondered if he was thinking of other ways they could work up an appetite big enough for a Thanksgiving feast. "Then we can come back here and have a small, quiet, intimate dinner."

"Sledding?" she said, cocking her head to one side.

He shimmied closer, placing his hands on her hips. "You got something against sledding?"

"No, but it sounds suspiciously like fun." She grinned and coquettishly raised one eyebrow. "I didn't think you did fun."

His mouth twisted mischievously. "I'm starting to see its allure."

Chapter 16

Back inside her cabin, Lacey practically floated to the couch and collapsed onto the cushions. Butterflies fluttered in her stomach as she recalled Scott's body against hers, her legs around his waist, his lips on hers. Damn, but Scott could kiss! And not just kiss, but make love to her lips. And if tonight had been any indication, he'd be earth shattering in bed. For someone who hadn't dated in ten years, he had major leg-trembling moves.

Her journal caught her eye from the coffee table. Without thinking, she picked it up, along with the pen beside it, flipped to the next empty page, and began writing.

Dear Diary,

Scott and I reached a new level in our relationship tonight. It was incredible. I've never felt like that before. Like I was more than just an afterthought. Like I was actually part of something. I never felt that way with Doug. With him, I was a means to an end. He got off on cheating on me. Scott makes me feel special. He makes me forget who I used to be and helps me realize what I want to become. With

Scott, I don't feel like an afterthought. I feel like a woman. A normal, sexy, desirable woman.

For. The. First. Time. In. My. Life.

And—Oh, God, I can't believe I'm actually thinking this—but I'm falling in love with him. I know I am. My heart beats harder every time I see him, and I feel like he needs me as much as I need him.

We have so much in common. We both bear the battle wounds of our pasts. He's scarred both physically and mentally from what happened to him, and so am I by what happened to me. This means we understand each other. Or at least, we would if I could just be honest about who I am.

I hate lying to him. I hate that he doesn't know the truth. I almost told him again tonight, but then he kissed me, and my brain shut off. All I could think was "more!" If Savannah hadn't been upstairs, I would have made love to him. Right there in his living room. I would have given my whole self to him, body and mind.

He's so amazing, such a good man. A noble, moral man with principles. He would never cheat on me. With him, I would never have to worry that I'm not enough. He already makes me believe that I am. I already feel like I've known him my whole life. He makes me laugh, and I forget all about the shit I'm running from when I'm with him. He's like this wonderful, sexy grounding rod that diffuses all the lightning and tension from the air.

And he's got this beautiful little girl. If I were to have a daughter, I'd want her to be just like Savannah. So perfect. So talented. So strong and courageous. She got hurt today, and I helped take her to the emergency clinic. She needed stitches, but she took them like a trooper. Like a pro. I'm almost jealous of Scott because she's his. Isn't that crazy? But she's really such a terrific little girl.

What am I doing? I need to tell him who I am before this goes much further. But I'm scared. For the first time in my adult life, I know what I want. Him. And I'm terrified of losing him. What if he hates me for keeping the truth from him? What if he tells Savannah, and then Savannah tells her friends, and then someone finds out that I'm here. Then I'm screwed. The press will be on me in a matter of hours, and then I'll have to leave.

And I don't want to leave. I want to stay here. And Scott's the reason why. I want to be with him.

God, did I really just write that?

But it's true. I see a future in Hope Falls. With Scott. He wants to be with me because of ME. Not because I'm Lacey Moon. He really, genuinely likes me. ME! Most of the time, I never know if someone is truly interested in getting to know me or my celebrity persona. I've had so many people, men and women alike, who simply wanted to use me to get close to the celebrity life. They've lied to me and told me that they're my friends, but they really aren't. Look at all of them who turned their backs on me during the last Olympics. Look at Doug. If I'd been just another regular citizen and not some superstar, Doug wouldn't have given me a second glance.

It's hard to know who to trust when I'm Lacey Moon. But as regular girl Mattie, I don't have to worry about whether or not someone is being nice to me because they want something or because they're just genuinely nice.

Which makes this whole situation one gigantic Catch 22. If I'd been honest with Scott from the beginning, I never would have known how he really felt about me. By lying about who I am, I know that Scott isn't using me like others have.

But that doesn't make me feel any better about being dishonest. I suppose that's because I do care about him. If I didn't care, it wouldn't bother me, right? But I didn't come here to care about someone. I didn't come to Hope Falls to fall in love. I came here to find myself.

Lacey stopped, pen poised over the paper, as a scary revelation burst into her mind. So powerful was the thought that, for at least a minute, all she could do was stare at the next blank line in her journal. Finally, she pressed her pen to the paper and began writing again, although more slowly, as if it scared her to put her thoughts into words.

Then again, maybe falling in love is part of finding myself. Maybe that's what's happening here. What if I was meant to come to Hope Falls? What if I was meant to meet Scott that first day? Not because he would inspire me to figure myself out, but because he was part of the solution. What if fate brought me here because Scott and I were meant to find each other?

And now I have to tell him the truth. What if that ruins everything? What if that destroys this whole journey and voids everything I've accomplished in finding myself? I'm not sure I could recover from that.

She set her pen aside, staring at what she'd written.

As if fessing up to Scott wasn't hard enough, now she'd

just voiced—albeit in the written word—one more tremendous fear to make it that much harder. Because now that she'd found him, what if she lost him after telling him the truth? It was one more reason to encourage her to keep the truth hidden. Damn, but fear was a powerful motivator.

But there was so much more to the situation than that.

Things were moving so fast. He'd asked her to spend Thanksgiving with him. That was a holiday for families. You didn't ask just any arbitrary someone to spend Thanksgiving with you. Sure, she and Scott had been spending a lot of time together. They obviously had off-the-charts chemistry and were attracted to one another, but this was just one more indication things were moving faster than she was ready to let them.

She needed some perspective.

She grabbed the phone off the coffee table and dialed her mom.

"Lacey! Hi, honey. How's your search for self coming along? Are you starting to figure things out? Are you coming home for Thanksgiving?"

"Jeez, Mom. One question at a time." Mom was like a machine gun.

"I'm sorry." Mom laughed at herself. "It's just been a couple of weeks since we talked, and I'm excited to hear your voice. And I was just thinking about you."

She'd talked to her mom a few times since arriving in Hope Falls, but the conversations had been short, mostly check-ins to let her mom know she was okay. She had yet to tell her mom about Scott.

"I've been thinking about you and Dad, too." She missed her family, but she wanted to finish what she'd started before going home. *If* she went home. And she was beginning to think she wouldn't.

"So," Mom said more calmly, "how are you?"

"I'm doing okay. I started snowboarding again."

"How was it? And I hope you're taking it easy on your leg."

"Yes, Mom, my leg's gotten much stronger. And..." She tried to find words to describe how snowboarding again made her feel. "It felt surreal, Mom. Amazing, incredible, off-the-charts. It felt really good to be back on the snow. Back on my board." She puffed out a quiet laugh. "I felt like I did when I was a kid. Remember how I used to kiss the snow?"

Her mom laughed. "Oh, goodness, yes. I remember that. You were so little and so fascinated."

"Well, I did that again. I actually kissed the snow."

"Oh, honey...see, you're finding your way back."

But that was the thing. What was she finding her way back *to*? Competing? Snowboarding? She'd recaptured the joyous innocence snowboarding had given her when she was a kid, but did that mean she was ready to hop back on the competition circuit? Or even if she ever *would*?

"Yeah, but I still feel like I'm not ready. You know? Like I'm still missing something. Some key ingredient." She felt like whatever she still searched for was right there, though. Just in front of her but obscured by fog. If she reached out, she might be able to feel it.

"You'll get there," Mom reassured.

"I hope so."

"What are your plans for Thanksgiving?" Her mom didn't miss a beat.

"Um…"

"You're not coming home?" She sounded concerned, maybe even a little disappointed.

"I'm not finished, yet, Mom. I can't risk derailing myself by leaving before I'm ready. If I go home, the paparazzi could see me, and then they'd follow me back, and that would be a huge mess." A bigger one if they published pictures of her new look. Talk about letting the cat out of the bag before she was ready. No, going home right now wasn't a good idea.

"But it's Thanksgiving, honey."

Lacey scrunched up her face, realizing she needed to tell her mom about Scott. "I sort of have plans already." And there was the real reason she didn't want to go home.

"Plans? With whom?"

"I met someone, and he's invited me to spend Thanksgiving with him."

Silence beat through the connection, then, "*Him?* Mathilda Lacey Moon, you met someone and didn't tell me?"

"I'm telling you now."

Her mom's smile blared through her voice. "This sounds serious."

Lacey bit her bottom lip and glided the tip of her index finger over the most meaningful sentence she'd written in her journal tonight as if she were reading Braille. *What if fate brought me here because Scott and I were meant to find each other?*

"Lacey?" Her mom's interest piqued. "Are you serious about this boy?'

Lacey blinked at Scott's name in her journal, smiling as she thought about the way he kissed her. "He's not a boy, Mom. He's a man. A handsome, wonderful man named Scott."

"This *is* serious."

Lacey sighed. "He's incredible, Mom. He and his brother own this cabin rental place where I'm staying."

"How old is he?"

"Twenty-eight."

"Does he have any kids?"

"A little girl named Savannah," Lacey said fondly. "She's nine years old and utterly adorable. Reminds me of how I was when I was her age."

"How so?"

"She's into skateboarding and recently got into snowboarding, too. She says I'm her idol."

"Awe, I bet she's eating this up then. You know, you and her dad being an item and all."

"Well...um..." Lacey nibbled her bottom lip.

"What's wrong?"

"That's just it, Mom. They don't know who I am."

"What?" Her mom's voice shot through the phone.

Lacey dropped her feet to the floor, bent forward, and pressed her hand against her forehead. "I know, Mom. I know, but—"

"How does this guy not know who you are?"

Lacey cringed. "Because I didn't give him my real name."

"And they didn't recognize you?"

"I cut my hair and colored it, remember? And I wear brown contacts now. I mean, Mom, I look completely different. *You* wouldn't even recognize me."

"Lacey! I can't believe you."

"Mom, stop. Don't make me feel any worse than I already do."

"But, Lacey, you're lying to him."

"Not technically." She winced.

"Why? Who does he think you are?"

By now, Lacey was up and pacing, hand over her face. "Just some girl named Mattie, but that's not technically a lie because my real first name *is* Mattie. Well, Mathilda, but Grandpa always called me Mattie."

Her mom huffed. "But he doesn't know you're *the* Lacey Moon, Olympic snowboard gold medalist and X Games champ, does he?

God, when her mom said it that way, it almost sounded profane, as if she should wear a scarlet letter on her chest to broadcast she was to be shunned.

"No," she said feebly. "He doesn't." Then she straightened and pulled strength back into her voice. "I told him my name was Mattie, but that was before I knew things would grow the way they have. Before I fell—" She cut off and dropped her hand to her side as she stared out the window at the snow-covered lake.

"Oh my God, Lacey. Did you fall in love with him?" Mom's voice rushed out on a shocked whisper.

"Mom..."

"Did you?"

She sighed, took a deep breath, and blew it out. "Yes. I'm in love with him."

"And you're sure this isn't just infatuation, honey?"

Lacey searched her heart. She had never felt anything like this. Scott was *it*. He was the guy. The One!

"I'm sure, Mom. I love him."

"Does he love you?"

She thought about the way Scott looked at her when they were together. *I've never felt this way before*, he'd said tonight. "I think so."

Her mom blew out a heavy breath. "But he's in love with Mattie, not Lacey. What happens when he learns the truth?"

She dropped back down onto the couch, unsure how to answer.

"Honey, you have to tell him the truth," her mom said. "Sooner rather than later. Because the longer this goes on, the more likely he is to find out another way, and it would be best if he found out from you, not some news report or what have you."

"Do you think I haven't already thought about that a hundred times? This is eating me up, Mom."

"Then why haven't you told him?"

"I've tried, but every time, we're interrupted or I just

chicken out at the last second." She frowned and dropped her gaze to her feet. "And I'm scared." Bingo! And there was her final answer.

"Of what?"

"Losing him."

"Then you'd better tell him soon, or you will."

"It's just...complicated." She knew how Scott felt about lies. After what Theresa had done to him, it was clear honesty was a hot button. How would he react when he found out she'd been lying to him, too? Or at least that she hadn't been entirely truthful?

"The longer you wait to tell him, the harder it will be."

"I know. I need to tell him, and I will. I promise. I never meant to let it go on this long, and I never meant to lie. I just...God, I never knew when I made this journey that I would meet someone and fall in love."

"Life works in mysterious ways, Lacey."

She heard the proud, maternal smile in her mom's voice.

"Yes, it does." Lacey sighed and checked the time just as her stomach growled. "I'd better get going. I need to figure out dinner." She was supposed to have had dinner with Scott and Savannah, tonight, but that was nixed, given the circumstances. Looked like leftovers were on the menu instead.

"Okay, honey. Thanks for calling. And I hope Scott understands when you tell him the truth. But I'm here if you need to talk, okay?" In other words, if Scott blew a gasket when she told him her real name and that she had been lying to him all this time, Mom would be there to listen to her cry.

"Thanks, Mom. That means a lot."

They said their good-byes.

She trudged to the kitchen, opened the fridge, and stared blankly inside. She was making such a mess of her life. She needed to tell Scott the truth, but the moment she did, her journey of self-discovery would end. Because once the truth got out, she would become a target.

Then there was Savannah to consider. She would be ecstatic, but if Scott got angry, or if she had to leave, it would break the little girl's heart.

There was also Shirl. Once she heard who Lacey really was, the whole town would know. There were so many variables to consider, all part of a giant web. A web she had woven, even though that hadn't been her intention.

She dropped her face into her palms. God, this was getting complicated.

Chapter 17

By Thanksgiving morning, Lacey still felt conflicted, but she was determined to enjoy herself. If an opportunity opened, and the time felt right, she would tell Scott the truth.

She had decided to rely on her intuition and fate to guide her. The same way it had guided her to Hope Falls. Whether her grandpa was responsible for that, or some other mystical force, it had gotten her here, so maybe it could direct her in this, as well.

At ten o'clock, Scott's truck rolled into her driveway. Dressed in three layers to protect against the cold, she met him on the porch. He leaned in and kissed her cheek.

"You ready for the most fun you've ever had?" He was like a kid experiencing his first snow.

She giggled. This was not the same man she'd seen that first day at Pappy's. That man had been scowling and serious, all business. The man in front of her was all smiles, open, and warm.

"What?" he said.

"Just...you. You're so different."

"From...?"

She followed him to the truck. "From the first time I

saw you."

"When? You mean at Pappy's?"

She nodded, climbing into the cab. "Yes. You remember?"

He grinned as he slid behind the wheel. Something in his expression seemed to be saying, "Are you kidding me?" As he backed out of her drive, he said, "Of course I remember. You made quite an impression on me that day."

"Well, you made quite an impression on me, too."

"I did?"

"Well, yeah. You were so scary. Scowling and quiet."

He shot her a sideways glance. "I was not," he said doubtfully.

She laughed. "Then you gave me that tiny smile as you were leaving. That's when I knew you were okay."

"You saw that, did you?"

"Yes. The duality made you that much more intriguing."

He pulled onto the main road and headed north. "And then Shirl told you about what happened to me."

"Yes. Then I understood."

"What?"

"Why you were so guarded."

The air in the cab stilled, and for several long moments, nothing was said. Then he reached for her hand. She slid hers around his.

"Well, I'm not so guarded now." He took his eyes off the road for a quick second to meet her gaze then turned back to the front, squeezing her hand.

She smiled out the passenger window for the rest of the drive, her hand warm and comfortable inside his.

The sled hill, which was at the golf course, was packed. For an hour, the two of them sledded alongside kids of all ages. Many knew Scott from his volunteer work at the skate park and as the referee for the high school football games, as well as for all the other work he did around town. And, let's face it, Hope Falls was a small community. The kind of town that published a paper only once a week. Cozy. Everyone knew one another.

Scott took his share of verbal jabs for being there with a woman. This was the first time many of them had seen him with the opposite sex, and the kids teased him relentlessly. Most likely, they had all thought he would grow old alone, but now here he was on a date. For them, it was ample reason to give him a hard time.

A couple of the moms appeared affronted, as if they resented that Lacey had caught his eye when they couldn't. She could bet there were a lot of slighted women in Hope Falls right now. According to Shirl, Scott was one of the town's most eligible—and desired—bachelors...but the most unavailable.

How everybody responded to seeing Scott with her made their relationship all the more real. This wasn't a casual fling for him. To take her out publicly meant something. She could see it in his eyes, so full of pride. It was as if with every glance, he was saying, "I'm with her, and she's with me, and I want the whole world to know it."

Her heart swelled. It was almost erotic to see how

Donya Lynne

proud he was of their relationship. In that moment, Lacey knew without a doubt that she loved him. She had suspected as much a week ago, but now she knew for sure. Scott was the man she'd always wanted but thought she would never find.

He took her hand at the top of the hill as they waited for their fourth run.

She looked up at him. His cheeks were flushed from the cold.

"You having a good time?" he said.

"Yes." Just gazing up at him made her lightheaded. Was this how the realization of love was supposed to feel? Like she was lifting off, floating, carried by the clouds? "You?"

From the intense yet dreamy look in his eyes, he was feeling the same way. "Yes." Without preamble, he bent and kissed her. Not lewdly. Not like he kissed her the other night. It was just a simple caress of his mouth on hers. And yet, the effect was the same. Her knees went weak, her pulse raced, and she gripped his hand more firmly.

She knew his intent hadn't been to show the townsfolk physical proof of just how much he liked her, but the message was clear nonetheless. The air around them sparked with awareness. Like fire tearing through dry brush, all eyes turned on them. Lacey didn't have to see them to know they were watching. She could feel it.

Someone let out a wolf whistle, and Scott broke away as if he hadn't realized he'd actually been kissing her. His face flushed a deeper shade of red, and he glanced to the side then over his shoulder before clearing his throat and straightening.

"Oops," he said under his breath, giving her a sheepish grin.

Lacey's cheeks and neck were in flames, and she ducked, hiding her face against his coat as he put his arm around her and chuckled.

"Scott and Mattie, sittin' in a tree," someone singsonged from off to the side. Most likely one of the kids he knew from the skate park. "K-I-S-S-I-N-G."

She peeked over her shoulder as Scott let her go, bent, and grabbed a handful of snow. When he stood, he threw a snowball at the kid, laughing. "No teasing, Matthew!"

"Oh, no you didn't!" The kid named Matthew let out a whoop, spun away from another snowball as he ducked and dug out a handful of snow.

Next thing Lacey knew, the top of the hill ruptured into one massive snowball fight. Kids were screeching in laughter, running and ducking as white missiles flew in every direction like wayward asteroids. Several of the parents got in on the action, too, while others escaped on their sleds down the hill.

A few minutes later, with snow melting in his trimmed beard and dripping off his hair, Scott grabbed her around the waist and pushed her toward their sled.

"Come on! Let's go!"

She hopped on, and he jumped behind her, arms around her waist. Snowballs flew past them, and she heard a couple explode against the back of his snowsuit. They started down the hill, picking up momentum and speed, flying by the time they reached halfway.

Lacey screamed in laughter as they careened on the verge of out of control.

"Hang on!" Scott gripped her more tightly, letting out an adrenaline-laced shout.

They reached the bottom and shot over a small lip in the snow. The sled flew out from under them, and they tumbled off, rolling and laughing until they finally stopped in a heap of tangled arms and legs.

Laughing, he pushed to his feet and helped her up. "You ready to head home?"

She dusted snow off her clothes. Casting a glance to the top of the hill, where the snowball fight was still in full force, she nodded. "I'm ready if you are."

Being here with him, in public, and seeing the way he'd responded to her, as well as to all the attention, she felt closer to him in a way that touched her deep in her soul. In a way that made her want to be alone with him, where she didn't have to shyly hide her face after kissing him.

He dropped her by her cabin so she could clean up before heading over for dinner. She showered, put a few curls in her hair, which had grown out some, and dabbed on a bit of makeup. Then she changed into a nice pair of denim trousers and a navy-blue button-down sweater over a black camisole. With one final check in the mirror, she slid on her coat and locked up.

A few minutes later, she was taking the steps to his porch when he opened the door and blew her mind.

She'd never seen Scott in anything but jeans, sweatshirts, and T-shirts. But tonight he wore black slacks and a light-blue button-down. The collar was open, but he still looked breathtaking.

He smoothed his palm down the placket of his shirt almost self-consciously, as if hoping to make a favorable impression.

"Wow," she said, pausing on the top step to take him in from head to toe.

"Is this okay?" He stepped back to allow her in. "You don't think it's too dressy?"

With a shake of her head, she eased past him. "I like it. You look...nice." Try intoxicatingly sexy. She liked a man who looked good in a pair of jeans, but there was something alluring about seeing an outdoorsy guy like Scott dressed up.

A pleased smile spread over his mouth as he shut the door. "Thank you. So do you." He took her coat and hung it on the rack as she meandered farther into his home.

In a way, it felt like they were back to first-date jitters, as if this was her first time in his cabin instead of the second. Lacey imagined that was only because they both knew how important tonight was. Not only because it was Thanksgiving, and he was spending it with her instead of his family, but because of what had happened the last time she was here, as well as how their morning of sledding had played out. There was definitely a different energy between them now. One that was supercharged and hypersensitive...full of sexual undertones.

A fire crackled in the stone fireplace, and the flat screen TV was turned to the football game, the sound low. The aroma of roasting turkey, homemade cranberry sauce, and pumpkin pie drifted from the kitchen.

"You've been busy for the past two hours," she said, taking a seat at the breakfast bar. Bowls and pans scattered the counters.

"Naw, I actually prepared most of the food last night. This is just phase two." He nodded toward the pie. "Baked that this morning before we went sledding."

The guy was a regular Chef Ramsey, obviously comfortable in a kitchen.

"If you're such a great cook, why do you eat at Pappy's so much?"

He tied on a dark-blue apron and shrugged. "I don't know. I guess I just like their food." He opened the oven and basted the turkey. "They're sort of a town monument. Been here for fifty years. They renovated back about six years ago." He shut the oven and set the baster on the counter. "What about you? You seem like a pretty good cook yourself."

Clearly, he was remembering her one and only attempt at tackling the Julia Child cookbook.

She held up her hands and shook her head. "That was a one-shot deal."

With a chuckle, he opened the refrigerator and pulled out a bottle of wine. "So I take it becoming a chef isn't on the short list of things you've come up with as you continue your quest to find yourself."

"Definitely not. Too much work. But at least I know I'm dangerous enough to roast a mean chicken."

He unscrewed the cork of the wine bottle and removed it with a pop. He took two glasses down from the cupboard.

"By the way, how's that going? Your soul-searching or whatever you want to call it? Have you made any decisions, yet?" His voice held a hint of concern, as if he worried that as soon as she had her answers, she would leave.

"Nothing definite." She took the glass he held out to her. "But I'm getting close. I've been reading this book that's helped clear my head and put a few things in perspective."

He stood across from her, one hand on the counter, the other holding his glass of wine in front of him. "Oh?"

"It's by Apolo Ohno. You know, the speed skater?"

He nodded. "He wrote a book?"

"Yeah. His autobiography. It's really inspiring." She trailed her fingers up the side of her glass. "Did you know that he almost quit short track before making it to the Olympics?"

"Really?"

She nodded in emphasis. "After he failed to make the 1998 Olympic team, he almost quit."

"Wow, just imagine how that would have changed the face of speed skating." Scott sipped his wine, and, for a moment, he looked like he was reminiscing over his own missed opportunity to play football. "He made a difference to the sport, not just by setting records, but in just about every way. He was a testament not just to speed skating, but to the Olympics, too. You can't watch speed skating now and not think of Apolo Ohno."

"I know, right?" She took a drink and set the glass on the counter. "He sort of went through what I'm going through now. You know, soul-searching, trying to figure himself out and what he wanted to do with his life. After he failed to make the team, his father took him to this isolated cabin in Washington."

"Kind of like you, huh?" Scott leaned onto the counter in front of her, his eyes sparkling as he grinned.

She gave him a lopsided smile. "Yeah, kind of like me. Except for that whole isolated thing."

"Except for that." His gaze danced over hers as he slowly spun his glass with his fingers.

Tiny crackles burst inside her belly. Scott had her senses on fire with just a glance.

Forcing down the flutters of excitement, she continued with her story. "Okay, so for nine days, Apolo stayed in solitude. No phone. No computer." She rested her arms on the counter, around her glass, leaning toward him. "He took long runs and started writing in a journal." She looked up. "Did you know I've started writing a journal, too?"

Scott shook his head, grinning. "Is it helping?"

"Yes. It's helping me organize my thoughts and see what's important." And right now, she was looking at the most important thing she'd written about. Him.

"So, how did Apolo figure out his life in those nine days inside an isolated cabin?" The tone of his voice implied he was asking about more than just Apolo.

"Well, he wrote in his journal, took long runs—even in the rain—and long rides on his stationary bike, and began watching tapes of short track competition. Nine days later, he went from wanting to quit speed skating to committing himself one hundred percent to being the best. Nine days!" she said emphatically.

"You sound like you're in the middle of some kind of revelation."

She felt that way, too. For the last couple of weeks, she'd been inching closer and closer to what she had come here in search of. The fog in her mind was gradually clearing, and what she sought seemed to be right there. Just out of reach but so close she could smell it.

"Maybe I am."

If Apolo Ohno could figure out the rest of his life in just nine days, surely she could do it in two months. Maybe her focus wasn't as tight as Apolo's, and maybe she wasn't completely isolated, but she was almost there.

She sat back and gently clapped her hands on the counter. "Whether I'm revolutionizing myself as we speak or not, his book is really helping me not feel like I'm so alone." That had been a big part of her problem. Before, she'd felt like the one lone sheep in a pack of hungry wolves. "Like, maybe no matter what's happened to make me lose sight of who I am and what I want, it's not that difficult to get back on my feet and rededicate my life to a purpose...to help me rediscover what I love and to remind me that maybe the path I'm on is the one I needed to follow."

She thought back to something Apolo had written in his book. "You know, Apolo questioned what would have happened if he'd actually made the '98 team. He wondered if everything else would be different. Or was that just how everything was supposed to happen? If he'd made the '98 team, would he have gone on to become the greatest speed skater the sport has ever seen? Would he have found the hunger to be the best and dedicated himself to a regimen that would make most people insane? It was those nine days he took to find himself that changed everything and gave us the greatest short track skater in the world. In his mind, that was the path he needed to take to find his purpose."

"I think he's right." Scott gave her a meaningful look, his eyes drinking in her face. "Because if you hadn't felt the need to find yourself, Mattie, I never would have found *you*. And right now, you're what *I* need."

Chapter 18

Scott's words burned inside Lacey's mind throughout dinner, during dessert, and even now as she sipped wine in the living room as he finished cleaning up. He'd refused to let her help.

You're what I *need.*

She gulped down a swallow of wine as the words echoed in her mind once more. He'd made his declaration then turned away from her to work on the potatoes while she sat stunned and speechless at the bar.

From that point forward, conversation had been thick with...what? How did she put into words what she'd sensed hovering around them for the past hour? She could barely discern her own feelings. All she knew was that the mood that had sprung to life the last time she was here, when they'd shared their battle wounds with one another, was back with a vengeance. She couldn't really say the atmosphere was sexual, though, because it was so much more than that. Sexual, erotic, hopeful, expectant.

Intimate.

Unable to focus, she wandered his living room, blindly scanning the books on the shelves, the pictures of him and Savannah, the knickknacks he'd picked up over the years.

Turning, she spied a corner curio cabinet and wandered closer. Inside were several models of ships...like the ones Columbus sailed to discover America, with the big white sails and wooden bodies.

She looked closer. One was labeled *Mayflower*. Another, *USS Constitution*. One was clearly a pirate ship, with the traditional skull and crossbones on one sail. Scott even had the *Santa Maria* among his collection.

In the reflection off the glass, she saw the light turn off in the kitchen. A moment later, he approached behind her.

"Did you make these?" She kept her eyes on his in the reflection.

"Yes." He stopped close enough that she felt his body heat against her back. "I used to enjoy building models when I was younger. Now..." His voice trailed off as his hands eased over her hips. His nose nuzzled her hair, and his eyes closed. "Now, I'm just too busy." He spoke slowly, his voice breathy.

The tension that had been hanging over them all night finally broke, and Lacey swayed back as his hands crept around to the front. It was suddenly hot inside Scott's cabin. Blistering to the point she felt dizzy.

"Your hair's longer," he murmured absently, swirling his nose in a slow circle before kissing the back of her head.

She licked her lips, losing her grip on reality. Behind her, Scott was mounting an untenable offensive she had no hope of stopping, even if she wanted to. Which she didn't. In front of her, she watched the play-by-play in their reflection.

Every sense was engaged or soon would be. She could see him, feel his touch, hear his breath whisper through her hair, smell the gentle, clean scent of his shampoo. And she knew if this kept up, she would taste him.

But for now, he seemed content to remain behind her, caressing her stomach, kissing her hair, pressing closer.

Her focus waned as her eyes closed. Somewhere in the recesses of her awareness, she felt him take her wine from her hand, heard the base of the glass clink quietly on a nearby shelf, and felt his fingers begin unfastening the buttons of her sweater.

She opened her eyes as he took a step back and slowly dragged her sweater off her arms. She didn't care where he put it. The floor, the back of the couch, the trash. Just as long as he kept touching her, kept kissing her, kept making her feel like a treasured relic.

His nose dipped into her hair again, and his chest rose against her back as he inhaled and laid his hands on her bared shoulders, right over the straps of her camisole.

"Stay with me tonight," he whispered, his warm breath filtering through her hair to her scalp.

She drew in a barely controlled breath as his fingers hooked one strap and slid it down her shoulder. His other arm wound around her waist and pulled her snugly against him so that the hard angles of his body molded into the soft curves of hers.

"Spend the night with me." His whispered words lilted like a question, not a request. A moment later, his fingers trembled on her shoulder as he teased the strap of her camisole. The tiny quake rippled up his arm, through his torso, and down his other arm, which tensed around her waist. She felt the tremor's entire journey against her back.

He exhaled a shuddering breath that sounded like a light attempt at a chuckle. "I can't believe I'm so nervous."

She found his disquiet sexy and strangely flattering. What woman didn't want to feel as special as he was making her feel this very second? She was the first woman he'd dated in ten years. That alone was enough for her to believe she was a cherished treasure. But to witness his barely contained anxiety in the moment was extraordinarily intimate. Erotic even.

"I like it." She spoke softly, keeping the mood intact. "It's...charming." She bowed her head, biting her lip as he played with her hair.

His deep voice rumbled quietly. "Charming enough to say yes?"

The embers in the fireplace sizzled, adding an apropos soundtrack to Scott's intoxicating seduction.

Her soul sang for his touch, his lips on hers, his warmth.

The ethereal moment stretched, his breath going still as he waited for her reply.

Placing one arm over his, she inhaled his clean scent. Then, smiling impishly, she said, "I like hot tea with my breakfast."

He exhaled then brushed her hair aside. "Is Earl Grey okay?" She heard the relief in his voice.

Butterflies lit in her stomach. "It'll work."

A moment later, the most tender of kisses heated her nape, followed by the fiery, moist stroke of his tongue.

They'd danced around this for weeks. All the kissing, the touching, the suggestive stares...everything culminated into this. The now. The only thing left keeping them from being fully together. Last week had merely been a prelude to the main event. An appetizer that had only temporarily sated their hunger, whetting their appetites for the main course.

And she wanted to be devoured. Heedless of her secret and what would happen after she told him the truth, she wanted this one incredible night with him. If she could have this, at least she could hold onto that forever if everything else fell apart.

He released her, and she heard the soft rustle of fabric as he unbuttoned his shirt and let it drop to the floor. A moment later, he gently pushed his hands up the back of her camisole and around to the front, lifting the formfitting wisp of fabric until he reverently drew it from her body.

Their eyes met in the reflection as his palms grazed her breasts, making her nipples tighten and a moan escape her throat. Again, he circled his hands over her supple curves, increasing the pressure until she couldn't stand the onslaught of sensual pleasure.

Laying her head back on his shoulder, she reached around to clasp the back of his neck and drew his face to hers until their mouths met.

If it had been hot in the cabin before, it was beyond tropical now.

Scott claimed her mouth like a man deprived of affection for far too long. And he had been. Ten years was a long time to wait to be with a woman again.

He shivered as he gripped her sides and twisted her around to face him, deepening the kiss as he exhaled tremulously through his nose. As his body trembled again, Lacey sensed he was on the verge of losing control, scarcely containing himself.

She forced herself to pull back. If she didn't slow things down, it would be over before it began. Holding his face in her hands, she held his gaze as his fingers dug into her hips.

"I don't know why I'm shaking," he said, breathing hard. His gaze blazed into hers before burning a path to her mouth and breasts, feasting on her nudity, before returning to her face.

"Sshh." She knew why he was trembling. Because it *had* been so long since he'd made love to a woman. Because he didn't sleep around. Because he took physical intimacy seriously. Scott was a moral man, principled and gracious. For him to ask her to spend the night meant he respected her and saw her as more than a casual affair.

Taking a step back, she slid the fingers of one hand through the dark hair on his chest with deliberate slowness. She needed to calm him while keeping the fire burning, but she also wanted to drink in his physical beauty.

The scar on his biceps was matched by one on his shoulder and another on his chest. She ran her fingertips over them, paying each badge of honor the respect it deserved before moving to the next. Scott didn't move, barely breathed, hardly made a sound. Only stood there, chest pumping, muscles tensing under her touch, watching her as she stepped to the side and ran her hand over his shoulder and down his arm.

Almost as if he knew she was admiring his body and locating the scars from his past, he remained still, facing the curio, as she eased behind him and dragged the tips of her fingers over the solid, supple curves of his back. He had no scars here, just smooth skin over hard muscle. The manual labor involved in running the resort and performing his volunteer work obviously kept him in tip-top shape.

He was a physical god.

Leaning forward, she placed a sultry kiss at the top of his spine, then came around the other side and smoothed her palm up his arm to his shoulder before trailing it down his chest and stomach to the dark treasure trail that disappeared into his slacks.

"Did I pass inspection?" he said, markedly calmer but still seething with need. His eyes glinted in the firelight.

She pursed her lips together and, with only a moment's hesitation, slid her palm over the bulge under the smooth fabric. He hissed, and his hands curled into fists as the muscles in his upper body flexed.

"Yes." She felt drunk. "You definitely passed."

Now she was the one falling under his spell. Again.

She liked this give-and-take they played with each other. First he'd enraptured her. Then she'd done the same to him. And now it was her turn again.

All she wanted was to keep touching him. She wanted to feel the dips and valleys of the muscles of his abdomen, on up to his chest, which was covered with the same thick, dark hair that formed his treasure trail. His nipples hardened against the tips of her fingers, and her own tightened in response when a quiet, staccato moan broke from his throat.

"You're killin' me here," he said softly, closing the short distance between them.

She blinked up to his face. "I've never...you're...I..."

"Sshh." One side of his mouth lifted in an affectionate smirk.

Obediently, she quieted—she couldn't gather her thoughts, anyway—and he lifted her off the floor.

She wrapped her legs around his waist and collapsed against him, arms around his neck, as he headed up the stairs, down the hall, and into his bedroom.

The only light came from what had to be a night-light in the attached bathroom.

He set her feet on the floor and sat on the edge of the bed in front of her. His fingers trembled as he unfastened the button on her jeans and released the zipper.

"You're beautiful," he said, pushing her jeans down her legs so she could step out of them. Then he pulled her onto his lap, finding her mouth with his, holding her with one arm as he used the other to blindly fish inside his nightstand for a condom.

Thank God he was prepared. Obviously, he'd given

tonight some forethought. Bless him for that.

Pulling her down on top of him, he crawled backward to the center of the bed and reached under her as she continued feasting upon his lips. She heard his belt buckle jangle free, felt the fabric loosen as he unfastened the fly. The bed jostled as he pushed down his pants and kicked them off, and then his arms were around her, his hips thrusting hard.

Gasping, she broke their kiss as he rolled against her again, groaning as he did.

His fingers slid under the elastic waist of her panties, pushing them down to expose her bottom.

Lost to lust, she ground herself against him, undulating forward and back, running her breasts down his torso and back up as the physical connection between her legs intensified.

"Make love to me." Lacey had never wanted a man more, and not just because he turned her on sexually, but because he turned her on in every way imaginable.

In a flash, he tore her panties from her hips and rocked beneath her as he fumbled to roll on the condom.

Coaxing her to rise up on her knees, he reached down between them, grabbed his cock, and then exhaled as she began to lower herself on him. As the tip of him pressed inside, the skin of his face grew tight. His jaw clenched, and he let out a strained burst of air.

"Jesus, Mattie." His fingers dug into her hips.

He was a tight fit, but not a painful one, and as she continued to slowly take him in inch by glorious inch, she wondered just how long Scott would last. He was clearly struggling already to keep himself in check.

Finally, she took in the final inch and seated herself fully against him as they both groaned. He drove so damn deep, filling her completely.

"Don't move," he said, trying to breathe steadily, gaze locked to hers. "Give me a second."

Lacey kept her hips as still as she could but caressed his face. "Do you know how good you feel?" She kissed him, licking his lips.

He smiled against her mouth and closed his eyes. "That's not helping."

"Sorry." But she really wasn't.

He exhaled and opened his eyes. "No, it's just...you feel good. So..." His hands smoothed up her back, and then his arms wrapped around her and held her flush against his body. "So perfect. Like your body was made for mine." He lifted his head and kissed her.

Who would have thought the tough, brooding man she'd met two months ago was really a romantic hidden in wolf's clothing?

He thrust into her then, slowly, tenderly, with deliberate self-restraint.

She moaned into his mouth as he withdrew and drove into her again, this time with less inhibition.

The front of his thighs cradled her bottom before opening wider, spreading her legs farther apart, allowing him deeper penetration. With each upward surge, he grew more confident, his body tuning back into the animal drive he'd abandoned a decade ago. Like riding a bike, his instincts knew what to do, rediscovering the motions that had given him a daughter.

And as he continued to gain momentum, gripping her more tightly, awakening Lacey's long-dormant G-spot with each invasion and retreat, her awareness that she belonged with him grew even stronger. She hadn't come to Hope Falls by chance. She had come here to find him. In doing so, she found herself. This was where her future lay. In his arms, in his bed, in his life.

"Scott..." Tears formed in her eyes as she felt her orgasm ease out of confinement.

"Mattie..." He growled and buried his fingers in her hair, pulling her head to the side so he could violate her neck with his mouth.

I love you! I want to be with you!

Raw emotion bruised her veins, laying waste to her insides as she began to come.

"Scott...!" She cried out in desperation, driving her nails into his shoulders as she swiveled her hips in perfect rhythm with his thrusts. "Don't stop! Please..."

His embrace tightened. His teeth nipped her flesh as he gasped. His body seemed to quickly fall out of his control.

"I'm coming, Mattie." He grunted, his body going rigid.

Just as he cried out and slammed his hips into her one last time, Lacey's own orgasm blasted through her. Her hips rocked against him of their own volition, milking them both, drawing out his release as well as hers, until finally she collapsed on top of him. She was still secured in his arms, and her face was buried against his chest.

For a long time, neither said a thing. They didn't move. They simply lay in each other's arms, breathing heavily, letting the rapture layer over and around them as the pleasure slowly dissipated.

After a while, Lacey was aware of Scott's fingers lazily combing through her hair. It was a loving, comfortable sensation. One she never would have guessed him capable of that first day at Pappy's. But now that she knew him, his tenderness seemed right in every way.

"I'm in love with you," he said quietly, his voice a deep purr.

Lacey's eyes blinked open, and she held her breath for a heartbeat before exhaling and curling more securely into his arms. If she spoke, she was sure she'd break down. She wanted to tell him she loved him, too, but until she admitted her identity, she couldn't. It just didn't feel right.

His hand opened against the back of her head, and he kissed her temple. "I've fallen in love with you, Mattie."

Squeezing her eyes shut to hold back the tears, she nodded and hugged him harder.

I love you, too.

Chapter 19

The next morning, after making love again, Lacey lay tucked against Scott's side, her head on his shoulder, her arm slung lazily over his stomach. She couldn't think of a time in her life she'd ever felt so content. In one night, they'd crossed over from merely tiptoeing around their relationship to being fully submersed inside it.

"This is a much better way to spend Black Friday than going shopping, isn't it?"

Lacey smiled. "Yes. Much." She never had been one for shopping, and not just because of her celebrity status.

His fingers traipsed back and forth on her forearm. "Maybe you should stay here."

"Do you see me in a hurry to go anywhere?" The last thing she was thinking about right now was leaving.

"No. I mean, maybe you should stay in Hope Falls. You know, for good." He spoke cautiously but hopefully.

She had already begun to think this was where she belonged, so his suggestion didn't throw her. But there were still too many open ends and unanswered questions.

"What would I do?"

That was the only thing she couldn't reconcile with her desire to stay. For one reason, she was still weighing the pros and cons of retirement. She was strongly leaning toward one more run at the Olympics, which meant if she stayed in Hope Falls—and with Scott—it would be with the understanding that the next three years would be crazy busy with training and competitions.

So, there was the ultimate answer to her question. She would be a professional snowboarder again. But now there were more questions to answer, especially where Scott was concerned. She still hadn't told him who she was. Once she decided just how far into the competition circuit she wanted to immerse herself—and before she embarked on the rest of her life—revealing her identity had to be at the top of her to-do list.

In other words, she had herself in quite a conundrum, compounded by her strong feelings for him.

He chuckled and pulled her more firmly against his side. "Your job would be to let me kiss you every day."

She laughed and pushed up on one elbow. "I'm serious."

"So am I." He dragged her down and pressed his mouth to hers.

When she pulled away, she placed her chin on his chest, maintaining eye contact. "Well, kissing you every day's a given. But what would I do for a job?"

Even though she already had a good idea what lay in her professional future, she wanted to hear his thoughts on the subject. Where did Scott see her fitting in?

He thought for a second. "You used to be a snowboard instructor, right?"

"Well, yeah."

"We have a snowboard park in Hope Falls where you can work and teach kids to be bigtime champions."

How close to the mark he was. "I can do that in the winter. What about the summer?"

His eyes swept toward the window. "In the summer, I lead nature hikes along the trails here. You can help. I can teach you." His crooked grin creased one cheek as he turned his gaze back to hers. "Hey, and if that doesn't work, there's always Pappy's."

She rolled her head with a subtle shake. "I think helping two hours on a busy Friday night tapped me out on the idea of working at Pappy's."

His fingers plucked through her hair, combing the tangled strands off her face. "Well, there's always something to do around here. We can figure it out. Just...think about it. I'd really like you to stay." His hand cradled the side of her head. "Look, I know you didn't come here in search of a new home and that you probably just thought this would be a temporary stop along the way, but...Mattie...I'm not sure I can let you go."

She smiled and dropped her gaze to her fingers swirling through the hair on his chest. What she needed was some time alone to think through the last bits still eluding her. She was so close to obtaining the answers she'd sought when she'd started this expedition at the end of September, but she needed to take these last few steps alone.

She also needed to determine the best way to finally tell Scott who she was.

And she couldn't do either with him so close, distracting her.

One way or another, it was time for her odyssey of self-discovery to end and for the truth to come out. And she knew exactly where to go to find the necessary perspective to put the final pieces into place.

Chapter 20

Whistling to the Christmas song on the radio, Scott checked his e-mail then began running through his accounts payable report.

After spending the morning with Mattie, showering with her, making love to her twice, and sharing an extra large piece of pumpkin pie with her for breakfast, she had told him she wanted time to think about what he'd said about staying in Hope Falls. He got the impression she was more or less sold on the idea, but remaining here was a big decision, so he respected her need to think about it before agreeing to stay.

"I know it's a lot to think about," he had said. "And maybe I shouldn't have hit you with the idea like I did. It just...I don't know...it felt right."

She shook her head. "Hey, you've already warned me that you tend to say what you think when you think it."

He chuckled, sweeping his hands around her waist. "Yes, I do. It's a character flaw."

"It's not a flaw. It's nice. I like that you don't put your thoughts through a filter."

"Well, I don't want to scare you away, either."

"Do I look scared?"

She didn't. Maybe a bit wary, and maybe a tad hopeful, but not scared. More like she knew she couldn't simply give him a yes or no without giving his idea serious thought.

"You're the most amazing woman I've ever met, Mattie. I just can't stand the idea of seeing you leave."

Her cheeks flushed as she demurely bowed her head. "I'm pretty crazy about you, too."

His heart beat a little harder.

She continued, "That's why I need to take some time and think about this."

"Take all the time you need." If it took a month for her to decide, he just wanted her to stay in Hope Falls.

She nibbled her bottom lip then said, "I was thinking I could go to Sun Valley. Do a little snowboarding." A whimsical smile broke over her face. "You know, clear my head and see what Grandpa thinks."

He totally got the grandpa reference. She believed he'd led her to Hope Falls. Now she wanted to determine if he'd meant for her to stay here for good.

"If that's what it takes, then I'm all for it." He kissed her. "And I'll be here waiting for you when you get back." If a few days away was what she needed to make her decision, he would gladly let her go.

She snuggled into him, her faced etched with hope. "There's just a few last pieces I need to sort through. Things I want to tell you. I just need a few days to put everything together in my head." She gave him a playfully shy smile. "And I can't do that with you around. You're too much of a distraction."

Then she had kissed him. The kind of kiss you give someone you want to spend the rest of your life with. And he'd kissed her back the same exact way. Because, in Mattie, he saw his future.

Sure, they'd only known each other two months, but sometimes that's all it took. Sometimes you just knew. And Scott just knew with Mattie.

She'd said her grandpa had given her a sign that first day at Pappy's. Whether or not he had, Scott was just glad she'd come to Hope Falls. If she hadn't, he would never have known how happy he could be.

Liam appeared in the hall, breaking Scott from his thoughts of this morning.

"What's got you in such a good mood?" Liam said as he unlocked his office, looking over his shoulder. "Wait. Let me guess. She finally gave it up." He pushed open his door and switched on the light.

Scott frowned and let out a disapproving sigh, not liking the crude manner in which Liam talked about Mattie.

Liam stopped with his arms still halfway in the sleeves of his coat. "Is that it?" he asked. "That's why you didn't want to come over for Thanksgiving? Because you were getting laid. Nice, little brother." He flung off his coat and tossed it on his coat rack with his scarf.

"You know what? Screw you, Liam. I'm happy. For the first time in a long time, I'm happy. How about you just shut the fuck up and be happy for me instead of giving me such a hard time?"

"If you're so happy, how about introducing me to her.

You know, officially. You can bring her over tonight. I've got plenty of leftovers."

"She's not here."

Liam crossed his arms and leaned against the doorframe, scowling at him. "How convenient. Where is she?"

"She's taking a few days to herself. She left for Sun Valley this morning."

"Alone?"

"Yes. Is that a problem?"

Liam ran his palm down his face. "So, she left. Alone. And you think she's just going out there by herself."

"Get to the point, Liam."

He took one of the chairs at the small conference table in the corner. "Little brother, she's playing you. She's probably going out there to rendezvous with the guy I heard her on the phone with."

Scott shook his head. "No."

"What makes you so sure?"

Ever since Liam lost his wife, everything was doom and gloom. He no longer saw the good, only the bad. Scott supposed that could happen after losing the love of your life. He'd only known Mattie two months, but he already knew he'd be lost without her.

"She said she needed some time to think."

"And you believed her?"

"Yes."

"For God's sake, why?"

Scott burst from his chair and slammed his palms on

his desk. "Because I love her!"

The air in the room turned to ice. Everything locked down. Scott didn't think Liam was even breathing.

"Are you happy now?" Scott shoved off his desk. "I love her, Liam, and people who love each other trust each other. I trust Mattie. So, when she tells me she wants a few days to make some important decisions about her life, I'm going to believe her."

Liam grumbled into his hand then chuffed. "Yeah, and we see where that got you last time you believed something a woman said."

"Mattie is not Theresa. She would never lie to me. She's not that kind of person."

"You barely know her, Scott!" Liam flew out of his chair and thumped his fist against the wall as if trying to wake him up.

Scott slapped his hands against his desk again then paced to the side. "I know her better than *you* do!"

"Something is up with that girl, Scott. I don't know what it is, but it's *something*."

"It's always *something* with you, Liam. You haven't been able to see the good side of *anything* or *anyone* since Lisa died."

Liam ricocheted backward as if Scott had pushed him. "Fuck you, Scott."

"Fuck *you*. This is *my* life. Maybe you should worry about your own life and get your own shit together, because I'm done with you getting into my business with your lousy attitude."

Part of him hated throwing Liam's past in his face, but the man Liam had become was not the brother Scott had moved to Hope Falls to live with. And it was because Liam had never fully accepted what had happened. Instead, he'd fallen into denial and let bitterness consume him. And he was only getting worse. Liam needed to find love again and find it soon or he'd cross the point of no return and die a lonely and caustic old man.

Liam glared at him for several long moments. Then he turned toward the door. "Fine. It's your life. But you need to open your eyes. There's something off with that girl and you're too love-blind to see it." He stormed out of Scott's office without waiting for a retort, entered his own office, and slammed the door.

Scott let out a heavy sigh and lowered himself into his chair.

Hopefully, Mattie was having a better time than he was.

Chapter 21

Lacey stood at the top of the mountain on the opposite side from where the superpipe was and adjusted her lowlight goggles. The day was overcast, and she needed the special lenses to help see the ridges and ruts, otherwise the snow-covered run in front of her would look flat. And flat equaled dangerous in winter sports.

It was Monday. Three days since Scott had told her he was in love with her. Three days since they'd made love.

And Lacey finally knew what she wanted to do.

For three days, she had communed with the snow in Sun Valley. She'd ridden the superpipe for the first time since the Olympics. She hadn't thrown any fancy tricks, but she'd felt the desire to. But she wasn't ready for that, yet. She'd need several months of reconditioning before she was ready to throw a double cork. Besides, throwing mad tricks down the pipe would have been like wearing a neon, flashing sign that said, "Hi, I'm Lacey Moon" to the crowds hitting the slopes and the pipe at the mountain resort.

When she hadn't been riding her boards through the pipe, down the freestyle course, or just down a hill, she'd been in her room meditating. Well, maybe not exactly meditating. But she sat quietly, staring out the window at the mountain, at the people milling around in their colorful snowsuits. And she wrote in her journal, releasing the last of her fears and embracing her future and the excitement that went along with it.

Yes, she was excited again. She'd rediscovered her love of the sport. Between falling in love with Scott and hitting the slopes, she had found what she'd lost more than two years ago. Except for one last task, she was ready to be Lacey Moon again.

It's time to tell Scott. Past time, she'd written in her journal this morning.

Tonight. I'm telling him tonight. I only hope he understands. I hope he sees why I kept my identity a secret. It was as much to protect him and Savannah as it was to protect me, especially after we started spending so much time together. The press would have rained down like the Great Flood if they'd found out, and that was a risk I wasn't willing to take.

And revealing my identity sooner would have short-circuited the whole reason I took this trip in the first place. There's no way I would have found myself again and reached the conclusions I have if I'd told him who I was. My name would have gotten in the way. It would have caused problems I wasn't ready to handle. And it probably would have led to me leaving weeks ago to avoid what would have been soul-crushing pressure. I wasn't ready then.

Everything happens for a reason, right? Everything happens in its own time. That's why I haven't told Scott the truth, yet. Because I wasn't ready. I couldn't handle it. And the universe knew it, which is why it kept throwing up roadblocks and excuses. Why every time I tried to tell him, something interrupted us or stopped me. The weight and expectations of the people in Hope Falls once they learned who I was would have been too much. And there's no way word wouldn't have gotten around. And even if it hadn't, I would have worried constantly that it would. I didn't have the mental power to deal with that at the time.

But now I do. I'm ready. And at least I know that Scott fell in love with me. ME! Not "Lacey Moon." No matter what happens, I'll always have that.

She'd called Scott that morning and left him a voicemail telling him she would be home tonight and that she needed to talk to him. That it was important. And this time, no matter what happened, she wouldn't chicken out. She would tell him who she was.

Lacey gazed down the hill and clapped her gloved hands together. This was her final run before heading home.

Home.

In her heart, she knew Hope Falls was home now. She belonged there. They had a snowboard park where she could train. There was a skate park where she could practice and stay conditioned in summer. As far as the pipe was concerned, she could train out of Sun Valley. A couple of the other female Olympian snowboarders did, and it would be nice to train with them. A little healthy competition between friendly adversaries never hurt anyone. In fact, training with fellow Olympians often pushed all to excel.

She might have to relocate for a few months out of the winter, but Hope Falls would be home. She could work out the logistics and living arrangements later. There were a lot of arrangements that still needed to be made, but now that the pieces had fallen into place in her mind, she was ready to move forward, all cylinders firing.

She shifted her weight and ratcheted her board around so that it was parallel to the hill. Gravity took over and pulled her forward. As momentum turned to speed, she raced smoothly down the mountain, her board easily carving into the packed snow. The wind whistled past her, stinging her exposed cheeks and mouth, but the cold refreshed her. This was the day her life would change, and she knew in her heart that it would change for the better. Her gut told her that Scott would understand. He would be surprised, but he would understand. That was just how he was. A year from now, they would look back and laugh at how they had met, and maybe he would always call her Mattie. She didn't care. She liked that he called her Mattie.

All she cared about was finally telling him the truth.

The shout of someone in trouble came out of nowhere.

Lacey's head swung around just as the kid careening down the slope like an out-of-control madman struck her at full speed as she crested a small bump in the snow. The small bump became a cliff, and she flipped, landed on her side on the snowpack, and then gravity did the rest until she skidded off course and slammed into a tree.

Shit!

Pain shot through her left wrist and down the entire left side of her body. She'd wiped out plenty of times, so she knew what the different kinds of pain felt like. Her left arm and wrist had taken the worst of the fall, but she was pretty sure she didn't have any broken bones. Then again, her head was ringing like a church bell.

The rush of boots beating against the snow drew closer, as did the hurried swoosh of skis, and then gawkers, along with a couple members of the Sun Valley patrol, surrounded her. One was radioing that they needed a medic.

"No, I'm fine..." She tried to sit up, but she was too dazed and flopped back into the snow.

"Just take it easy, Miss." One of the patrol guys placed his hand on her shoulder. "You need to stay down, okay? Can you tell me your name?"

"Lacey Moon." As soon as her name left her mouth, she froze. Oh God. Had she given her real name? She'd meant to tell them it was Mattie. Not Lacey. Shit. Oh shit, shit, SHIT!

The guy's eyes went wide behind his goggles. "Excuse me?"

She closed her eyes and fought back her tears. "I'm Lacey Moon." She knew what this meant. She had about five seconds left to enjoy anonymity.

She heard someone whisper behind her. "Oh my God, it's Lacey Moon." Then the whispers grew louder. Within seconds, people were shouting all around her, gasping and snapping pictures and taking videos with their phones, all of them pushing forward, eager to get a look at the fallen Olympian.

"Tell them to stop taking pictures," she said, cringing as the patrolmen helped remove her helmet. She didn't want pictures flooding the internet. This wasn't how she wanted Scott to find out who she was, and she knew that within the hour, the story of how Lacey Moon had taken another massive fall in Sun Valley would be everywhere. With all the pictures being taken of her as she lay helpless on the ground, there was no way she could protect her identity, anymore. The cat was out of the bag.

"Hey!" One of the patrolmen shouted to the onlookers. "No pictures! Move away. Now!"

Few listened, and Lacey dropped her helmetless head back into the snow with a groan. There was nothing she could do. One out of control snowboarder who looked like he'd had no business outside the flats of the training area had just changed everything. In a split second, she had gone from anonymity to viral.

The crowd surged closer. Cell phones rose in the air in

ungloved hands. Everyone craned for a closer look. A few cries of "Lacey, can I get a picture? Can I get an autograph?" rang out above the growing upheaval of celebrity-hungry fans massing around her.

"Move!" the patrolman barked as the stretcher was hurried in and placed beside her. They quickly lifted her onto it and strapped her down, but the mass of humanity was swiftly becoming a riotous swarm.

Lacey covered her face. "Get me out of here," she said, starting to cry. She didn't want to cry in public, where everything was captured with the click of a button and posted online for everyone to make fun of and mock.

"Hold on, Lacey," the man said. "We're moving as fast as we can." He and his team lifted her and pushed through the crowd to the waiting snowmobile.

Cell phones shot out over her. The snap-click of pictures being taken rang out by the dozens. Hands pawed her arms and legs.

"Get back!" the man shouted at the crowd.

Lacey couldn't believe how selfish and rude these people were being. She was hurt. Nothing serious, as far as she could tell, but still, these people didn't know that. She could require swift medical attention, but the mob intruding into her personal space would be preventing it. All they saw was a celebrity. A piece of meat to consume. To them, she wasn't even human.

And so the machine began churning again. She'd thought she was mentally prepared to defeat that piece of shit, but she hadn't been expecting to be blindsided on a

Donya Lynne

mountain while enjoying a leisurely ride.

After several long, agonizing minutes of unbearable psychological torture, Lacey was finally secured to the snowmobile and whizzed down the mountain to the first aid center.

A news crew had already been on site filming a story, but apparently word had gotten out that she was there and had fallen, because the crew rushed toward her, cameras rolling. The reporter shoved a microphone in her tear-streaked face.

"Lacey, what happened on the mountain?"

She turned away, trying not to cry as anger exploded inside her. "What's it look like happened? I fell."

"Lacey," the reporter said, "you've been out of the public eye since your fall in the Olympics. Where have you been?"

Where did these guys learn how to ask such stupid questions?

"Can't you see I'm hurt?" she said imploringly. "I need medical attention, and all you care about is where I've been?" No way would she tell them about Hope Falls. She would do what she could to protect Scott and Savannah from these vultures, but she knew it was only a matter of time before they found them.

"Will we see you return at the next Olympics?"

Seriously? Were these idiots so desperate for a story that they were already talking about the next Winter Olympics?

"That's three years away." She frowned at the

242

reporter, who wore a fur coat and a matching fur cap that sat high on her head, as if she didn't want to mess up her hair.

"Lacey, can we expect you—"

She'd reached her breaking point. "Can't you fucking vultures leave me alone for two goddamn seconds so I can get medical attention!" Outrage spilled from her veins.

The reporter hesitated for only a second before pushing forward.

"The public deserves to know—"

"The public doesn't deserve to know anything right now other than I'm injured, need medical attention, and have a right to my privacy. Now fuck off."

Okay, so two f-bombs in one interview wasn't her finest moment, and her publicist was going to have to conduct emergency fire control, but right now, she didn't care. She was laid up on a stretcher, being carted into the first aid center, with pain shooting through her wrist, her head spinning, and about a hundred mobile downloads of her flying out into cyberspace, running down Twitter and Facebook feeds even as she lay there staring up through tear-filled eyes at the overcast skies.

So much for telling Scott the truth. With her name going viral this very second, if he didn't already know, he soon would.

Chapter 22

Scott carefully inspected every rose before selecting a dozen perfect blooms.

Mattie had left him a message this morning that she would be home tonight with her decision and something important she wanted to talk to him about. He wanted everything to be perfect.

He took the roses to the checkout, where the clerk wrapped them in green tissue paper then inside heavier paper of a light-blue shade.

"Thank you, Clara," he said, exchanging cash for the flowers. He'd known Clara for almost ten years. Her husband had helped build some of the cabins at the resort before being killed in a forest fire out-of-state four years ago. She'd decided to stay in Hope Falls after his death, and while she always wore a smile, he could tell his death still haunted her.

"It's about time I saw you come in for red roses, Scott. Must be one special lady."

"She is." He waved the bound roses at her, smiled, said good-bye, and headed out.

Next stop, Pappy's. He needed to pick up lunch before heading back to the office.

Donya Lynne

The fact that it was cloudy didn't dull his happiness one bit. In fact, nothing could kill his good mood today. For the first time in years, he could see a future that didn't include a lot of lonely nights and emptiness. He had his daughter, which filled some of the gaps in his life, but a man needed more than that. *He* needed more than that. And now, with Mattie, he could have a richer, more meaningful life. And children. More children. He wanted Savannah to have a little brother or sister, maybe both. And Mattie was so good with kids. The way she related to Savannah was incredible.

Maybe he was jumping a little ahead of himself, but he couldn't keep the hope he felt from pouring forth. Everything was falling into place, his future stretching in front of him, and he couldn't wipe the smile off his face.

"Hey, sugar," Shirl said as he entered the diner. "Those for your girl?"

He glanced down at the flowers. By now, the whole town knew he and Mattie were together. There was no stopping the rumor mill. "Yep, they're for Mattie."

Shirl smirked. "Mattie," she said with a chuckle and a wink, sounding amused. "You don't have to keep it a secret, anymore, sugar. Everyone already knows."

He stepped up to the counter. "I know that everyone knows we're together. There's no way I can keep a secret in this town." He flipped over the cup on the saucer in front of him.

Shirl gave him a funny look as if she were trying to figure him out. "You don't seem too worried," she said, pouring coffee in his mug.

"Worried? What would I be worried about?"

"About your girl, of course. *Mattie*." Shirl winked conspiratorially again and giggled as she set the decanter down. "I mean, it's all over the news."

Scott was beginning to get the feeling he and Shirl were talking about two different things. "The news? What are you talking about?"

She looked up and frowned. "Didn't you hear?"

Now Scott was starting to worry. What did Mattie have to do with the news, and why would she be all over it? "Was there an accident?"

"Well, yeah. I thought you'd heard. Isn't that the reason for the flowers?" She pointed to the roses he'd placed on the counter. It was too cold to leave them in the truck.

"No. I didn't hear about any accident. What happened? Is Mattie okay?" His heart raced. He needed Shirl to tell him everything she knew so he wouldn't worry, and then he would get in his truck and go to wherever Mattie was. If she was hurt, he needed to be there.

Shirl sighed. "You don't have to keep calling her Mattie, Scott. I know the truth. I mean, I can understand why you didn't want the whole town to know, but now *everyone* knows, so the jig is up."

"What the hell are you talking about, Shirl? Is Mattie okay or not?"

"*Lacey* is fine," she said with a huff and a dismissive wave. "It's just a wrist sprain."

"Lacey?"

She tsked him. "Quit playing." She picked up a bar towel and started wiping down the counter.

"I'm not. Why did you call her Lacey?" A bad feeling bloomed in the pit of his stomach.

"Because that's her name." She eyed him like he was crazy.

Like *he* was crazy?

"No it's not. It's Mattie."

Shirl stopped and narrowed her eyes. "Wait a minute. Did you seriously not know?"

"Know what?" If Shirl didn't level with him in about five seconds, he was going to lose it.

"Scott, you've been dating Lacey Moon. That's her real name."

He shook his head. "No...no, that can't be..." Why was Shirl playing such a cruel trick on him?

"Holy shit." Her mouth fell open. "You really didn't know, did you?" She gasped and leaned on the counter. "Scott, the woman who came into town two months ago, who is renting one of your cabins, and who you've been involved with, is Lacey Moon. The Olympian. I thought you knew."

"No, I didn't..."

Looked like the joke was on him. Scott stared into the distance as his mind raced through the memories of all the time he had spent with Mattie. She had been so secretive, as if she'd been hiding something. And then Savannah had said she looked like Lacey Moon, and Mattie had hesitated before answering that she got that a lot. The skateboarding. The snowboarding. The way she knew how to handle an injury. Even the fact that she had read a book by a fellow Olympian. There had been so many signs, and he hadn't seen any of them. Mattie had—no...*Lacey* had lied to him. She had fucking lied to him. Why? Why had she lied? To him? To Savannah? To everybody?

"It's on the house today," Shirl said quietly, handing him his order. Her face was the picture of worry and sympathy, but Scott knew that as soon as he walked out of the diner, she would be on the phone to everybody she knew.

Within hours, he would become the laughingstock of Hope Falls.

Without a word, he picked up the bag of food and the roses then left. Unable to feel his hands or his feet, numb to everything but the blinding realization that Mattie—*Lacey*— had lied to him, he somehow made his way to his truck, climbed into the cab, and drove home.

Not the office. Home. Because no way could he deal with work right now.

Not even fifteen minutes ago, he had thought nothing could kill his happiness, but he had been wrong. The reason for his elation was the very reason for its demise. Lacey. She had gutted him. With one stupid, fucking lie, she had killed it all.

Just like Theresa.

Nothing would ever be the same again.

Chapter 23

At almost midnight, Lacey pulled into Scott's driveway. The lights were on, but the curtains were drawn. He hadn't taken any of her calls all afternoon, and he hadn't returned them, either. Not a good sign.

After being tended to at the first aid unit at Sun Valley, an ambulance had picked her up and taken her to a nearby emergency facility. They'd X-rayed her wrist, determined there were no broken bones, and then wrapped her arm and put it in a sling. Then they gave her some ibuprofen with instructions to take it as needed and took her back to the ski resort, where she battled through the gathered media circus, hid inside the lodge for a while, and then was finally given a ride to her SUV by a member of security who snuck her out to his car.

Driving home in a sling had proven too risky, so she had taken the sling off and driven with her right hand unless she needed to use her left around turns, but the damn thing ached like a bitch.

The kid who had slammed into her on the mountain had apologized profusely for running into her, and then had asked for her autograph. Of course. She had given it to him, but what she really wanted to do was lecture him about taking hills he wasn't prepared for.

But that didn't matter now. What mattered was the man inside the cabin with curtained windows. The man who was probably trying to figure out why she had lied to him.

Parking her SUV, she winced as she pulled the sling back on then used her right hand to open the door. Snow crunched under her boots as she walked toward the open garage door. It was as if he'd been expecting her and this was an invitation for her to come in so they could get this over with.

She slipped inside the garage, past his parked snowmobile, and then took the concrete steps up to the door that led into his kitchen.

What waited for her on the other side? Would he tell her to get out? Would he be angry? Or would he understand? Something told her that last option wasn't going to happen now. Maybe it was the ominous cloud of negative energy hanging over the cabin that clued her in that Scott wasn't going to be happy to see her, or maybe it was just a gut instinct, but what waited inside wouldn't be fun.

She took hold of the cold doorknob, breathed in and out a few times, fought back her tears, and opened the door.

The first thing she noticed when she stepped into the kitchen was a dozen red roses in the trash can.

Oh boy. Oh shit. This was worse than she imagined.

As quietly as possible, as if that would lessen the damage she'd done, she closed the door behind her.

Scott was sitting on the couch, motionless, the TV on but the sound down.

"I was beginning to think you weren't coming," he said flatly. He didn't turn around to greet her.

"I just got back." She gingerly entered the living room.

"Savannah called," he said. "She was so excited to learn who you really are."

Lacey's heart fell into the pit of her stomach from the emptiness in Scott's voice. She stepped cautiously around the couch.

His gaze lifted accusingly to hers. His eyes were rimmed in red. "I can't say I'm as excited as she is." Anger and hurt seethed from him, and he glanced only briefly at the sling around her arm, but it was long enough for a flicker of concern to flash across his expression before he turned away resentfully.

"Everything's the same, Scott," she said quietly, still standing. "The only thing that's different is my name."

"No, Mattie—" His jaw clenched as he closed his eyes. When he spoke her real name, it hissed out on an angry breath. "*Lacey.*" Accusing eyes shot toward her again. "It's not just your *name* that's different. *Everything's* different. Don't you see that?"

"Scott—"

He leaped off the couch. "You're a goddamn champion snowboarder, Lacey!" He flung his arms out to his sides. "A two-time Olympic gold medalist, for God's sake! How is that *not* different from the woman I got to know as Mattie? Huh?"

Tears stung Lacey's eyes. "I'm sorry." Even to her own ears, her apology sounded lame.

"You're sorry?" He gave her an exasperated glare. "Sorry? You've lied to me about who you are for two months, Mat—Lacey! You lied to my daughter. You made a fool out of me! You've played with my emotions..." He paced to the draped window, his back to her, and jacked his hands up on his hips. "I...I fell in love with you, but..." He spun around, daggers flying from his eyes. "But it wasn't really *you*, was it? I fell in love with this sweet, adorable woman who glided into town and simply wanted to find herself. Who I thought needed me. But..." He frowned. "You don't need me at all, do you? You're goddamn *Lacey Moon*." His arms shot into the air as if her name was cause for fanfare. "What the hell would you need from a guy like me? What? Was I just some idiot you wanted to play with for a while? Some poor clod you got a kick out of lying to? Was this some kind of game to you?"

His words sliced into her like jagged rocks, and Lacey stopped trying to hold back her tears. "No, this wasn't a game to me, Scott. I *did* come here to find myself." She swiped her fingers over her cheeks. "After what happened to me at the Olympics...after what I've been through.... You don't know, Scott. You don't know what it was like. How awful it was. How hard it's been not to tell you the truth." Tears rolled down her cheeks. "I never intended to hurt anyone. And I certainly never expected to meet a man like you and fall in—"

"A man like me? What's that mean? Gullible? A

pushover? Someone you could play with while you tried to figure out 'who you are'?" He made air quotes with his fingers as if he didn't believe for a second that she had come to Hope Falls to figure out her life. "Of all people, you know how important honesty is to me."

Her of all people. She was the only one he'd opened up to about his past. The only one he'd told his version of events to about what Theresa had done to him and of the accident that had stolen his football career.

"I know. I'm sorry..." How many times did she have to apologize?

"I don't want to hear it. You don't need me. You don't need anyone."

His anger kept him from being sensible and hearing her, and the longer they talked, the angrier he grew. Lacey could see the hurt and frustration simmering just beneath the surface, fueling his outrage.

But she couldn't leave without trying to make him see the truth. *Her* truth. Not what he assumed he knew because of what he'd seen on the news.

"Scott, it's not like that! I do need you. You weren't just some game to me. You're the reason why I needed to come here, don't you see?" Her cheeks were soaked with tears, and she could barely speak through her sobs. "*I love you!*"

Silence engulfed them as he grew still as stone, his face a block of ice. For a heartbeat, she thought that maybe she had gotten through, but then he sadly shook his head. "How can I trust you, Lacey? How can I believe anything you say to me now?"

The breath rushed out of her, and her heart broke. She had lost him. She had waited too long. "Because it's true," she whispered. But it was too late. The damage was done. She should have been honest with him from the beginning. In a weak voice, she added, "And my first name really is Mattie. Well, Mathilda. I've just never used that name publicly. My middle name is Lacey. My grandpa was the only other person besides you to ever call me Mattie." She felt she needed to at least tell him that, to let him know it hadn't all been a lie. At least not technically.

Scott turned his back on her and walked to the window, where he stopped, hands on hips again, and refused to look at her. After several long, silent seconds, he said, "You need to leave, Lacey." His voice was tight.

Nearly gagging on a choked-back sob, Lacey nodded and let her tears fall openly as she turned and walked with leaden feet back to the door that led to the garage. With her hand on the doorknob, she turned halfway around but kept her gaze on the floor.

"Scott, I didn't tell you who I was because..." She paused, sniffled, and drew in a ragged breath. There were so many reasons why she had kept the truth a secret. For one, *she* hadn't even known who she was when she arrived in Hope Falls, and she had been so worried about staying anonymous that the lie of omission snowballed from something innocuous into a disaster. But the other reason was more personal...and more tragic. "Scott, if I had told you I was Lacey Moon, would I have ever known how you really feel about me? *Me?*" She lifted her gaze to find he was still facing the window, but his shoulders sagged. "As Lacey Moon, it's hard for me to know who to trust. Who really likes me for me and who just wants a piece of me because of who I am. If you had known who I was, would I have ever known how you really feel about me?"

He waited a long moment before replying. "You'll never know now, will you?" His voice cracked as if he was holding back an outpouring of emotion he didn't want her to witness.

Hiccupping through a sob, she opened the door. She sniffed and took a deep breath, "I'm so sorry. About all of this. I never meant to hurt you. Or Savannah. God, I'm…" She sighed. She could only apologize so much before the dead horse was nothing but a bloody pulp. "I really did fall in love with you, Scott." She sniffled, forcing back her tears. "Thank you for giving me that. I've never known what real love felt like until I met you." She took a deep breath then turned away. "Good-bye, Scott." She stepped out, closed the door, and cried herself into her SUV and all the way down his driveway.

She had just lost the one man she had ever truly loved.

Chapter 24

December 2 - 1:00 in the morning.

Dear Diary,

I blew it. I blew it with Scott.

I only wanted to clear my head and gain a little perspective, and maybe gain a little courage, because I was going to tell him the truth tonight. I couldn't live with the secret, anymore. I should have told him from the beginning, anyway.

God, look at the mess I'm making. I'm crying all over the page.

Lacey stopped writing and tried to dry the tears off the paper with a Kleenex, but all she did was smear the ink.
Shit.
She could barely see the page through the tears pooled in her eyes, anyway. With a sigh, she set the pen tip on the dampened paper and kept writing.

Screw it, you'll just have to deal with my tears, because right now I can't stop crying, and to be honest, I don't want to. Maybe after I've left here and put a little time and distance between me and the cluster fuck I created, and can finally forgive myself for hurting him, I'll stop crying. But that's not going to happen tonight.

For the next thirty minutes, she scribbled rapid-fire about what had happened in Sun Valley, from the reckless kid to the crowds to the reporter. No detail was spared, not even the ones pertaining to her emotions.

After they examined me and sent me off to get X-rays and patched up, all I could do was lie on the stupid doctor's table, miserable because I knew Scott was going to hear the truth from the media and not me. I was lying there, my arm in a sling, a fucking gigantic purple bruise forming along the entire left side of my body, the press gathering like vultures outside the doctor's office, and all I could think about was Scott. I didn't care if my arm was broken or whether or not I would ever get on a snowboard again. All I was worried about was how Scott was going to see me on the news and learn through some sensationalized report that the girl he knew as Mattie Moon was actually Lacey Moon.

I wish I *were* Mattie Moon, because then my life

would be so much simpler. I wouldn't have to dodge the media everywhere I go. I wouldn't have to question the intentions of every single person who comes into my life. Do they like me or do they just want a piece of me, like the motherfucking media?

Mattie Moon didn't have to worry about that shit. She didn't have to worry about ducking cameras or finding a quiet moment to herself. She didn't have to worry about whether Scott wanted to get to know her or if he just wanted to get *with* her? The only thing Mattie Moon had to worry about was how long it would take for Scott to ask her to marry him.

If I were Mattie Moon, I'd be with Scott right now, sleeping in the safety of his arms after he made love to me, feeling protected for the first time in my life, because that's how Scott always made me feel. Safe. Protected. ME. As Mattie, I got to be me for the first time in years, but my selfishness ruined it. I ruined everything, because I'm NOT Mattie Moon. I'm Lacey Moon.

Lacey Moon doesn't get such simple luxuries as normalcy, love, peace, and safety.

So, I guess I finally figured out who I am. But now I can't even look at my own reflection in the mirror.

Because I destroyed a man's life. I lied to him, and
I lied to his daughter, and I only hope that one day
he'll forgive me, because I'm not sure I can forgive
myself.

Lacey slammed the journal closed and tossed it aside on the
bed, then rolled to her stomach and sobbed into her pillow
until she finally cried herself into a fitful, restless sleep
around two in the morning.

But she didn't sleep long.

At six o'clock, with her arm and left side aching like a
bitch, she woke up, eyes swollen and bloodshot,
unceremoniously threw all her things in her suitcases, and
lugged her bags one-at-a-time to her SUV. It took a little
effort, and her entire body protested, but she got her bags
and all her equipment loaded in the back, then climbed
behind the wheel.

She wanted to get out of there. There was nothing left
for her in Hope Falls, anymore. Later today, the press
would rain down on the town like a hurricane. She didn't
want to be here when that happened. That would just make
everything worse for everybody. If she was gone when they
got there, they wouldn't be inclined to stay. Besides, Scott
had told her to leave, and it was clear from his tone that he
hadn't just meant from his cabin. He wanted her to *leave*-
leave.

At a quarter of seven, Lacey backed out of cabin thirty-
six's driveway, shifted into drive, and drove quietly out of
Scott's life. As she cruised by his cabin, she slowed, gave

one last look at the darkened windows, and then started crying again as she pressed on the gas.

He hated her for what she had done to him. Probably for what she had done to Savannah, too. And Lacey didn't blame him.

Maybe she just didn't fit into Scott's world, or he didn't fit into hers. Perhaps being Lacey Moon was a curse, and she needed to get used to things being how they were.

If she hadn't lied, she never would have known how Scott really felt about her, but by lying she had sealed her own fate and doomed their relationship. Talk about a Catch 22. She was damned if she did and damned if she didn't.

North of Boise, she pulled through a McDonald's drive thru for breakfast, and by ten she was on I-84 heading toward Salt Lake City. If traffic held up, she would be home this afternoon.

Only, Utah didn't feel like home, anymore. She had left to find herself, and she had. In Idaho. With Scott. In Hope Falls. In only two months, she had come to think of Hope Falls as home. Now she would have to rethink everything and find herself all over again.

Scott woke up and blinked at the glowing numbers on the digital clock on the nightstand.

Eight o'clock.

He rolled back over and pulled the pillow over his head, not ready to get up and face the day. Had yesterday really happened? Had he really learned that he had fallen in love with *Lacey Moon*? Why hadn't she told him?

After the exchange with Shirl at the diner, he had come home and turned on the news, and there she was, his Mattie. Only it wasn't Mattie, it was Lacey. She'd been in an accident at Sun Valley. Nothing serious, but the pictures of her on the stretcher being carted away cut to the quick of him, anyway. Even through the anger and hurt, he had still worried about her and hoped she was okay. But that was because he still saw her as Mattie, the sweet, tender woman he had fallen in love with. But Lacey was a tough-as-nails competitor. She didn't need him worrying about her like some lovesick puppy.

Last night when he had seen her arm in that sling, he had just wanted to take her in his arms and tell her it was all going to be okay, but that was what Mattie would have wanted. Lacey Moon didn't need him doting over her. She didn't need to be protected. She had trainers and coaches and doctors to do that.

Lacey Moon didn't need him, and he didn't need a woman who would lie about who she was, especially not after he'd been lied to before with such dire consequences.

A shot of anger roiled through him. He threw off the covers and stormed to the bathroom, where he cranked on the shower. Damn straight he didn't need a woman who lied to him. To hell with Lacey Moon. He slapped the soap against his arms and raked it up and down like he could scrub her out of his body if he washed hard enough, but it was no use, Lacey was engrained inside him, lie or not. She had planted herself inside his heart, and it hurt like hell that she wasn't there with him, where she would have been if she hadn't gone to Sun Valley and gotten into that accident and her name hadn't been splattered all over the news.

She'd told him that she'd intended on telling him the truth last night. So, that was what she'd been referring to in her voicemail yesterday morning.

He wanted to believe she would have followed through, but did he really know for sure that she would have? She'd had ample opportunity to explain herself before and hadn't, so who was to say whether she would have last night or not. But if she had, would he have reacted differently? Would he still have been angry? He wasn't sure. But at least he would have heard her out with a clear head, not one loaded with endless, sensationalized news stories. They would have talked. She could have explained why she'd lied, and maybe that would have made all the difference in the world. But finding out the way he did, from Shirl and from the nonstop news reports, had been too humiliating.

What she'd said to him last night before she left still echoed in his mind. *Scott, if I had told you I was Lacey Moon, would I have ever known how you really feel about me?*

He didn't know the answer to that, but her question bothered him for some reason. Like a niggling headache sitting just behind his eyes, he couldn't stop rolling her words around his mind.

But it was what she had said right before saying good-bye and walking out the door that broke his heart. *I've never known what real love felt like until I met you.*

Now that he'd slept, something about what she'd said didn't sit right. How could she never have known love? Was there more to Mattie—*Lacey*—than he assumed?

What did he know about her? He knew that she had come to Hope Falls because she was trying to figure herself out? Why? What did *Lacey Moon* have to figure out? She had everything.

He remembered something she had said to him on one of their dates. Something about how sometimes you can feel alone even in a room full of people.

At the time, he'd assumed she was speaking in generalities. But now...? A sad picture of the kind of life Lacey led began to form in his mind. Maybe she had come here to get away from all that. To reclaim happiness.

To find herself.

Wrapping the bath towel around his hips, he exited the bathroom and drew a pair of long johns out of his dresser and tossed them on the unmade bed.

His thoughts continued to process the facts. What had driven her to leave and run away? Change her entire look, no less? He hadn't even recognized her. She'd cut and colored her hair. And now that he thought about it, Lacey Moon had blue eyes. The striking blue of her eyes was almost as popular as her red-streaked hair. Mattie's eyes were brown. Colored contacts? Obviously, Lacey had gone to a lot of trouble to keep anyone from recognizing her. Why?

She hadn't just come to Hope Falls looking for herself. She had fled. She had purposely disguised herself to escape. But escape what?

He pulled on his long johns and a pair of jeans, his brain dissecting the facts.

After what happened to me at the Olympics...after what I've been through.... You don't know, Scott. You don't know what it was like. How awful it was. How hard it's been not to tell you the truth.

That's what she'd said last night. What had happened to her before she'd come here?

For starters, she'd wiped out in the last Olympics and broken her leg. And she'd taken a beating from the media, as well as from her fellow teammates and competitors. He remembered how Savannah had gotten so angry at "the awful things" they said about her.

The mystery that was Lacey Moon began to take shape. A picture of a battered, worn-down person seemed more appropriate for Lacey than a well-put-together, in-control athlete. The pressure on her shoulders had to be enormous. No wonder she had fled her life. No wonder she had disguised herself and hid behind a fake name. Well, not fake, but not the one she was known by.

Scott could only imagine the circus that Lacey had to endure in her life. From what he'd learned from their time together, she preferred the quiet. She liked the calm moments, the tranquility of a peaceful walk in the woods.

Maybe that was the problem. She had wanted to get away from the media circus after the Olympics. Perhaps she really had been trying to figure herself out after her horrible fall.

And here he had said awful things to her last night and kicked her out of his home without even an ounce of compassion.

Shit.

He should go to her cabin and make sure she was okay. That was the least he could do. He was still hurt and angry, but he was a big boy. He would get over it. Right now she had to be hurting, too. He didn't have to be a dick. He could show her he understood.

And maybe...

No, he didn't want to think they could work things out. At least not yet. He was still angry at what she'd done and not ready to forgive. Maybe in time he would see things differently. Maybe.

He finished dressing, pulled his Oregon Ducks skullcap over his head and trudged out to the garage. A couple of minutes later, he pulled up to cabin thirty-six. Lacey's SUV was gone.

Ice unexpectedly chilled his heart. He hadn't expected her to be gone. When had she left? Where had she gone?

Jumping out of his truck, he rushed to the door and knocked. No answer. As if he expected one.

He hopped off the porch and peered inside the windows. Nothing. No signs of life. He had a terrible feeling about this.

Resorting to his master key, he unlocked the door and barged inside.

"Lacey!"

Surely, she had only just gone into town, but the chill

running down his spine and freezing his veins told him she hadn't...that her absence was of a more permanent nature. He couldn't believe she was gone for good. They needed to talk. They needed to work this out. Suddenly, that was more important than his anger and hurt feelings.

In the bedroom, he opened the closet. The hangers were empty. When he opened the dresser drawers, they were empty, too. Her bags were gone, and the bathroom was cleared of all signs she'd even been there.

He raced back through the living room. Her books weren't on the coffee table, but in the kitchen, he found her Julia Child cookbook abandoned on the counter.

His heart unexpectedly heavy, he picked up the cookbook and returned to the bedroom, where he sat on the edge of the unmade bed. What was this dreadful heaviness settling in his chest? It hurt. Ached. Gnawed and spread down his arms and into his gut.

She was gone.

"Damn it." He slumped then rolled back on the rumpled bed. As he did, his head landed on something hard. "What the hell?" He sat back up and pulled aside the covers. Lacey's journal lay in a nest of wrinkled sheets.

He picked it up and stared at the cover. It was black with one of those weird skulls—he thought he remembered hearing Savannah call it a sugar skull—on it. The thought that he was holding Lacey's innermost thoughts in his hands made for a surreal moment. He'd wanted answers. Here they were. But this was her journal. It was private.

But something made him turn to the first page,

anyway. He couldn't explain it, but it just felt...right. As if she'd left the journal there for a reason. For him to find.

Turning to the first page, he read what she had written.

My name is Lacey Moon, but I don't know who I am. I'm trying to figure that out...

Once he started reading, he couldn't stop. He suddenly needed to know everything about Lacey Moon, the woman he had fallen in love with. The woman he *still* loved.

Chapter 25

After stopping for lunch around two o'clock, Lacey pulled into her parents' driveway around five in the afternoon. Thank God the press wasn't waiting for her.

"Lacey!" Her mom burst through the front door, arms wide.

Lacey suddenly needed her mom more than anything and ran into her arms as the sobs she had fought all the way home readily spilled. Her arm still hurt, and her body ached like road kill, but she didn't care. She just wanted her mom. The physical and emotional trauma of the past twenty-four hours had rendered her eight years old again and sorely in need of the kind of comfort only a mom could give. The kind that came with hot cocoa, a bowl of chicken noodle soup, and an order to do nothing but watch cartoons in her pajamas.

"Mom!" She cried against her mom's shoulder, racking sobs hiccupping her body.

"We saw you on the news. Are you okay? Are you hurt?" She looked up and down the residential street. "Come on, let's go inside."

Against the brace of her mom's body, Lacey dragged herself inside and collapsed on the couch, defeated. She was physically and emotionally drained. She had only barely held it together for the eight-hour drive home, not including stops for breakfast and lunch, but now she could let herself go.

"God, honey, you look awful."

Lacey hadn't showered since yesterday morning, so she had to look and smell a mess, and then of course was the disaster of how her life had imploded in a matter of seconds yesterday on the slopes, and of the fallout last night at Scott's cabin, which had set her on what had to be a record-setting crying binge that had left her eyes dry, irritated, bloodshot and swollen beyond description.

Mom sat down on the chair across from the couch. "Honey, tell me what's wrong."

"I can't right now, Mom. Okay? I just need..." She rolled to her side and began crying again. "I just need to be here for a while. I promise, I'll tell you everything later, but right now, I just need..." What? She had no idea what she needed. No, that wasn't entirely true. She needed Scott. But he wasn't there, and he never would be again. He was gone, and she had to learn to deal with that, but right now, all she wanted to do was cry, and sleep, and then maybe when she woke up, this would have all been just a bad dream and Scott would walk in and make everything right.

"Sssssshhh," her mom said, leaving the chair to kneel beside the couch. "Just rest right now, okay? You can tell me what happened later."

Lacey nodded, tears streaking her face as she burrowed into the throw pillow. Her mom draped a blanket over her, kissed her cheek, and then quietly left the room. A moment later, Lacey heard her on the phone, talking in hushed tones. To her dad, from the sound of it.

"She's home." She paused then said, "I think so, but she's pretty upset." Another pause as she listened to whatever Dad was saying from his side. "I don't know." Short pause. "No, don't come home. She's resting...She seems okay, just shaken...Okay, I'll call you if I need you. Love you, honey."

Love you, honey.

Her mom and dad had been married for thirty years. She wanted that. She wanted what her parents had, and she'd almost had it with Scott. But she'd blown it.

The tears renewed once more until she finally cried herself out and into sleep a few minutes later. The stress of the last twenty-four hours, along with less than ten hours of sleep in two-and-a-half stressful days, finally caught up to her, and she passed out like a vampire at dawn.

Scott filled her dreams, and for that, she was grateful.

Chapter 26

Scott read the last sentence in Lacey's journal, turned the page to find it blank, and let out a shaky breath he hadn't realized he'd been holding.

Tears pooled on the brims of his eyes, and he quickly scrubbed his palm up and down his face as he dragged in a heavy inhale.

Lacey had been hurting so much, especially when she'd written last night's entry, and his heart broke for her. He should have listened to her. He should have pushed back his pride and listened, because then maybe she would have told *him* all of these things she had been forced to pour into her journal instead.

The ink was smeared and the pages wrinkled as if they'd gotten wet. It didn't take a genius to figure out why.

In two months, they had fallen in love, and it was clear from every word Lacey had written about him that she was as in love with him as he was with her. But now what? He couldn't just leave to be with her. He had responsibilities here. And just because they had these incredible feelings for each other, it didn't change the fact that she was who she was. He didn't want a long-distance relationship, and with Lacey, that's exactly what he would get. She lived in

Utah and would be traveling and competing, and where would that leave him? At home, alone, which was right where he was now.

But at least he would have known she was coming back if she were merely traveling. Right now, she wasn't coming back at all. And, yeah, that sucked.

God, why was he even entertaining such thoughts? She had lied. He couldn't forgive her for that. It was over, and it was better this way. End of story.

That evening, with Lacey's journal taunting him from the corner of his desk and a slew of news vans invading Hope Falls—and in particular McCord Cabin Rentals—Scott kept his nose in the books, even though he'd already paid all the bills and recorded all the payments.

But staring at his payables and receivables beat heading outside and dodging the vultures gripping microphones and aiming their cameras at everything that moved. No wonder Lacey had needed to get away. Just a few hours with these mongers, and he was ready to put on a wig and a hat if it would help him leave undetected.

"Knock-knock."

Scott looked up to find Liam standing in the doorway. He turned back to his computer, not interested in whatever Liam had to say. "I thought you'd left for the day." Which was why Scott had waited until after he'd left to come to the office. "Did you come to tell me you told me so?"

"'I told you so' isn't my style."

"Yeah, well, you're thinking it, aren't you?"

"Actually, no. You should have listened to me, on the other hand..."

Scott glared at him.

Liam held up his hands. "Only kidding. I didn't come here to rub it in. You weren't answering your phone, so I thought I'd check on you and bring you dinner." He tossed a bag from Pappy's on his desk.

"I'm not hungry."

"Bullshit."

"Damn it, Liam. I'm not. Hungry."

"Then I'll eat it. I'm starved." Liam reached for the bag, but Scott grabbed his wrist, preventing him from taking it. "That's what I thought." Liam pulled his hand away and slowly lowered himself into one of the chairs in front of Scott's desk.

Fine, so he was hungry. But he wouldn't give Liam the satisfaction of eating in front of him. He'd wait.

"Did I invite you to sit down?" Scott said.

Without answering, Liam leaned back and crossed his ankle over his knee as if he planned on getting good and comfortable and intended to stay a while.

"How're you doing?"

"I don't need a shrink."

"I didn't say you did."

Why couldn't Liam just leave him alone?

"Scott..." Liam's eyes fell to the small Oregon Ducks figurine on his desk, and he sounded subdued. "You've made me realize a few things about myself in the last couple months. Maybe your methods were indelicate, but you woke me up." His eyebrows pulled inward. "You're right, I *haven't* been the same since Lisa died." He let out a long, uneasy exhale. "Maybe it's time I got some help."

"Liam—"

He held up his hand, cutting Scott off. "I've been a jerk, and for that I'm sorry."

"You were hurting." If anyone knew how hard losing a relationship was, it was Scott. He'd lost Theresa and now Lacey.

Liam gave him a dubious look. "That's no excuse, and you know it." His eyes slid to the left. "What's this?" He picked up the journal and the Julia Child cookbook.

Scott took them back. "They're Lacey's. I found them in her cabin this morning. She left them."

"Is that a journal?"

Scott set them on the opposite side of his desk where Liam couldn't get to them. "Yes. I thought I could get her address off her rental contract and ship them to her." He turned back to his computer, wanting the subject dropped.

"Uh-huh."

"What?"

"You read it, didn't you?"

His silence was as good as an admission. A knowing expression spread over Liam's face.

Scott pulled out his financial binder, even though he didn't need it. "It doesn't matter whether I read it or not. She's gone. She lied. I'm done."

"You make it sound so cut and dry."

Scott blindly flipped through his binder. "She's not

who I thought she was. She's Lacey Goddamn Moon, not *Mattie* Moon. She's not the woman I fell in love with."

Liam sat forward and smacked his hand inside the binder to make Scott stop paging through it. "Isn't she?"

Scott scowled at him. "She lied."

"All she lied about was her name, Scott. Her *name*. That's it. Do you think the rest was just a lie, too? That she made up this alter ego to come here and fuck with your head and play games?"

"What is this? I thought you didn't like her. Now you're suddenly all up on the Lacey Train?"

"That's your fault for making me realize what a dick I've been." Liam sat back and crossed his arms. "You were right, Scott. I've seen how happy you are, and it pissed me off. Both of us have been in the same boat for so long. It felt...comfortable. Like I really wasn't all alone. Then she came to town, and you changed. Suddenly, I was on the outside looking in. You got happier every day, and every day, I felt shittier."

"I'm sorry. I didn't mean to upset you."

Liam shook his head in disregard. "Like I said, you woke me up. I see now how bad I got...and how bad I came after you." He uncrossed his arms and scooted forward to the edge of the chair. "The point is, you were happy with her, Scott. Genuinely happy. I tried to ruin that, but thank God I didn't. You fell in love with her, and you deserve to be happy."

"I don't know. Maybe." It was the anger and his wounded pride talking, because after reading Lacey's journal, he knew things weren't what he'd assumed barely twenty-four hours ago. "But none of that matters anyway, because she's gone."

"Then go after her."

"I can't."

"What is it you're really afraid of, Scott?"

"I'm not afraid." But now he was the one telling lies, because he was terrified he had chased Lacey away for good. When she had needed him the most, he hadn't been there for her. What kind of man left the woman he loved hanging out to dry like that?

A conflicted one, that's who.

He shouldn't have reacted on emotion. He should have waited until he was calm before facing her. And then he should have listened to her without judgment.

Ah, the gift of hindsight.

After letting all she'd said last night stew in his mind, he knew she had hit the nail on the head with her concerns about how he would have reacted had he known her identity from the start. Would he have taken the time to get to know her, or would he have been too caught up with the name and all it entailed to see past the celebrity to the woman? He would have liked to say the former, but he had a feeling it would have been the latter. Not knowing who she was had allowed them to get to know one another at a level her celebrity status never would have afforded.

Hadn't he made a dozen assumptions about her when he learned who she was? He had assumed that someone like Lacey Moon would have her shit together. That managers, coaches, and trainers dictated her life to the minute, and that she didn't need a damn thing from anyone. And that had only been for starters.

Now that he'd read her journal, he knew the truth was far from his assumptions. Lacey was a human like everyone else, and she came with the same baggage and desires all humans do, only hers were magnified by her celebrity status, making it harder for her to find peace and understanding from every corner of life.

But more than anything, he had learned that she *did* need him. And he had failed her.

So, yes, he was afraid. What if he had broken the spell that had brought them together and caused them to fall in love? What if he went to her and found only pain and rejection in her eyes instead of the love and relief he'd grown accustomed to seeing?

"How the tables have turned," Liam said, shaking his head knowingly.

"What?" But Scott already knew what. He had never been able to hide anything from Liam, despite getting at each other's throats the past two months. The two could have been twins for all the freaky mind meld mojo they worked with one another.

Liam leaned closer. "She was afraid to be honest with you for fear of your reaction, and you reacted just the way she feared, which was what held her tongue in the first place. And now you're afraid of being honest with her for fear of *her* reaction, and you're fucking terrified that she'll react the same way you did, aren't you? It's like you two have reversed roles."

Scott sagged. "Liam, I can't lose her twice."

"So, you're just going to accept that you've lost her and not even try to get her back?"

Scott hung his head. "I don't even know where to begin to get her back, Liam."

Liam stood, crossed the hall to his own office, and rummaged through the files. When he returned, he held a rental contract in his hand. "Here. Her address. Start with that." He placed it on top of her journal. "You said you needed to ship those back, right. Well, maybe you should."

"Why do I get the feeling there's more to your idea than that?"

Liam smirked. "Because you know me too well."

"What do you suggest?"

"I don't know. Maybe you should include a little something extra in the package for her."

"Like what?"

Liam shrugged. "That's up to you to figure out, little brother." He walked to the door, stopped, turned around, and pointed to the bag of food. "I'd tell you to eat before that gets cold, but I think it's already too late." With that, he disappeared, calling back, "Hey, I think the last of the news crews are finally giving up and heading out."

Scott stared at the address on the contract. "Thanks."

Then he pulled the food from the bag and ate his dinner as the first flash of hope he'd felt in twenty-four hours lit inside his heart.

Chapter 27

Lacey dropped her handbag on the couch and beelined for the kitchen.

"How did it go?" her mom said from the table, a cup of tea in her hand and her empty lunch plate in front of her.

She grabbed the milk from the refrigerator. "Fine." She'd met with Trent today to discuss her plans for training. After being home five days, it was time to look forward instead of back. She couldn't wallow forever.

"A package came for you today." Her mom pointed to the counter.

"For me?" Lacey set the milk down and spun the small box to read the mailing label.

When she saw that it had come from McCord Cabin Rentals, her heart skipped a beat.

"Is that from him?" her mom said.

She glanced across the kitchen then grabbed a knife from the drawer and sliced the box open. Peeling back the flaps, she was surprised to see her journal. She hadn't realized she'd left it behind. She lifted it out to find her cookbook underneath. Otherwise, there was no note. Nothing to indicate Scott had even sent it.

"No." She dropped the books back in the box, took

Donya Lynne

them upstairs, and set them on her desk.

Christmas came and went, then New Year's, and then
Valentine's Day.

After reaching out to a few other former gold medalists
who'd survived the fires of stardom and getting some good
advice about how to handle her career, Lacey set some new
parameters with Trent, as well as with her publicist and the
media. Instead of being a hapless bystander, she took
control of her own brand. No more makeup ads. No more
last-minute interviews. Her focus was going to be on
training and improving her skills. The rest could wait.

The first week of March, she was going through the
piles on her desk, trying to make sense of the chaos as she
decluttered her space and started packing things up to
move into her new apartment. She pulled the box from
McCord Cabin Rentals in front of her and took out her
journal.

It had been three months since she'd left Hope Falls. A
lifetime ago, but it felt like just yesterday. Her heart still
ached.

She opened her journal and began flipping through,
skimming the entries. Reliving the special moments,
smiling at the happy memories, and then tearing up when
she reached the recounting of that last day.

It was time to write the final entry in this journal so she
could retire it and start a new one. One that would
document her progress back into competition form.

She grabbed a pen and turned to the next page.

And promptly sucked in her breath.

The page should have been blank, but it wasn't. Placing her hand over her mouth, she read in stunned silence.

Mattie (you'll always be Mattie to me),

I've had time to think, and I realize now why you did what you did. You were right. If I'd known who you really were, I don't think I would have gotten to know the real you. And I liked the real you I got to know. A lot. I imagine not many have had the rare opportunity I've had to truly know you, and I'm honored you chose me to share yourself with.

But then I betrayed your trust. I accused you before I understood your reasons. Instead of listening, I put up a wall. Something I've gotten very good at in the last ten years, by the way. I need to work on not doing that in the future. But now that I know the why behind what you did, I would have done the same thing in your shoes. I get it now. Completely.

Mattie, you're the most incredible woman I've ever known. What you did took courage and strength. More than I think I could have mustered under the circumstances. I see that now. And I can only hope Savannah grows up to be half as strong and courageous as you.

I'm so sorry I hurt you.

I miss you.

I need you.

I love you. Still. Even more than before.

And I'd love to hear your voice again.

Wake up beside you.

Touch you.

Kiss you.

Hold you.

...if my actions and careless words haven't destroyed all hope for us.

If you want to try again, I'm here. I'm waiting. I'll leave it up to you and honor whatever decision you make. I know I hurt you, and for that I am truly sorry. Please forgive me. Please come back. Hope Falls isn't the same without you.

Yours,

Scott

Lacey blinked through her tears and reread Scott's note. Then she read it again.

He still loved her. He had forgiven her.

And his forgiveness had been here all along. If only she'd looked at her journal earlier.

Scott was the missing piece. The one thing she needed to be truly happy now that her life was moving in the right direction. The logistics didn't matter. The fact that he lived over seven hours away was inconsequential. She loved him, and if there was still a chance to make things right, she would grab it and never let go.

She snatched up her phone and dialed. When her coach answered, she said, "Trent, there's been a change of plans."

"What do you mean? Don't tell me you've decided to retire. I don't think I could ta—"

"No, I'm not retiring. Not yet." She smiled. "But I need a few days off. Maybe a week. And then I'll explain everything."

She was in control. And she knew exactly what she wanted.

Chapter 28

At five o'clock the next day, Scott followed Liam out of the office and locked up.

"Any plans tonight?" Liam said.

"No. Just...home."

"It's supposed to warm up next week." Liam looked toward the blue sky. "Maybe we should check the trails for fallen trees before the summer tourists come through."

Scott tossed his jacket in the cab of his truck. "Yeah. Sure."

Uneasy sympathy coated Liam's expression. "Still haven't heard from her?"

Her. Lacey. *Mattie*. It had been three months. Surely, she'd seen his note by now. The fact she still hadn't called spoke volumes. He'd blown it. The best thing to happen to him since Savannah, and he'd let her slip through his fingers because he'd been too proud and self-centered to try and see things from her perspective.

"No. Nothing." He halfheartedly pulled open the door and climbed behind the wheel.

Liam gave him a tight smile and nodded in understanding. "Well, maybe soon, huh?"

"Whatever." He cranked the engine. Then, with a

simple lifting of his hand that passed for a wave, he pulled out and headed for home. As he rounded the bend, his foot almost lifted off the gas when he saw a blue Ford Escape parked in his driveway.

Someone was sitting on the porch.

Someone with blond hair.

Hair that was longer than he remembered.

She stood as he drew closer, and his heart began to race and beat hard enough he could feel the vibration against his sternum. Thoughts whirred through his mind, and his hands trembled as he put the truck in park and released the door.

As he made his way up the sidewalk, their eyes met. In that moment, Scott knew what it felt like to look into the eyes of an angel. Mattie could still take his breath away.

He stopped in front of her, not daring to hope she was here to stay. "Mattie..."

Her pretty eyebrows furrowed, and her face contorted into a pained expression a split second before she rushed forward and buried herself inside his arms.

"Sshh." His heart nearly burst from his chest as he held her close, kissing the top of her head, fighting back tears of his own as she unburdened what felt like a lifetime of emotion.

Her fingers clutched his shirt, and she pressed her face against his chest as she cried.

Closing his eyes, Scott gave thanks to whatever had finally brought her back to him, whether it was fate, her grandpa, or nothing at all.

She was here now. Everything was right again.

Lacey hadn't intended to cry. She had thought she could stay composed. But then she saw his truck. Then him. And then he was walking toward her and looking at her with what she could only describe as awe. As if she had risen from the dead and he couldn't believe his good fortune.

But the moment he said her name—her real, given name—she broke. The culmination of everything slammed into her, bringing her out as if from a dream. Until now, none of this had felt real. Through the long drive north, returning to Hope Falls, pulling into his driveway and seeing his cabin, to walking up to his porch...it had all felt surreal. As if she were outside her body observing instead of actively participating.

Feeling his warmth, his touch...hearing his voice again...seeing him. Now it was real. She was here. With him. And he was holding her, kissing her hair, whispering loving words.

"You're here. You're really here." He gently rocked her. "I'm sorry, Mattie. I'm so sorry I hurt you. Just...stay with me. God, please stay. I can't lose you again." His strong arms shuddered as he squeezed her harder.

"You won't," she managed to choke out between sobs. "You won't lose me again. I love you."

A mangled sob ruptured from his throat as if he'd been fighting it. And then another as he drove his face into her hair.

Men like Scott didn't cry easily. It took something

monumental to bring this kind of emotion out of a tough, rugged guy like him. And even then, such men rarely if ever let others see them cry. Knowing that he trusted her to see him at his most vulnerable meant more than words could convey.

"I love you, Mattie."

"I should have been honest with you from the start."

He pulled back, shaking his head as he cradled her face in his hands. "No." His eyes were rimmed in red. "If you had, I never would have fallen in love with you."

How had she found such an incredible man? "Scott—"

His lips found hers before she could utter another word, and whatever she'd been about to say vanished. Over and over, his mouth crashed against hers, firm, insistent...yearning.

In an instant, her body responded, reawakened after three months of dormancy. Never had a kiss been more salacious, more evocative, more full of promise and love and freedom.

Because Scott was freeing. In his own way, he'd freed her from who she'd once been so she could realize who she was meant to become. The two of them together were synergistic, better together than apart.

In the months since she'd left Hope Falls, something had been missing. It wasn't just that she'd missed Scott. She'd missed who she'd been when she was with him. How she'd felt when they were together. He was her perfect complement, and she was his.

With what felt like unimaginable restraint, he released

her mouth and pulled back, his eyes penetrating hers.

"Blue," he said, almost refreshingly.

"What?" She blinked and swayed toward him, missing his lips on hers.

"Your eyes...they're blue. Not brown. I like them."

With a smile, she nodded. "I ditched the brown contacts when I got home."

"Why?"

"Because they weren't me. I figured it was time to finally embrace me. Not Lacey Moon, but Mattie." She caressed his chest through his shirt. "And Mattie doesn't have brown eyes or long, brown and red hair. She's a blue-eyed blonde."

"And she's beautiful."

She bit her lip. "And she's realized she likes the simple things in life a lot more than she thought."

"You calling me simple?"

Pressing closer and searching his face, she shook her head. "Absolutely not. In fact, you're one of the most complicated people I've ever met." She raised onto her tiptoes and placed a sweet, lingering kiss on his mouth. "But despite your crazy-busy schedule, you lead a refreshingly simple life."

He kissed her back then bent his neck so his forehead touched hers. "One you think you might like to share with me someday?"

Happiness bubbled inside her stomach as she gazed into his serious eyes. "One I'd like to start sharing with you right now if you'll let me."

"Done."

"That was easy."

"Now you're calling me easy?" His hands gripped her hips and pulled her against him.

"If the shoe fits..."

He gave her a heated grin as his fingers grazed her bottom. "Do you want me to show you how easy I am?"

"I thought you'd never ask."

With one final kiss, he took her hand and led her inside, up the stairs, and to his bedroom.

"I was beginning to think I'd lost you," he said, slipping her sweatshirt off her shoulders. Her skin was still as soft, still as pristine. "What took you so long to come back?"

"I just found your note yesterday." She pushed her hands under his long-sleeve Henley. He raised his arms and helped her pull it over his head.

His fingers trailed down her stomach to her jeans. "Yesterday?"

She ran her lips over his chest as she unbuckled his belt and pulled it from the loops. "Yes. I was too heartbroken to look at my journal sooner."

He groaned as her mouth pressed against his chest again. Her tongue teased his nipple. God, if he didn't get her out of her clothes soon, he would pass out. "If you'd read it sooner, you wouldn't have been so heartbroken."

She let out a soft laugh. "True, but then would this feel as good now as it does?" She unzipped his fly and eased her hand inside to cup his erection.

He gasped and nearly came on the spot. "No more talking."

In a flurry, they finished undressing then fell into each other's arms. He was already rolling on a condom. He'd waited three months to be with her again. He wouldn't wait another second.

She cried out and dug her fingers into his back as he plunged inside her.

In a rhythm as old as time, he rocked against her, falling more in love with every stroke. This was his future wife. One day, she would have his name. He knew in his soul she'd been sent to Hope Falls so he could find her...even as she was finding herself. Together, they'd found each other.

And as she shattered around him as he exploded inside her, he knew neither of them would ever be lost again.

Epilogue

Three years later

Mattie McCord stood at the top of the superpipe, focused with laser clarity on what she had to do to win her third and final gold medal. After this, gold or not, she was done. It was time to retire. At the age of twenty-nine, she was ready to begin the next chapter of her life.

She'd earned the highest score in qualifications, and down at the bottom of the pipe, the woman who had qualified second had just scored higher, which meant Lacey had to pull out perfection—and maybe a little something extra—if she was going to edge her out for the gold. She knew what she had to do. The trick she had fallen on in the last Olympics. The one with the highest degree of difficulty. The trick no other woman had been able to land. If she nailed that, she'd guarantee gold.

She had this.

Starting her run, she flew down to the deck, swooped down the side, pumped across the middle to gain speed, and exploded up the opposite wall. The crowd gasped at the big air. Solid landing, back to the other side, up into an alley oop with a back grab. Another perfect landing, and it was time to throw down the clincher. No way was that other woman going to take what belonged to her. She was Mattie McCord, formerly Lacey Moon, the greatest goddamn snowboarding bitch on the planet. Once more, she flew up the side of the pipe. She soared. She flipped, rotated, and grabbed the back of her board. She flew through the air and back down toward the pipe.

And nailed a perfect landing.

The crowd erupted. Just three more passes, and the gold was hers.

At the bottom of the pipe, she pumped her fist toward the crowd and skidded to a stop.

She had done it. She had completed her last run near perfection.

"Yeah!" She pumped her fist toward the crowd again and dropped to her knees, the elation overwhelming her as she kissed the snow. All around her, the crowd cheered at deafening levels. Chants of "U.S.A., U.S.A." rose into the air. Gold was a foregone conclusion, but when the scores came up, they cemented it. It was the highest score ever awarded to a female snowboarder. She was retiring as not only a gold medalist, but as the reigning all-time-highest-scoring women's record holder.

She and the silver and bronze medalists hugged and shared congratulations, and tears of joy moistened her eyes. For this one brief moment, she lifted the weight of a country on her shoulders and basked in the glory of delivering what she hadn't been able to four years earlier. And it was all because of Scott. Her wonderful, supportive husband.

As if on cue, Scott broke through the crowd and joined her, twelve-year-old Savannah hot on his heels. On his head, he wore a red, white, and blue Olympic skullcap, which she was sure would be replaced by his old, trusty Oregon Ducks cap with its cute little pom-pom as soon as they returned home. She had learned after moving in with him that his favorite winter headgear had been a Christmas gift from Savannah.

"Lacey, how does it feel to be an Olympic gold medalist again?"

Even though she'd changed her name back to Mathilda as part of her identity reinvention, everyone in the media, and most in the sport, still called her Lacey.

"It feels awesome! Go U.S.A.!" She waved to the fans wearing stars and stripes. They went crazy, jumping, waving, shouting, snapping pictures with their phones.

"After the last Olympics, you weren't sure you'd come back. What changed your mind?"

She glanced up at Scott, who smiled back at her, eyes full of adoration. "A lot of soul-searching," she said, still gazing into Scott's eyes. "A lot of tears. And..." She squeezed his hand. "This guy right here. I couldn't have done this without him." The last three years had been grueling, but it was Scott's unwavering support that had carried her through.

"What now? What's next for Lacey Moon? Are you still planning to retire, or will you come back one more time to defend your gold?"

She shook her head, glancing between Scott and Savannah. "No. No more competitions. This is it. I'm going out the way I always intended. On top. This is where I belong. This is where I'm staying."

"There are rumors you plan to go into coaching. Are those true?"

"Yes, I'm thinking about coaching." She winked at Savannah. "And I just signed a deal to design a line of women's snowboarding attire and boards."

"Sounds like you're going to be busy."

"Absolutely, but first, I have to celebrate this moment. Gold medal, baby!" She pumped her fist again for the fans.

The reporter finally let her escape with Scott and Savannah, giving them a few minutes before they had to prepare for the medal ceremony.

"Who's the busy bee now?" Scott said, pulling her to him for another celebratory kiss.

"Takes one to know one, right?" She pecked his lips then pulled back and drank in his heavenly face. "But there is one more thing I want to accomplish in the next year. One more grand achievement." She said it with a slight flourish in her voice.

His embrace tightened around her uniform. "Oh? What's that?"

Grinning from ear to ear as she leaned into him, she gazed into his perfect, kind eyes. "Motherhood."

A victorious smile spread over his face. He'd wanted this since they'd gotten back together. She wouldn't make him wait another day.

His gaze glided over her face, waking a fire deep in her belly. "Wouldn't it be a great story to tell our child he or she was conceived on the night you won gold?"

She raised an eyebrow. "What are you saying?"

"Let's get this medal ceremony over with, and you'll find out."

Something told her she'd be carrying a very special, very tiny, very cherished package on the flight home. One Scott would give her later tonight if all went well.

Let the next phase of her life begin. She was ready.

From the Author

Thank you for reading Finding Lacey Moon. If you enjoyed the book, please consider leaving a review at the retail site of your choice or on Goodreads to help other readers discover the Hope Falls Series, as well as my other books.

Now, turn the page for an excerpt from Good Karma, the first book in my Strong Karma Trilogy, which is already available for purchase.

Excerpt from Good Karma

Tuesday night, Karma sat on her couch, finishing a plate of homemade lasagna. The TV was turned to some random movie she was neither interested in nor paying attention to. She simply wanted noise to drown out the barrage of voices that echoed through her head. So many questions, so much confusion. And no answers.

Mark had left the office with Don at ten o'clock this morning to attend two off-site meetings and a client business dinner. She hadn't heard from him all day, and now that they had entered into what felt like a covert affair, she was antsy to see him.

At eight thirty, her phone dinged with a text. Snatching it from the coffee table, her heart skipped. The message was from Mark.

Are you busy?

She typed out her response. *No.*

Less than thirty seconds later, her phone chimed again. *Can I come over?*

Her mind screamed, *Yes! God yes!* Instead, she typed, *Sure.*

She stared at the blank screen, biting her lip, eyes wide. Something about the fact that he was texting her gave her a perverse thrill.

She actually jumped when her phone dinged again.

Be there in fifteen.

She hopped up, quickly cleaned her dishes, put away the leftover lasagna, rushed to check her hair, took a few deep breaths, and returned to the living room.

A few minutes later, he arrived with a quiet knock.

Butterflies took flight, angels sang, and rainbows and unicorns danced around her heart.

"Hi," she said, holding the door open.

"Hi." He had changed into loose jeans and a faded-blue T-shirt, and he held a small, gift-wrapped box in his hands.

She waved him in and gestured toward the couch. "I wasn't sure I would hear from you tonight."

"I would have called sooner, but dinner ran late, and I wanted to pick something up before coming over." He held out the box as he settled into the couch.

"What's this?" He was already buying her gifts? She had never received a gift from a man before.

"Just a little something I thought might be fun to help us get to know one another." His devilish smile told her this wasn't just any ordinary gift. "Go ahead, open it."

"Is this going to embarrass me?" She removed the bow on top.

"I guarantee it."

"Oh God." She hid her face in her hand, making him laugh.

"Oh, come on. It's not *that* bad."

She ripped off the paper, pulled out a four by five box, and read the front. *Cosmo's Truth or Dare: Our Naughtiest Game Ever!* Dumbfounded and speechless, her mouth flapped open, closed, and then opened again as she lifted her gaze to Mark's. Was he serious?

"Here, let me open that for you." Mark took the box

from her and lifted the side, which closed magnetically. The top opened like a book, and inside was a deck of cards.

"What exactly did you have planned tonight?" She gulped and eyed the cards as if they were scary intruders. It didn't take a genius to figure out by the cover of the box that this was a game for two consenting adults. And, yes, while she had agreed to move forward with Mark, consenting to whatever the *dare* portion of this game likely entailed wasn't what she had in mind this soon in their relationship...or whatever this was between them.

Mark thumbed through the deck—there had to be at least two hundred cards—then set them on the coffee table.

"Don't worry. I don't plan on daring you to do anything. I just thought we could go through some of the truths and learn a little more about one another, and maybe have a little fun and a few laughs."

"Why do I get the feeling you just want to make me as uncomfortable as possible?" She had felt the color drain from her face the moment she read the game's title.

"That's precisely why I bought the game."

"Huh?" Was Mark sadistic?

"What I mean is that, sometimes it takes uncomfortable circumstances for us to find ourselves. The more uncomfortable the better if change is what you want." He took her hand. "And I think you want change, or you wouldn't have worn that brooch today. Am I right?"

He made a good point. "Well...yes."

"Trust me. I just want to get to know you. That's all. So I can take better care of you." He searched her eyes for understanding.

She liked his choice of words. *So I can take better care of you.* How many women could say that the men in their lives held such attitudes?

"Okay," she said, feeling her nerves ease.

He let go of her hand and sat back. "So let's just play *Truth or Truth* with our game. No dares tonight." He nodded toward the cards on the table. "Just pick up a card, and ask me the question. I'll answer then do the same. How's that sound?"

Karma took a deep breath and eyed the cards. "Okay. But if I die from embarrassment, tell my family I loved them."

His deep, throaty laughter tickled her ears. She loved his laugh.

"I promise," he said, crossing his heart. "Now, go on. Take a card and ask me a question."

She picked up the top card. Just reading the question to herself made her face burn.

"Okay," she said, sighing, "Do you like your hair pulled during sex?" She couldn't even read it aloud with a straight face, let alone make eye contact.

"Hmm, I guess that depends on the situation, but yes, generally speaking, I like when a woman pulls my hair during sex."

Curious now, Karma looked up. "Really? Why?" She figured it would hurt if someone pulled her hair, whether during sex or otherwise.

He shrugged, and his left eyebrow shot up. "I guess I

like it because it shows me the woman is really enjoying herself. That she's completely lost to her passion." He paused. "I take it you've never had your hair pulled like that." It wasn't a question.

Karma briskly shook her head and set the card down like it was a hot potato. "No."

"Didn't think so." Mark reached for the deck and pulled off the next card. A crooked grin spread over his mouth as he read the question. "Who was the first person you ever kissed? Was it good or bad?"

Well, that wasn't too bad. A question like that wasn't likely to send her into a queasy fit. She reluctantly told him about kissing Tony in high school and how she froze up, which made him laugh.

"Okay then, how about the second guy you kissed?"

"Hey, that's two questions."

He crossed his hands in his lap. "Just getting to you know you."

"Fine, play by your rules." She took a deep breath and blew it out. "The second guy I kissed was named Brian, and..." She cringed. "That kiss was kind of bad, too."

"How so?"

Of course Mark would want specifics.

"He and I were both...um...virgins, and I kind of froze up with him, too. Just like with Tony."

"How did you and Brian meet?"

"At a movie theater where we both worked during senior year. Brian attended a different school than I did, but we got to be pretty good friends at work."

"Did you end up having sex with Brian?" Mark's eyes never wavered from hers.

Flames shot through Karma's face and down her neck, and she dropped her gaze to her hands, which rested in her lap. "Yes. Eventually."

"Was it good?"

She shook her head. "Not really."

"Tell me about it."

She knew what Mark was trying to do. He was trying to get her to open up and become more comfortable talking about this kind of thing—trying to enforce change. But right now, this had to be the most awkward, difficult conversation she'd ever had. Even worse than the time she got called to the principal's office in junior high for calling a classmate who was bullying her a skanky bitch. Not her finest hour.

She lifted her gaze to his and found warmth and safety staring back. Mark really did have her best intentions at heart, and he clearly wanted their time together—as little as they had—to mean something and make a difference.

She gathered the courage and moved forward. "Brian and I were virgins. We met at work." Each sentence felt labored, but as she forced herself to continue, it grew easier. "He was an usher, and I worked in the concession stand. After work, we often hung out together, and now that I think about it, he probably liked me more than I liked him." Brian had been a nice boy, and, at the time, she had felt like he was as good a guy as any to lose her virginity to. Now she wished she hadn't, but at the time, all she wanted was to get her first time over with in hopes it would make her feel more grown-up and help put her past behind her.

As she relayed the story, the memories of that night six years ago rushed into her mind, and they felt just as fresh, just as raw.

Brian's mom had been out for the evening, and he had stolen a condom from her bedside table before rushing back into the living room where Karma waited for him, half naked, on the floor.

He began to put on the condom, and then, "Damn it!"

"What?" Karma frowned as Brian scampered bare-assed out of the living room and down the hall toward his mom's room again. The only light came from the TV, which was fine by her. The less light, the better.

"Condom broke," he called back.

Karma sat up in the shadow-strewn room and straightened her work shirt, which smelled like buttered popcorn, then pulled her jeans over her lap, waiting for him to return. The only way she could do this was if she could keep on some of her clothes. No one had seen her naked before. Brian didn't seem to mind her shyness, though. Then again, he was an eighteen-year-old virgin, too. He was probably just happy he was finally getting laid.

She tucked her long, mousy brown hair behind her ears and looked around. Some B-rate monster flick was on TV, and the smell of two-hour-old pizza wafted from the open box on the nearby coffee table. This wasn't how Karma imagined she would lose her virginity. On a hard living room floor, which was covered with carpet that looked like dirt and felt like fuzzy tree bark, but at least tomorrow she could wake up and know she had finally done it.

She eyed the afghan tossed over the back of the couch. A blanket was a good idea. This carpet didn't exactly look sanitary on her bare bottom. She pulled the afghan to the floor and spread it out, sitting back down and covering up with her jeans again just as Brian returned from his mom's bedroom. He held two more condoms in his hand.

"Just in case I break another one," he said breathlessly, dropping to the floor in front of her as he tore one open.

Unlike her, Brian was naked, and his erection strained toward her. It looked a little too big to fit.

She gulped and took a nervous breath as he put the condom on.

"There," he said with a smile and wiped his hand on the blanket. "Did it right this time." He laughed nervously. "I tried to put the last one on backward."

"Oh, okay." Karma nibbled her lip. She hadn't known there was a right or wrong way to put on a condom, but now that she thought about it, it made sense. "So...now what?"

Brian clumsily lurched forward and kissed her, pushing her to the floor. She bonked her head.

"Sorry," he said, wriggling around on top of her.

"No, it's okay. Just..." Her leg was pinned, and she worked it out from under him. "There." She bent her knees on either side of his hips as he fumbled around, pushing against her like an excited bull charging a matador.

"Am I in the right place?" Brian grunted and shifted, and his erection bumped and pushed against her.

"I don't know...ow!"

"Sorry."

"That's okay. I don't think that's—ow!"

What were they doing wrong?

"Here, maybe if I..." Brian reached down, grabbed his penis, and began shoving it against her private parts as if it were one of those round blocks in a children's game and he was trying to jimmy the thing inside a square hole. "Can I move these?" He let go of his erection and tugged on her jeans, which still lay over her hips.

"Um...I don't..." She didn't want to lose her security blanket, but it was dark...and he wasn't looking at her down there...and she was more concerned with keeping her top half covered than her lower half, anyway...and maybe it would be easier for him to get inside her if her jeans weren't in the way. "Okay, sure."

He yanked them out from between their bodies and tossed them under the coffee table.

"That's better," he said, taking hold of his penis again.

He pushed, he prodded, and then, with a sigh of relief, he unceremoniously found where he had been trying to go for five minutes.

"Ow!" Karma winced and dug her nails into Brian's shoulders as he gained entry. *Ow, ow, ow!* Damn! Was it supposed to hurt this much? She'd read somewhere that a girl's first time could hurt, but she hadn't expected this kind of pain. In the movies, women usually looked like they were enjoying this, but there was nothing enjoyable about what Brian was doing to her. At all.

Brian bucked and looked like he was having a seizure as he began hammering away, and it felt like it, too. Her poor vagina. Would she even be able to walk tomorrow? God, what was he doing?

"Oh, uh-huh. Good...yes...is it good for you?" Brian was like an overly excited jackrabbit, and he spouted words in a way that sounded foreign on his tongue, as if he'd heard them in a movie—maybe the same ones she'd seen where the women actually *enjoyed* having sex—and thought he was *supposed* to say them.

Karma held on to his spasming body and tried to nod. "Yes." It wouldn't help to tell him the truth that this was the worst kind of pain she had ever felt, except for that time when she fell and cut her leg on a jagged rock poking out of the ground. But even that had lasted only a few seconds. This pain had gone on for almost a minute already, and it was getting worse.

Brian's eyes were closed, so he couldn't see the distress on Karma's face as he continued bruising her tender flesh with his penis of death. "Yes, so good...I can't stop...Karma...oh...oh...uh-huh...there..." Brian huffed, puffed, and made like a giant jumping bean as he pounded her fragile flesh even harder.

OOOOWWWW!

Her back and hip bones ground against the floor, and white-hot pain seared her insides. She wanted it to be over. Just hurry up already and be done. This shit hurt.

In less than two minutes from start to finish, Brian's body began to jerk. His breathing intensified and his animalistic grunts rose on a crescendo. Then he slammed his hips into her and fell into epileptic shudders. A long, ragged exhale poured from his open mouth. Then he collapsed on top of her. Done.

Thank God.

Afterward, Karma had stared at the water spot on the ceiling, numb, with flames licking the inside of her vagina as Brian remained on top of her, gasping for air. But the pain had been a small price to pay for achieving a rite of passage.

"I'd begun to think I would never have sex," she said, coming to the end of the story. "But there, on Brian's living room, with *Godzilla* roaring from the TV and cold pizza on the coffee table, I finally did it. I lost my virginity." When she finished, she glanced at Mark, who had grown so quiet it was almost as if he weren't there.

"That was your first time?"

She nodded and looked down at her hands, but not before she saw a flash of emotion pass through his eyes.

"Did the two of you have sex again after that?"

"A few more times."

"Did it get better?"

"No, not really. It didn't hurt as much, but it was always rapid-fire fast, like he didn't want to get caught or something."

"And you never had an orgasm?" Mark watched her closely, as if he were taking each of her answers and building a file in his head.

"No."

"And how many lovers have you had since Brian?"

She knew Mark already understood there hadn't been many, and now was the moment of truth.

"I'd like to say none, but there was one more, but I don't really count him."

Mark's eyes narrowed briefly, and he tilted his head slightly to one side. "Why not?"

"Because we only did it once."

"Only once? Was that your choice or his?"

"His, but after I found out why, it was mine, too."

Concern etched the lines of Mark's face as he shifted on the couch. He appeared both worried and concerned, as if he wanted to know what happened but wasn't sure he should ask.

"Richard was an ass," she said, making the decision for him. "He only wanted one thing, and I was too gullible at the time to know that. He seduced me, and I use that term lightly, because all he wanted was sex."

"How did you know him?"

"He was part of the crowd Daniel and I hung out with in college for a while. He got to know me, and after a couple of 'dates'..." she made air quotes with her fingers, "we had sex."

Mark sat forward. "Did you want to?"

"At the time, I thought I did, because, like I said, he seduced me. He told me how much he liked me, and how alike we were, and how he knew from the moment we met that I was special. Blah, blah, blah."

Mark chuffed. "He didn't seduce you. He lied so he could use you." He sounded disgusted, and didn't that just make him seem like her knight in shining armor.

"Yes, I figured that out the hard way." Silence stretched between them for several seconds. "A few weeks later, I learned that was Richard's MO. He moved in, targeted girls who were shy and quiet, then did his thing."

Mark pressed his lips together and his face grew tight, but he didn't voice whatever frustration she could tell sat on the tip of his tongue. A moment later, he said, "I'm sorry."

"It's not your fault," she said.

"I made you think about it."

She smiled. "I'm pretty tough. I can handle it."

He gestured toward the cards. "If you want to stop playing, we can—"

"No, I want to continue."

"You're sure?"

"Positive." Talking about all this was strangely freeing. She felt like she was molting, shedding old layers of herself to reveal more of the woman within.

He sighed and sat back. "Okay then, it's your turn. Pick a card and ask me a question."

She could tell that, at some point, Richard would come up again, even if only in passing or indirectly.

"Okay," she said, picking up a card. She snickered when she read it. "This is a good one. What's the most flexible sex move you can do? Tell me why it's *awesome*?"

She emphasized awesome even though it wasn't emphasized on the card.

Mark burst into laughter. "What? Seriously?" He grabbed the card and read it to himself.

Karma laughed, which was a nice change from the oh-so-serious line of questioning she had just endured. And maybe channeling all that seriousness was why she and Mark both continued laughing a little too hard for several seconds.

"I can't say that I have any flexible sex moves," he said, flicking the card toward the table. It fluttered and spun on the air before gliding to the floor. "Unlike you, I don't do yoga. I think I'd break something if I tried to get flexible. Ask me another," he said. "I didn't like that one and can't answer it, anyway. Besides, I owe you after that last round of questioning."

She snagged the next card on the stack. "Would you rather be lightly spanked in bed or have a feather run softly over your whole body?"

"Mmm." Mark sank into the cushions and looked up at the ceiling. "Definitely the feather. Or maybe hair." He turned his eyes on her. "I like a woman's hair to glide down my chest and stomach."

There was only one time a woman's hair would glide down his chest and stomach, and that was if she was taking her mouth *down there*. So, yeah, this game had just taken an interesting turn.

"Has anyone ever used a feather on you?"

He licked his lips. "Once or twice."

Her mind took the next logical step. "Have you ever used a feather on anyone?"

His single dimple dug into his right cheek. "Once or twice."

"And...?"

"It can be very pleasurable," he said. "Perhaps I'll show you sometime." Before she could say anything further, he grabbed the next card on the deck. "My turn." He read it to himself first. "What's the first thing that pops into your head when I say oral?" He lowered the card and gave her a slightly wicked smile. There was no doubt where his mind had gone.

And considering where her thoughts had just been a minute ago with the whole hair-on-his-body idea, her mind had gone there, too, because her first thought was of giving Mark a blow job. But no way was she going to say that, especially when she had never given one. There had to be a law that stated if you'd never given a blow job, you couldn't use the term.

"Hygiene!" she said a little too forcefully.

His left eyebrow rose as he narrowed his eyes. "Why don't I believe you?"

She shrugged and quickly picked up another card, trying to hurry ahead before he could entrap her into another long line of questioning that was sure to embarrass her. "Have you ever been aroused at work? Give me details."

"Yes," he said. "I have been aroused at work. Very recently in fact." He sat forward and leveled her with a look that held enough steam to hard boil an egg. "Friday, when I suggested that you unbutton your blouse, and when you did…?" His gaze swept her face, and a wistful smile played over his mouth. "That really turned me on."

Oh wow, okay, so…uh-huh. The game was definitely getting more interesting.

He held her gaze for a long moment then picked up the next card as he cleared his throat. His smile brightened as he read the question to himself. "I like this one," he said. "I can't wait to hear your answer." He looked up, eyes twinkling. "What physical trait of mine first caught your eye?"

Way to put her on the spot. She pressed her lips together, thought about it for a second, and tried to envision him sitting beside her at the blackjack table. She had turned toward him, and a split second before she looked at his face, she saw his hands. He had rugged, sure hands. The kind that when they held you made you feel like you were really being held. She hadn't known that at the time, but she'd found out soon enough.

"Your hands," she said definitively.

"My hands." He glanced at them.

"Yes. Then your eyes, then your mouth, and then your chest when we were dancing."

A glimmer of recollection crossed his face. "Ah, yes, I remember." He grinned, making her blush as she recalled feeling him up. "You did seem a little taken with my chest at one point."

Looking down, she forced herself not to laugh. "I guess

you caught that."

"Mm-hm. It was cute how you reacted when I caught you, too."

She sighed. "Okay, you can stop embarrassing me now."

He laughed and settled into the cushions again. "Are you a chest woman?"

"A chest woman?" She frowned in confusion. "What's a chest woman?"

"You know how some men are leg men, some are boob men, stuff like that. Are you a woman who likes men's chests? Do they turn you on?"

"I never thought about it that way, but yes, I guess so. I also seem to notice a man's arms and his hands, too." She gestured toward his. "Obviously, since that was the first part of you I noticed. Hmm...chests, arms, hands, shoulders. I guess I'm more of an overall upper body kind of gal."

"I see." The file he was building on her sounded like it had just grown a bit more interesting, much like the conversation.

She snagged the next card before she could dork out any more than she already had then almost choked as she read the question. "Do you think toe sucking is totally hot or really gross?" She started laughing. Toe sucking? Really? Who came up with these questions?

"Totally hot, for sure," he said without hesitation, cutting off her thoughts.

Karma's mouth fell open. "What? Really?"

He nodded emphatically. "Oh God, yes." He glanced down at her sneakered feet. "I'm what is called a foot man." As evidence, he lifted hers and unlaced her sneakers without pulling them off, even though it looked as though it took all his willpower not to as he caressed her ankles. "I thought you would have figured that out already. I haven't done a very good job hiding my interest in your feet."

She remembered how he'd looked at them last Friday at the department store, how he'd moaned just a little, and how he'd seemed so affected when he'd told her she had beautiful feet, but the thought had never occurred to her that there were men in the world who got turned on by feet or that he was one of them. Discovering this little nugget about Mark was like finding a chunk of gold in her carpet, and his reasoning for asking her to wear the black peep-toe pumps to the concert suddenly made more sense. Finally, this game had given her something she could slip into her mental Mark file.

"You mean, if I took off my shoes right now..." She gently pushed her toe against the heel of one sneaker so that it pushed halfway off her foot. His eyes instantly flared as he dropped his gaze. "Does this distract you?" She grinned daringly as the vixen side of her personality shoved her conservative persona into the shadows.

He moaned and laid his head back, taking a heavy breath. Then he cast her a warning glance. "Yes, that distracts me."

"Oh, I'm sorry," she said as innocently as she could muster as she began to tuck her foot back into her shoe. "I'll just put my shoe back on and—"

He grabbed her foot and pulled off her sneaker. "No. Don't." His heated gaze raked her face. "Please." He dropped her sneaker to the floor, pulled off the other, and dropped it as well. "If you don't mind, I'd like you to keep your shoes off." His breathing sounded labored, as if he was forcing himself to calm down, and his eyelids drooped, giving him a sexy, drowsy appeal.

His expression lit something primitive and debased in the pit of her stomach. "My feet really turn you on that much?"

He blinked heavily, and as if he were holding a sacred gift, he lifted her right leg by the ankle, opened his legs, and nestled the sole of her foot against his crotch. He was hard. Very hard. An airy moan broke in his throat. "Yes. Your feet really turn me on that much." He took a heavy breath and blew it out like he was trying to meditate. Then he swallowed and, holding her sole against him, leaned over and picked up a card. "Your turn." He took a moment to compose himself then read the question. "Which do you think is hotter: sex standing against a wall or bent over a table?"

Karma had never done either, so how could she answer honestly? "I don't know."

"Let me guess, you have no experience with either way, right?" He still sounded sexually bent but a bit calmer.

She bit her lip and nodded.

"Does one sound more interesting than the other?"

She thought about it for a moment then shook her

head. "Not really."

Mark grinned as if making a mental note. "Well, we'll just have to help you figure that out, won't we?"

Gulp.

"I guess." She grabbed the next card. It certainly was getting warm in here, especially with her foot still pressed to his erection. After reading the card to herself, this next question wasn't going to cool things off, either. "On a scale of one to ten, how sensitive are your...uh...your nipples?" The words caught in her throat, and she coughed before reading the second half of the question. "How would you like me to...um...touch them?" She slowly lifted her gaze.

He looked like a wolf ready to devour her.

"My nipples are pretty sensitive, so I'll say about an eight or nine." His voice had grown deeper. "I like when a woman touches them or licks them. Or bites them." He cleared his throat and shifted on the couch, making her foot rub down the hard length of him. "And you have sexy teeth."

"Sexy teeth?"

He nodded. "Oh yes. Very sexy. I want you to do naughty things to me with your teeth. No drawing blood or anything like that, but..."

She felt light-headed. "No, of course not."

"It's just that..." He licked his lips. "I like the idea of your mouth on me, Karma."

And she liked the idea of his on her.

Mark waited a moment before grabbing the next card from the deck. The corner of his mouth ticked upward. Oh boy, this was going to be a good one. She could just tell.

"Describe exactly what it feels like when you orgasm."

Thud!

"Um, well..." She exhaled heavily through pursed lips, making her cheeks puff out.

Mark set down the card and casually sat back, waiting for her answer, a patient smile on his face.

"Okay, so..." Her fingers twisted in her lap. "You already know I've never had an orgasm during...um...sex."

"From what you've told me, I assumed that was the case. But you have had an orgasm, haven't you?"

If she said yes, she would be admitting to masturbation, and something about that felt too personal.

"Karma," he said, his voice lilting as he rocked himself against her foot. "Do you give yourself pleasure?"

"Oh hell," she said, huffing as she rolled her eyes. "Fine. Yes. Yes I do. God, this is so embarrassing."

"And...what does it feel like?"

She set her jaw and slapped her hands on her thighs. "Good, okay? It feels good."

He threw his head back and laughed so hard his whole body shook. "Fine, I'll take that. But..." He held up his index finger as if making a point. "An orgasm you give yourself rarely feels as good as one someone else gives you, and almost never as good as one you have during sex."

"Oh, and you know this how?" She plucked the next card off the pile. "Oh wait, let me guess. Lots of practice, right?"

His single dimple creased his cheek. "Something like

325

that, yes. But I've also read a lot on the subject." His eyebrows shot up as if he'd had a Eureka moment. "As a matter of fact, I'm going to build you a reading list. I have a few books in mind that I think you'll enjoy."

She lowered her face into her left hand and groaned. "I feel like Luke Skywalker being trained in how to use The Force."

Mark burst into laughter again. "Are you calling me Yoda?"

She had to admit, it was pretty funny. "No. You're better looking than Yoda."

"I certainly hope so." He pointed to her card. "Okay, ask me."

She read the card. Her heart performed another perfect swan dive into the pit of her stomach, and she glanced warily at him.

"Go ahead," he said. "I can already tell this one's good."

He had no idea.

"Okay, um..." She looked back down. *Here goes.* "Take me to a place in the house where we haven't had sex." Her gaze flicked nervously to his before she continued. "Kiss me...and then whisper what you would do to me if we were to...get it on there." She lowered the card to her lap and kept her head down.

Mark waited a moment then lifted her foot from between his legs, leaned toward her, and reached for her hand. Without looking at him, she took it. As he moved into the middle of the couch, he tugged her onto his lap and situated her so that she faced him. Her legs straddled his thighs.

Her heart beat like a wild drum in her chest.

"Come here," he whispered, caressing her cheek in such a way that drew her face to his. His lips found hers and held them in a static kiss. He didn't move, and neither did she. All that mattered was the simple, chaste connection and the way a thousand tiny starbursts exploded throughout her body. His kiss seemed so innocent, and yet it sent shards of erotic desire into her blood.

He broke away, but held her close. "Since we haven't had sex, yet, I choose here." He patted the couch. "And as for what I would do to you here, I would make you stand in front of me, where I would slip my hands up your skirt and pull off your panties. I would invite you onto my lap and whisper how sexy you are…" He bent around and kissed her earlobe. "You're *very* sexy."

A shiver raced down her spine.

His lips skimmed down her jaw to her chin. "I would kiss your neck." And he did, letting his tongue sneak out to lick a fiery trail from one side to the other.

Karma felt like she was in a vicious state of sensory overload. She was practically panting.

"And I wouldn't stop making love to you until you came." His breath washed over the skin of her neck, and his lips closed over her shoulder as he licked her. "Your first orgasm with a man inside you," he said a moment later when he met her gaze again.

As badly as she needed oxygen, she could hardly

breathe.

"Oh," she whispered breathlessly. Apparently she could barely speak, too.

His gaze dropped to her mouth, and a heartbeat later, their lips meshed again, this time with more force. A quiet groan broke from deep in his chest.

She wrapped her arms around his neck and shoulders. No way was she letting this moment go. All night, they had talked about sex. Visions of him in various states of undress had taunted her throughout their game, and she had felt his magnificence against the sole of her foot for at least ten minutes. They had fallen under the very spell the game was designed to cast, because they were unraveling into lust faster than a stripper takes off her clothes.

"Bite my lip," he muttered against her mouth. "Let yourself go."

She thought she *had been* letting go, but clearly he knew her better than she knew herself, because the moment he told her to let go, she found a fifth gear she hadn't thought possible. Her tongue danced with his, and he groaned low and loud, and when she did as he asked and took his bottom lip between her teeth, he practically growled, and his fingers curled into claws on her back, pulling her closer.

"That's my girl," he said when she released his lip. Then he assaulted her mouth again, nipping her lip as if to show her the pleasure she had just given him. And it *was* pleasurable. Being bitten, even if only lightly, knocked her good side clear out of the picture, leaving only the vixen she had discovered in Chicago.

Passion rose in her blood, turning her into someone else. She was no longer sweet, shy, good Karma. She was lusty, sultry, bad Karma. A woman lost to her desires, driven by erotic need, who wanted to experience pleasure only a man could give. That only *Mark* could give.

He pulled away, and she opened her eyes to find him grinning at her, his gaze hooded.

"What?" she said, breathless.

His left eyebrow twitched. "You're pulling my hair."

She glanced up and found that her hands had curled into fists, and tufts of his dark brown hair poked out between her fingers. She quickly opened her hands and let go.

Of course, this made Mark laugh. "I wasn't complaining. Remember, I like when a woman pulls my hair."

"Uh, yes..." She sheepishly looked away. "I got a bit carried away."

He pulled her down so that her forehead rested against his. "I know. And I liked it. A lot."

For a long moment, nothing was said as Mark ran his palms slowly up and down her back. "I want to be the first man to show you what you've been missing, Karma," he said softly. "I want to succeed where others have failed."

Her bashful side made a subtle reappearance, and she curled in on herself. "Why?"

He caressed her cheek. "For one, I think you deserve to know what a really good orgasm feels like, don't you?"

When he put it that way, how could she say no?

His fingertips brushed back her hair. "Second of all, I'm a man. And, like most men, I'm proud and have a big ego. I'm not afraid to admit it. And when I make a woman feel good...when I give her such intense pleasure that she screams my name as she's falling into the most unbelievable orgasm she's ever had, I take great pride in that." He hesitated and narrowed his eyes. "Especially when I know she's never felt anything like that before." He paused to let his words sink in.

Karma's entire body heated. They had most definitely sunk in.

Who says egomania is a bad thing?

Mark shifted against the couch, and she felt his erection press against her. "To know that I awakened that part of a woman gives me tremendous satisfaction, Karma. It's the best ego boost in the world." His gaze danced back and forth between her eyes. "So, the most direct answer to your question is that I want to feel you fall apart and come undone under my touch." He took a shaky breath and closed his palm over her cheek. "My God, but just the thought of that...to see you, head thrown back, that heart-shaped mouth open as you cry out..." He rubbed his thumb over her bottom lip. "Let's just say the idea turns me on very much."

The idea turned her on, too, as in way on.

"There's something undeniably sexy about you, Karma," he said. "You intrigue me, and I want the pleasure of discovering you, and of helping you discover yourself if you'll let me. Will you? Let me?"

As the air in the room froze and her heart beat in a wild rhythm, hope and anxious anticipation broke over Mark's expression. His intense stare never wavered.

The most lascivious aspect of their pending affair pressed solidly against the apex of her body, and she had to force herself not to rotate her hips. How would he feel inside her? What would it feel like to finally have an orgasm—a *real* orgasm—during intercourse? Mark promised to answer all those questions and more.

What he was offering was more than she ever could have imagined. He was handsome, charming, intelligent, and confident in his abilities. He was the kind of man women dream of. And he wanted to be with her. *Her!*

If you want to change some things in your life, you need to change some things in your life.

"Yes," she whispered. "Yes, I'll let you."

She bit her lip and a shudder danced up her spine as he smiled.

Mark had to be a magician, because only a magician could have made her behave the way she had tonight.

This was going to be good. So very, very good. She didn't regret her decision to wear that gold brooch to work today one bit. Not one damn bit.

About the Author

Donya Lynne is the author of the award winning All the King's Men Series. Making her home in a wooded suburb north of Indianapolis with her husband, Donya has lived in Indiana most of her life and knew at a young age that she was destined to be a writer. She started writing poetry in grade school and won her first short story contest in fourth grade. In junior high, she began writing romantic stories for her friends, and by her sophomore year, they had dubbed her Most Likely to Become a Romance Novelist. In 2012, she made that dream come true by publishing her first two novels and two novellas. Donya has many more novels and novellas planned for years to come.

Donya loves to hear from her fans. You can e-mail her at donya@donyalynne.com

Sign up for Donya's newsletter on her website: www.donyalynne.com

Find Donya on Facebook (Author Donya Lynne) and Twitter (@DonyaLynne)

Also by Donya Lynne

All the King's Men Series
Rise of the Fallen
Heart of the Warrior
Micah's Calling
Rebel Obsession
Return of the Assassin
All the King's Men - Prequel

Strong Karma Series
Good Karma
Coming Back To You

Hope Falls Series
Finding Lacey Moon

Stand Alones
Winter's Fire